LETHAL CIRCUIT

LARS GUIGNARD

fantastic press

Published by Fantastic Press

fantasticpress.com

Copyright © 2011, 2012, 2013 by Lars Guignard

ISBN 978-0-9877753-4-4

ALSO BY LARS GUIGNARD

Blown Circuit

LETHAL CIRCUIT

Jade must be chiseled before it can be considered a gem.
Chinese Proverb

1

HONG KONG

CHUNGKING MANSIONS. EVEN the name sounded decrepit. Twenty-seven stories of decaying concrete apartment block that made the worst housing project in America look like the Hilton. The truth was, Chungking Mansions wasn't so much a residence as a third world city stuffed into a condemned building occupying some of the most valuable real estate on the planet. Why it still stood was a bureaucratic mystery, but the prevailing theory was that it had taken the place of the old Kowloon Walled City which had been razed years previously.

The old Walled City had been a historical anomaly: an unclaimed property lying in the no man's land between Chinese and British jurisdiction that had grown into a tangled web of vice and commerce the likes of which the world had never seen. There was no law. There was no order. There was only humanity run amok in a group of structures that had slowly but steadily grown into one another until they became one and the same: six and a half acres of madness, fourteen stories high. The old Walled City had finally met the wrecking ball, but its displaced residents had needed some place to go and that place was Chungking. In a word, Chungking was hell, Hong Kong style. It was also home to some of the finest South Indian curry on the Pacific Rim. It was this curry and the ice cold beer that accompanied it that added up to the long trough-style urinal Michael Chase now stood before.

Michael stifled a cough as he undid the fly of his cargo shorts. He'd stepped off the plane from Seattle less than four hours earlier and already he thought he might have picked up a case of tuberculosis. No worries, he thought, he was twenty-six and in the best shape of his life. A run of antibiotics and he'd be fine. What mattered now wasn't what disease he might have contracted, or how quickly the beer had run through him, or even how sharply the climbing pack he wore over one shoulder dug into the small of his back. What mattered was that he focus his attention on the task at hand.

Because Michael hadn't flown eight thousand miles to take a leak. He had much more serious business to attend to and right now every ounce of that business revolved around his urinal mate, the man slouched over the trough two feet to his left. One hand poised on the grimy cracked subway tile, the other in his pants, the older man went by the name of Shanghai Larry, and as he stood there, his tired Eurasian features twisted into an alcoholic stupor, Michael reflected that the moniker could hardly be more appropriate. Salt-and-pepper hair curling just above the tops of his ears and a perfect mole on his chin, if anybody had one foot on Bond Street and the other on the Bund, Larry was the man. The restroom door opened, flooding the shadows with light, and Michael steeled his nerve. It was now or never. Zipping back up, he turned to Larry and uttered the words he'd traveled so far to say.

"I know what you did," he said. "I know that you killed my father."

• • •

Outside the restroom door, the woman listened intently. She was tired, but she suspected that if there was any truth to what she had overheard, her evening had just begun. She stepped away from the door as a third man entered the restroom. Unlike the men inside, this man moved deliberately. As if he had something important to do. Something more than relieve himself. The woman knew she needed to get closer. She slipped in the swinging door before it shut. Now, as she stood in the outer vestibule, a five-foot partition wall providing just enough cover to hide her from where the men were lined up at the trough, she praised her instincts. Even if she was wrong about the third man, there was definitely something up with Michael. Something a whole lot bigger than he had previously let on. She listened intently to Larry's reply.

"That's a hell of an accusation, Sport."

"It's not an accusation. It's a fact. You were the last to see him alive. You two had some kind of issue. You owed him money."

"Doesn't mean I killed him."

"Get real, Larry."

"Listen, Sport, I know this is a difficult time for you."

"Cut the Sport shit. If you didn't do it, who did?"

Larry ran a hand through his thick head of hair. "Pay attention, I'm serious here. It's looked bad for me from the beginning. But I'm not your man. I never was. And I can prove it."

"How?"

"Your dad—"

"Yeah, Larry?"

"He sent me this."

Michael forced himself to breathe as Larry zipped up and reached drunkenly into his jacket pocket. He had noticed their new urinal mate, a powerfully built Chinese man with a pock-marked face and zebra-striped hair, but paid him little heed. His concern now was Larry— Larry who had pulled a cell phone from his pocket and was lazily tapping its dirty touch screen. When a video finally began to play on the phone's display, the first thing Michael noticed was the lack of sound. Apparently the volume was off. The next thing he noticed was that the man on the screen was his father. He was bearded and looked very tired, black circles under his eyes, but it was his dad, anybody could see that. Then, before he could get a better look, all hell broke loose.

Michael had caught a glimpse of the lean, tan woman entering the restroom behind him. He was well aware that her name was Kate, but that didn't concern him at present. What concerned him was how quickly the man with the zebra-striped hair had managed to interject his stout frame between Larry and himself. In that moment, Larry seemed to recognize that something was very wrong because he pulled the cell phone back. Then, Zebra bent to his side and Michael saw what looked like a tattooed snake wrestling a tiger inked to the base of his muscular neck. A quarter second later Zebra had produced a black alloy butterfly knife from the depths of his long leather jacket. Michael stepped back. Zebra unfolded the knife in a smooth flick of the wrist, pressing the two halves of its handle together to form a lethal weapon.

What happened next was fragmented. Michael saw the glint of the blade under the flicker of the fluorescent light. He heard Larry let out a blood-curdling moan. Then he saw the phone slide across the grimy tile, followed by Larry's collapse to the floor. Blood covered Larry's white French-cut shirt and more was flowing out. Even in the poor light Michael could see that he had been stabbed in the heart, and though he immediately brought his hand to Larry's chest to stem the bleeding, his attention was torn. Zebra, a mere ten feet away, had stooped down to pick up the cell phone. He wrapped his fingers around it, idly scooping it up like he had all the time in the world. And that's when the woman smashed him on the head.

Zebra went down in a slow-motion thud. Like he'd been switched off. And then for a second, maybe more, all was quiet. Michael couldn't be sure what the woman had used to hit him, but it was irrelevant. The net effect was that Zebra was now splayed out unconscious on the filthy bathroom floor beside Larry, blood trickling down from behind his left ear. Michael was uncertain of the number of men who next entered the restroom. All he knew was that they wore turbans and that upon seeing the carnage they ran out as quickly as they had come in. The men gone, Michael knelt on the floor. He lifted a blood-soaked hand from Larry's heart and placed two fingers on his neck to check his pulse. He was silent for a long moment before looking up at the woman who stared down at him from the corner of the room.

"He's dead," Michael said flatly.

The woman nodded, eyeing Zebra warily as she stooped down to pick up the bloody cell phone. She had barely grasped it in her hand before the sound of her breath was drowned out by a shrill fire alarm. It was followed by what sounded like movement on the floors below and then the pounding echo of jackboots in the stairwell. She cast her gaze at Zebra's tiger-snake tattoo before redirecting it to the broken bathroom window.

"Follow me," she said. "Follow me or die."

2

I was a good twenty-five-foot drop from the broken bathroom window to the trash-strewn roof below. But it was survivable. Michael knew because the woman had already jumped. So he jumped. Off the window ledge. And down. Michael didn't know how long he was airborne, probably just over a second, but the landing was as he had expected, jarring but manageable. He landed on his feet, hitting the refuse pile just as the woman shook herself free of it.

The trash was maybe two feet deep and damp. It had obviously rained recently. Michael had no idea why Chungking's residents chose to dispose of their refuse as though the Middle Ages were alive and well, but he didn't care. Not right now anyway. Besides, it was mostly packaging and fast-food wrappers; the odor emitted not so much fetid as sweet, creating the illusion that whatever he was trudging through was no worse than a freshly fertilized field. A long-tailed rat scurried through the trash in front of him and Michael made every effort to turn his mind to pleasanter thoughts than the plague.

Michael was six-three and weighed in at about a hundred ninety pounds, but even with his lean strength, trekking through the deep trash was no cake walk. He picked his way after the woman carefully, thankful for the heavy-duty trail running shoes he wore. Then, as the woman stopped abruptly at the far wall, he followed her gaze down. Between the masonry wall of the adjoining building and the roof he stood upon was a fourteen-inch crack extending at least twelve stories down. A drain pipe threaded down the crack to what Michael could just make out as the alley below.

"Tell me you're kidding."

The woman simply eyed the bathroom window. There were voices up there. Movement. Then a beam of light swept the roof.

"Get down."

Michael ducked under a wet cardboard box, but he wasn't quick enough. The flashlight beam hit his back and a shrill scream rang out in Cantonese. The woman didn't bother waiting. Michael looked up to see that she had already disappeared into the crack between the buildings. Then, without further warning, the report of a pistol cracked through the night air. Michael rolled toward the roof's edge. Though he was loathe to do so, he saw little choice but to descend. Pulling the backpack from his back, he tossed it between the buildings. The pack was too wide at first, but with a good shove he was able to get it to fall. The beam of light bounced back and forth across the roof. There were more shots now, but they were scattered. Obviously the shooters didn't have a bead on him yet, but Michael didn't want to stick around until they did. He pulled his lanky frame up and over, grasping the cast iron drainpipe as he slipped his body into the crack. A natural athleticism had always been a part of Michael's life, but the bullets were something he hadn't experienced in a long time. They added an element of urgency to the proceedings he could happily do without.

The drainpipe was wet, water overflowing from the gutter above. He had heard his backpack hit the ground, the four or five seconds it had taken it only emphasizing the length of the descent ahead of him. He could no longer hear the shouting above, but now, as Michael crept down the crack foot by foot, gray water streaming down the walls, he felt like a river was closing in around him. Michael had an issue with tight spaces. He didn't like the label claustrophobic, but it didn't make it any less true. Nine years ago now, Michael had endured an experience that had changed him. That event still haunted him and even though he knew rationally speaking that the walls on either side of him were fourteen inches apart and barring any unexpected earth movement, they would stay that way, it didn't matter. What would happen if the walls narrowed to the point that he would no longer be able to move down? Working against gravity, he'd no longer be able to climb up either. He would be stuck there, caught between two slabs of wet concrete twelve stories high, and the feeling chilled him to the bone.

But Michael also knew that he had to get to the bottom before the men with guns. Add to that, the woman was nowhere to be seen. He had to assume she had made it to the street below. It couldn't be far now. So, taking hold of the drainpipe with both hands, he retired the downward stepping motion he had been using and simply hung in the crack, lowering himself down the drainpipe hand over hand. It was quicker this way. Much quicker. And just when Michael began to fall into a rhythm, he felt the world open up around him. The rear wall of the crack fell away and Michael found himself in a covered alley. He slid down the last few feet of the drainpipe landing next to the woman who stood immobile, the noise of the street audible from the end of the alley.

But it wasn't over yet. Because the woman didn't stir. Didn't even flinch. And when Michael followed her gaze to the end of the passageway, he saw why. They had been quick, but not quick enough. Somehow Zebra, sporting a nasty gash above his left eye, had gotten down before them. Michael suspected he had found a fire escape, but it didn't much matter now. He was there. And he had put away the butterfly knife in favor of an automatic weapon.

Michael knew his way around a gun. Not just because he was a red-blooded American, but because his father had taught him how to shoot and more importantly how to respect firearms. It was something he had always been thankful for, regardless of what side of the debate was popular amongst the company he found himself in. Right now, though, the debate had gone from the academic to the visceral. He was facing down what looked like a machine pistol, probably a fully automatic TEC-9 capable of spraying lead from one side of the alley to the other. It wasn't a terribly accurate weapon, but it was vicious, and Michael knew that it packed enough of a punch to leave both him and the woman dead before they hit the ground.

Michael considered their options. Running was always a good one, but with a brick wall behind them it meant sprinting headlong into a spray of bullets. The other choice was to fight. Fight or flight, he thought. It always came down to one or the other. Except on those odd occasions when another predator entered the fray.

A set of powerful xenon headlights lit up the alley. They were closely followed by the low growl of a big block engine as a vehicle bore down on Zebra from behind. Michael and the woman took to either side of the alley wall, but strangely Zebra didn't flinch. He simply glanced back at the speeding car as if he expected it, as if he were counting on it. He then turned his attention forward and fired the gun.

Michael could tell by the muzzle flash that the shots went high. Way high, because what Zebra obviously hadn't anticipated was the fact that the vehicle would run him squarely over. The car, now clearly visible as a black Mercedes S-Class sedan hit him with such force that Michael was sure he heard the crack of bones. Zebra rolled up over the front bumper and down the right fender, taking the hood ornament along with him for good measure. Then a strange thing happened. The car didn't lurch forward or away, it didn't spin its tires, or rev its engine menacingly. It simply crawled ahead, giving them ample berth, the rear passenger window rolling a smooth three inches down. There was a silence before a cracked voice spoke from the darkness within.

"You owe me a favor, Mr. Chase."

Michael peered through the gap in the glass, but could make out no more than the shadowy outline of an old man.

"How do you know my name?"

Michael's only response was the sound of heavy boots on the tin roof above, flashlight beams scouring the edges of the covered alley. Then, the window closed and the sedan reversed away.

"Friend of yours?" the woman asked.

"I never saw him before in my life."

"He seemed to know you."

"Yeah, I got that."

The woman seemed to think about it. "We'll worry about that later," she said. "For now, you stick with me."

The way she said it, like they were already old friends, Michael couldn't help but cast his mind back on how the evening had begun.

3

CHUNGKING MANSIONS - TWO HOURS EARLIER

THE REASONS FOR Michael's trip to Hong Kong were complicated, but they boiled down to this. His father had disappeared unexpectedly while on a business trip to China just over six months earlier. The official investigation into his father's disappearance had been short but sweet, netting nothing but a one-line explanation and a death certificate. Per the official report, his dad's speeding vehicle had plunged into a river gorge, and though the body was never recovered, it was determined that no one could have survived the fall. That was it. It was all Michael and his family got. When it became evident that no remains would be found, they had held the funeral just over a month later. To say it had been a difficult time for Michael would be to miss the point entirely. It had been devastating.

The news had come one night while Michael was cloistered in his garage apartment in Seattle's old Belltown neighborhood. He had just gotten off his shift at Starbucks, the original store down by Pike Place Market, and was now at work on a proprietary piece of computer code.

Michael had been floundering, just treading water for awhile now. He had no idea what he wanted to do with his life and it showed. His apartment, like his plan for the future, was a mess. He had done a double major in computer science and history at college, but instead of going to work for the Facebooks of this world he had decided to try life on his own terms for awhile.

His own terms meant a variety of jobs and locales. No commitment, but no real progress either. With the code he was working on, he hoped to break free from the cycle of twenty-something malaise he found himself in. He knew it himself. If he could just commit to something, anything, things would work out for him. With this little piece of code, Michael thought he might just get on track. It could be something big. Maybe not Google big, but big nevertheless. If he could just get the application up and running, he had planned to present to venture capitalists in the coming weeks. Instead he had found himself picking out caskets.

Michael was fairly certain his father would have rather burned, but the lack of remains made the choice of cremation problematic. Both his younger sister and mother wanted a symbol, a coffin to lay to rest, even if it was empty. So as the eldest son, Michael had dutifully obliged. He picked out a coffin, he picked out a headstone, he even picked out the flowers, all while his mother sat lost in her La-Z-Boy, staring at the rain.

The funeral had come and gone and Michael decided that the quickest way to get back to normal would be to act as though everything was normal. He rang up customers, he frothed cappuccino, he even presented to the venture capitalists, but as much as he wanted it to be, his heart wasn't in it. They passed on the project. And that's when Michael got the call.

It wasn't a call really, it was a text, but its meaning was clear. His father's death hadn't been an accident. There was foul play involved. The message had come from a guy named Ted Fairfield, an old family friend and business associate of his dad's. The text didn't say much else other than the fact that Ted would contact him again. Six months later and here he was, half a world away in the back room of a broken down Indian restaurant about to come face to face with the person who would change his life.

"Come here."

Ted Fairfield rose from the table. As always, Ted's smile was as wide as an airplane hangar, his thinning gray hair tied back into a sparse ponytail. Ted opened his arms and Michael reciprocated with a hug. Ted had not only been a business associate of his father's but was also his dad's closest confidant. He was in his late fifties and lean and fit, his enormous toothy grin belying the fine lines on his face. Ted had always been there for Michael. When the news of his father's death had come, it had been Ted who had brought it. Ted had been a pallbearer. Ted had spoken at the funeral. And Ted, of course, had arranged for tonight's dinner. Seeing him now, in this strange place, caused Michael to feel a warmth he wouldn't have thought possible under the circumstances, the warmth of family. Ted released Michael from his bear-hug grasp, allowing a second man to speak.

"You're late, Sport."

The man was in his mid-forties, and though Michael hadn't actually met him before, he knew this had to be his father's business associate, Larry Wu—or as just about everybody knew him—Shanghai Larry. Larry worked for a multinational company that manufactured in the region and had also been a colleague of his dad's.

"Take a load off," Larry purred, rising from his seat unsteadily to shake Michael's hand. "You're your father's son all right. Your father's son all over."

Larry released Michael's hand, giving Michael the opportunity to drop his pack and cast his glance down the length of the rickety table. Larry was without a doubt the most formally dressed of the bunch that sat there, and judging from appearances, the least able to hold his liquor. In fact, Michael thought, if one of these things was not like the other, it was definitely Larry with his thousand-dollar pin-striped suit and perfectly clipped salt-and-pepper hair.

As Ted made introductions around the table, it didn't take long to realize that the rest of the group screamed of a wholly different aesthetic. They were younger, of course, but that was far from all of it. They seemed somehow connected. As though they belonged to some kind of secret club Michael could never join. There was a lanky Scotsman sporting dreadlocks and a pork pie hat who went by the name of Crust; a bubbly, tanned Australian girl by the name of Song; a shorter guy with some serious facial hair and a French accent whose name Michael didn't quite catch; and last of all, a low-key brunette who was introduced as Kate. It was Kate who sparked Michael's interest.

About five-ten with a clear complexion and an aquiline nose, she was somewhere in her mid-twenties, her wide almond eyes lending her an air of sophistication that Michael couldn't quite put his finger on. When she spoke, her accent was to Michael's ear completely neutral, suggesting a solid Midwestern lineage, but something about the way she held herself told Michael that though her accent might be American, she wasn't. She wore a rough-cut white linen blouse, a long skirt, and a copper bracelet which seemed to be, as near as Michael could make out, yoga-hiker chic. It was the kind of ensemble that would be just as at home at work as it would be at play, but Michael knew he was applying Seattle standards to what was undoubtedly a very different kind of woman. Fortunately, Larry interrupted before he could gawk any longer.

"So, Michael. Fresh out of Chek Lap Kok, I hear?" Chek Lap Kok was Hong Kong's ultramodern airport and, given its ease of use, a preferred gateway to the East.

Michael checked his watch. "Ninety minutes and counting."

"Well you couldn't have picked a better place to land." Larry pushed a big plate of curry Michael's way and signaled the waiter for another bottle of beer. "When Teddy said I should come out and say hi, I didn't know he'd have a whole table of fresh faces for me to meet." He looked around the table, eyes glazed over. "Now where in the world were we?"

"Malaysia," Kate said.

"Ahh, yes. Malaysia."

"I wouldn't be caught with a lone spliff in that God-forsaken country," Crust said. "Those buggers will hang you for humming along with Bob Marley." Crust must have read the incredulity on Michael's face because he went on. "But the good news is, your gruel, the months of imprisonment during your trial, even the length of rope they use to string you up, none of it will cost you a penny." Crust took a swig of his beer. "If, however, you were to step out of this fine city of Hong Kong, into China proper, you'd be looking at a whole new cricket match. You do the crime, they throw you in prison, and not only do you have to work twenty-one hour days vulcanizing rubber to pay your way, your family gets the bill for the bullet after the firing squad."

Crust lowered his voice to a whisper. "I've heard from a reliable source, and not some gap-year tourist by the way, but someone in government, that some of these executioners are such bad shots that the poor families end up paying twice. Two bullets. Sometimes even three. Best case scenario, you get busted, they imprison you in a munitions factory and your family gets a trade discount on the shells."

Larry laughed drunkenly but Crust went on, "I kid you not, the court hears daily requests for imprisonment in armament factories, hence Crust's number one rule for round-the-world travel: something goes down...."

To Michael's surprise, a chorus sounded around the table: "Don't stick around."

As tall bottles of beer were toasted in the air, Michael reflected that this was it—the Circuit—the round-the-world backpacking trail upon which travelers of all ages and stripes met up time and time again. There were a thousand variations to it, but a typical broad strokes tour on the Circuit might mean working up the required traveling funds in London, catching a cheap flight to Kenya, maybe hopping a safari before lounging on the island of Lamu, then jumping to India for a stint in Goa, followed by a sabbatical in Thailand, or a brush with Bali. Circuit-goers were ever working their way eastward for a little urban entertainment, which is where Hong Kong entered the equation. From there they might double back into South Asia, or head out across Siberia before refueling for funds in a suitably affluent Western land. It was a big world, and there were a million ways around it, but a good backpacker could always count on running into his cronies in the local hot spots, the ones only the other backpackers knew about. Michael had first heard about the Circuit years before, but he'd delayed actually getting on it until he at least had college behind him. Or he had a reason. Now he had both.

The Frenchman must have been about done with Crust's sermonizing because he put his arm around him and said, "This man has been traveling for too long, no?"

Michael wasn't sure if the question was rhetorical, but the Frenchman quickly followed it up with another query; one that was bound to come up sooner or later.

"So, tell me, Michael, where are you backpacking on our lonely little planet?"

Michael had already sensed that travel itineraries were more than a simple A to B with this crowd. What he was about to find out, though, was how much more. He coughed to clear his throat, reflecting back on the Chinese geography he had picked up from his guide book. "I was thinking," he said, "I'd kick around Hong Kong a bit, then ease my way north up the Pearl River Delta to Guangzhou, before heading a ways west to Guilin and Yangshuo, then maybe onto Kunming."

The table lapsed into silence. Finally, Kate asked, "Why Yangshuo?"

"My father spent some time there years ago. He always used to talk about it."

"That's," Crust said with little enthusiasm, "interesting."

Kate sprung to Michael's defense. "Lay off, Crust."

"What? I'm talking about the route, not his dad."

"So am I," Kate said. "The Hong Kong-Yangshuo Express. It's a great route. A classic. We've all done it."

"Like I said, it's interesting."

"You said interesting like it was day-old bread."

"Okay, you got me. It's just that Yangshuo, so early in the game, I don't know if Michael here is ready for its simple pleasures."

Kate slid a palm over Crust's mouth. "It's a great route, Michael. A good first leg in China and Crust is just jealous. He'll be getting his ass bit off by malarial bugs, drinking from tire treads in Tibet when he could be joining you."

Crust rose to his own defense. "Not true."

Kate didn't back down. "Tell me you wouldn't prefer to kick back with a banana pancake contemplating your next rubdown instead of bribing some corrupt PSB official to sign your permit so you can set up your frozen teepee on the leeward side of Mount Kailash."

"Kailash is in the Himalayas."

"Hmm, banana pancake," Kate weighed out the options like the scales of justice, "frozen balls." She looked Michael in the eye. "It's a good route. You're going to have a great time."

It was at that moment that Shanghai Larry, whom Michael was convinced had been slumbering in the corner, came to life.

"Great time. Fantastic time. Tickly-boo like a pussy tourist in Patpong." Looks were exchanged around the table, but Larry went on. "But it doesn't really matter, does it, Michael? Because he hasn't told you what he's really doing here." Larry pulled his shoulders up from a full body slouch as he stretched his arms high, lowering his voice conspiratorially. "Sport, here, has come to find his father."

He followed his grand pronouncement with a belch before rising from the table. "Piss anyone?" A moment later Larry's knees buckled out from under him and Michael knew in earnest that the evening had begun.

4

KOWLOON 0100 HKT

Two murders and forty minutes later and they were lost in the neon crowds of Nathan Road. Michael had removed his bloody t-shirt and pulled on a clean white one from his backpack. He was running on adrenalin and he knew as much. You couldn't be shot at, roll through the trash, and watch a man die without taking some of that with you. And right now, Michael felt as though he had taken it all.

In truth, Michael was acquainted with violence. At his father's behest he had trained in the Shito Ryo style of karate since he was a kid, earning his junior black belt at the age of sixteen and going on to get his first real belt and Second Dan in college. Oddly, in the age of ultimate fighting, karate had a bit of an old lady image to it, but it was a martial art and martial meant war. It was meant to prepare you for battle.

That was the theory anyhow. In practice, real violence, the kind where your opponent wasn't bound by a set of tournament rules, was a whole lot more visceral than any martial art. Michael knew this first hand, even though he often wished he didn't. And so, even though he felt a strong desire to slow down and clear his head, now wasn't the time and he knew as much. The police were no doubt already scouring the city. Given the quick escalation of the evening's events, what mattered in the near term was that they get away.

The electric intensity of Hong Kong wasn't helping Michael's state of mind. There were people everywhere. It wasn't like Seattle, or even a busy evening in Manhattan; here it was the middle of the night and it looked like a coliseum had emptied on every glittering block.

Following Kate through the crazy crowds, Michael noted that they stopped and started frequently, Kate checking her back constantly to determine whether they were being followed. When, after a series of circuitous stops and starts, they finally arrived outside a hulking residential skyscraper, Michael had the distinct feeling they weren't far from where they had started. Kate took him around a side entrance and they entered a swinging security door marked in flaked gold leaf with the words *Mirador Mansion*. Michael knew they needed a safe place to regroup and as such didn't question Kate as she led him up the dingy concrete steps of the tenement.

When, however, they stopped before a dirty pink door that read *Happy Tom's*, Michael had to wonder. Kate must have read his look, because her reply was absolute.

"We'll be safe here."

"With Happy Tom?"

"You need to trust me."

Kate opened the metal door with a grating squeak and Michael was served his second look at the international backpacking scene. Happy Tom's was a guest house, a hostel where travelers of all sorts put up for the night, and even at this late hour they were everywhere. A blonde Swede brushed her teeth while studying the notices tacked to a decaying corkboard; a black backpacker with bright-red braids kicked back reading a *Lonely Planet* guidebook; and a waif of a girl who looked like she couldn't have been more than sixteen pecked out an e-mail at an aging computer terminal.

Kate nudged Michael forward into the narrow hall leading out of the tiny common room. He passed a communal bathroom, followed by an open doorway. Inside Michael saw backpackers snoring on racks of floor-to-ceiling metal bunks. Kate continued forward another two steps and inserted a key into a door at the far end of the hall. Ensuring that no one was watching, she opened the door. It wasn't a regular room at the hostel, that much was clear. Brooms and cleaning supplies lined the walls. But there was also a single metal cot complete with trundle bed. She shut the door and flipped on a light.

"We need to talk," Kate said.

"Here?"

"You have a better idea?"

Michael drummed his fingers on a jug of bleach. "Yeah. We could go to the police. Tell them what happened."

Kate almost laughed before lowering her voice to a whisper. "This isn't America. There's no innocent until proven guilty. There's only guilty and more guilty and as far as I could tell, you had blood all over you."

"I didn't kill him."

"You fled the scene."

"It was your idea to leave."

"To save your ass."

"And why would you do that?" Michael asked. "You don't even know me."

Kate took a seat on the drooping cot. "Call it a character flaw," she said. "You were in trouble, I helped out. All I want in return is an explanation."

Michael averted his eyes, glancing around the closet-sized space. "Look, it's not you personally. I just don't want to pull anybody else into this."

"You don't think it's kind of late for that?"

It was true. She was involved now. Almost as involved as he was. "What do you want to know?"

"You accused Larry of murdering your father."

Michael felt a lump grow in his throat. "Are you sure we're good here?"

"For now."

"Then here goes." He dropped his pack, taking a seat on the far end of the drooping mattress. "My dad worked for a big athletic shoe company. The kind with lots of Madison Avenue marketing and product manufactured wherever it was cheapest to do it."

"Nike? Adidas?"

"It doesn't matter. The point is, he traveled a lot. While I was growing up, my dad spent a lot of time out of town. He was always there when we needed him, but work kept him away a lot of the time."

"Somehow I don't think two dead guys are about a lack of quality time with dear old dad."

Michael rolled his tongue inside his mouth and said, "About six months ago, he didn't come home at all. The official explanation was an automobile accident west of here in Guangxi Province. They say his car plummeted to the bottom of a river gorge. His body was never recovered."

Michael unzipped the top compartment of his backpack. "Larry was the last to see him alive." Michael removed a letter-sized envelope. "Five days ago I got this in the mail."

Opening the envelope, Michael pulled out a paper airline ticket for travel between Seattle and Hong Kong. Across the back of it was a simple message scrawled in a violent hand.

It read: "LARRY DID IT."

Kate examined the envelope. "It's postmarked Kowloon Central. No return address. You took this to mean that Larry murdered your father?"

"How would you take it?"

"Probably like that." Kate considered the implications. "What do you think now?"

"Now I don't know what to think."

"So the backpacking bit, the route you were going to take?"

"In the event that Larry was a dead end," Michael winced at his choice of words, "I knew my dad was last seen out here. I came to find out what happened to him."

"So what are you waiting for?"

Kate reached into her daypack and without another word tossed him Larry's bloody cell phone. It was an Android smartphone, probably less than a year old, and if you looked past the blood, barely used. After a moment's hesitation, Michael woke the device from sleep mode. Then he hit play.

The first thing about the video clip Michael noticed was the room. It had stark concrete walls, almost like a cell. A battered metal door was visible in one corner. An incandescent bulb hung from the ceiling above a gray metal table. To the side of the table was a gray tubular metal chair. Michael's father stood between the table and chair. He had several days' growth of gray beard and his wispy hair was greasy, falling haphazardly over his forehead. From the video, he looked to be in his mid-sixties, though Michael knew him to be younger than that. His father's eyes burnt like hot embers, despite his obvious fatigue. He wore a simple oxford shirt, the collar open. Michael paid special attention to his neck, because even in this medium shot, he recognized the pendant—three small stars offset in a silver ring—that his father wore.

"What's he saying?"

Michael realized that the volume was still turned off on the phone. He turned it up.

"One, two, four, six, one, three, eight—"

"Start it from the beginning."

Michael replayed the message, this time with the volume on.

"Eight, five, six—"

"It's like he's reading off the weekly lotto draw."

His father finished uttering the digits, sixteen of them, all a number between zero and nine, and the screen went blank. That was it. Michael checked the phone, but there was little else. No outgoing calls, nothing in the address book, no cached web pages, no apps, no games, nothing except a record of a single incoming call.

"Either Larry's really unpopular—"

"Or he purged the phone."

Michael shared a glance with Kate and did the most expedient thing in the book. He tapped the redial button. There were the telltale tones of digits being dialed, followed by the sound of a connection being made, followed by nothing at all. Dead air.

"Who are you?" Michael asked.

The connection was cut. Michael immediately dialed again, but this time the call wouldn't go through. He tried for a third time, but it was the same story. Frustrated, he tossed the phone to the bed. Even at this late hour, horns and traffic were audible outside the old building. To say Hong Kong never slept was a cliché. Hong Kong didn't even slow down to catch its breath.

Michael watched as Kate picked up the phone. Maybe she thought she could find something else. Something he hadn't seen. She hit the play icon again, watching his father's video message one more time. Then, about halfway through, she paused it and hit another key. Then she just stared. As if she had seen something unexpected. Something impossible.

"What is it?"

Kate turned the screen toward Michael. There was an information window opened over the still video frame of his father's gaunt face.

"The message is dated April 25."

"That makes no sense. He didn't go missing until October."

"April 25th of this year."

Michael took hold of the phone and looked himself. It was true, the time stamp read 1:36PM HKT, April 25th of the current year.

"You know what that means?" Kate said.

Michael just looked at her. He wasn't a fool. He knew what it meant.

"As of five days ago, your father was alive."

5

THE FIRST THING *Michael's father taught him was courage. Michael remembered it well. He was just five years old. They had moved to a new town and Michael was scared. He had just gotten used to his old kindergarten and now he had to go to a new one. To make matters worse, today was Halloween. All the kids were to report to school in costume. Michael's mom and dad knew about Halloween and they made sure that Michael had a costume to wear that morning. But Michael didn't want to go. All of a sudden his green dinosaur costume seemed really lame. All the other kids were probably princesses or pirates. They would laugh at a dinosaur.*

So Michael's dad made him a deal. He said Michael didn't have to go if he didn't want to. The school would always be there. He could stay home all week if he wanted. But Michael's dad also reminded him that dinosaurs were an important part of Halloween. Maybe the most important part. Dinosaurs stopped the princesses and pirates from tearing each other to pieces. If Michael didn't go to school, he might have a fine day playing Play-Doh and watching cartoons, but who would protect the pirates? Michael saw the logic. Somebody had to keep the peace. He attended his first morning at the new kindergarten in full dinosaur regalia. Happily, not a princess or pirate was lost all day.

As of five days ago his father was alive. Kate's words hit Michael like a hot poker. It wasn't that Michael hadn't hoped it, hadn't dreamed it even, but to have another human being utter those words just made them that much more real. Even if they turned out to be a lie. And it was for this reason that upon hearing Kate say the words, Michael made it his business to get as far away from her as possible. Even if everything changed, he wanted to keep the illusion alive. Besides, she'd already seen the video. He didn't owe her anything more than that.

But getting out of the tiny room without alerting Kate turned out to be more of a task than he'd imagined. She seemed to sleep with one eye open and his first visit to the washroom amounted to her practically showing him the way. Only after a mumbled explanation regarding the flaming curry and three subsequent trips to the can was Michael able to shake the interest of his ever-vigilant roommate. On his fourth trip to the washroom, less than half an hour before dawn, Michael retrieved his backpack from the storage locker in the hallway and continued out of Happy Tom's and into the twilight.

Michael suspected that he had little time before Kate realized he wasn't coming back, but his bigger concern was that the police were still looking for him. After all, the debacle at Chungking had taken place less than four hours earlier. They might be winding down their search, but he doubted they'd have completed it. For this reason Michael was pleased to note that the Westrail Station he needed to reach was less than a twenty-minute walk away. The mass transit map he'd picked up at Chek Lap Kok clearly indicated he could take the MTR, Hong Kong's highly efficient subway, to the station, but he knew he'd already be taking a risk riding light rail out of the city. There was no reason to compound the problem by walking into a subway station where the police could well be checking identification.

As it was, the brisk walk in the pre-dawn light gave Michael the perspective he had been craving. Neon signs faded gently against a gradually lightening sky and before he knew it, Michael had located the Westrail Station. He purposely chose not the main concourse which was located in a shopping mall, but a smaller elevated outdoor platform about a five minute walk past. There, after a wait that couldn't have lasted more than a minute on the already busy platform, the white train whooshed to a stop and he stepped aboard, taking his stainless steel seat.

Soon, the dense urban jungle of Kowloon proper was behind him, replaced by the lush landscape of Hong Kong's New Territories. The New Territories were so named because they were the last piece of colonial Hong Kong to be leased to the British. They were also the last stop before China proper and the answers that country held hidden. Michael mulled on the thought as the tin-roofed shanties on green hills flew past. He wanted to believe that his father was alive. He wanted to believe it so badly that it hurt. It was, after all, this secret hope that had driven him to fly across an ocean. But he had also buried his father. He had thrown the last handful of dirt as the empty casket was creakily lowered into the rain-soaked ground. To have to reevaluate those fundamental assumptions, to have to truly consider that his father might still be living was a difficult proposal. Not because Michael didn't want his dad to be alive. But because he didn't want to go through the pain of losing him all over again.

Michael also realized, however, that what he wanted was largely irrelevant. He knew that if there was even a chance that his father was out there, he needed his help. And it went without saying that Michael would go to the ends of the Earth to help him, which is why upon hearing his father recite the sixteen-digit number, Michael knew exactly what he needed to do.

Number one was to immediately commit the number to memory. It was something he'd been able to do ever since he'd learned to count. He didn't know if he had an eidetic memory or not, he'd never been tested, but running the number over in his mind he had recognized what it was. It wasn't a lottery number, or a telephone number, or even a code. It was much simpler than that. It was a simple GPS waypoint—coordinates that designated a precise latitude and longitude and one look at Kate had told him that she knew exactly what it was as well, however well she might have tried to hide it.

It wasn't an accident that his father would send him a message like this. Some of Michael's fondest childhood memories were of times spent hiking with his father in the back country of the Pacific Northwest's Cascade Range. They'd hike in the mountains for days, sometimes even venturing up to the Coast Range in Canada, always excited about what the new day would hold and always carrying a GPS receiver en route. They'd never needed to rely on it per se, but it was nice to know that absent a map, there would always be a way back.

Now, a sixteen-digit number was telling Michael that there was a way back to his father. According to the Suunto GPS-capable watch he wore on his wrist, the coordinates were just over the mainland Chinese border, about fifteen miles east of the city of Shenzhen. That revelation had been enough for Michael to leave Kate behind and forge ahead.

Michael steeled his nerve as the train crawled toward the Chinese border at Lo Wu Station. When the train's doors finally opened, he slung his backpack over his shoulder and continued onto the platform and down a crowded set of stairs into the bowels of passport control. Despite his well-masked anxiety, neither he nor his passport attracted undo scrutiny, and after a slow but methodical pass through two congested immigration checkpoints, one to leave Hong Kong, and another to enter China proper, he found himself on a bridge, crossing a barbed-wire-enclosed drainage ditch toward the early morning lights of the city of Shenzhen, Hong Kong's nearest neighbor and arch rival.

Michael wasn't halfway across the pedestrian bridge before the automatic doors on the other side of it opened, revealing a shopping arcade filled with everything China had to offer. Electric dusters competed for space with scooters and robots and gift-boxed chopsticks. As he strode through the arcade, the sheer mass of product threatening to overwhelm his senses, Michael kept his eyes on a second set of deeply tinted automatic doors at the far end of the corridor. Those doors were his goal. The reason he was there. Five paces out, the deeply tinted panes slid smoothly open revealing the largest outdoor square that Michael had ever seen. It was then that it hit him. The border he had just crossed was much more than a simple line on a map. It was a line in the sand. A division between East and West, and as Michael contemplated that fact, he realized that here, alone in this vast square, far from home, the search for his father was about to truly begin. And so, Michael crossed not only his fingers, but the threshold of everything he had ever known, and entered the East.

6

Li Tung didn't like to travel. If you were to ask him why, he would probably say that he was old now and preferred the comforts of home, but the truth was, he had never much liked it. It was a fact he had, out of necessity, gone many places in his youth, but now, in his golden years, his once thick black hair a mottled snow gray, Li preferred to stay close to the quiet home he had created for himself atop Hong Kong's Victoria Peak. He still had to go down the hill occasionally, if only to let his underlings know that he was still very much in charge, but he rarely ventured farther afield than Kowloon, and never beyond the borders of Hong Kong's Special Administrative Region. Life was, after all, short and Li intended to employ what few years he had left, the way he liked, at home, in his garden, having the world come to him.

Today, however, was different. Li was preparing for, of all things, a trip. The very thought of it made him anxious, so anxious in fact that if there had been any other way, he would not have entertained the idea of going. But sometimes life's circumstances dictated even to powerful men like Li and in this case they dictated that he must leave the comfort of his home. As such, his items of a personal nature already packed by his loyal staff, Li made his way down the marble hallway of his elegant home toward his waiting limousine.

The car was a stretch S-Class Mercedes, the second of three he kept in his fleet, and much more suitable for a long journey than the damaged vehicle from the evening before. Many months of planning and negotiation had led up to this day, but as Li walked, his attention turned not to the details of what he was about to do, but to the reason he was about to do it—his only son. It was for his boy, now a grown man in his own right, that Li was setting off on this journey today, and it was for his boy that Li would do much more should the situation demand. He hoped that it would not come to that, but if it did, he would be ready. For the present, though, Li was pleased to see that his car was warm and waiting. He only hoped that the rest of his journey would go as planned.

7

SHENZHEN SPECIAL ECONOMIC ZONE

THE BUS LOOKED normal enough. It was the ride that felt like something out of a sick video game. The madness was apparent even before Michael had stepped aboard. The bus didn't stop on the busy street, it simply slowed, disgorging its passengers as others ran breathlessly on. But getting on, Michael came to realize, wasn't the problem. The problem was staying there once he was aboard, because the driver, as near as he could tell, was insane. He drove with one pedal, the accelerator, seemingly believing that the mere presence of his giant battered vehicle was enough to scare anything and everything else out of his way. And in this case everything ran the gamut from three-wheel tractor trucks to water buffalo pulling motorless truck cabs to bicycles hauling loads twenty times their size.

The weirdness wasn't limited to the traffic. Shenzhen's downtown core safely behind them, it wasn't long before Michael saw what appeared to be the Eiffel Tower poking its head out of a field. Moments later they passed under a near life-size replica of the Golden Gate Bridge, before motoring past a pyramid, and then a whole swath of unfinished skyscrapers, soaring skyward, still covered in their flimsy bamboo scaffolding.

Michael didn't know if he was passing theme parks or office parks, but whatever the explanation he knew that he had only been to one other place remotely like it in his life, and it wasn't in China. It was in Nevada, Las Vegas to be precise, and as far as Michael could tell, China's glittering economic miracle of Shenzhen was like Las Vegas on speed. For a town that had been little more than a fishing village not many years before, it was hard not to marvel at how far the city had come. Where it was going, of course, was anybody's guess, but Michael had more pressing concerns. The bus was scheduled to pass his father's waypoint near the end of its route, and eyeing his GPS, Michael knew he was close. He raised his hand and, after some frantic waving, the bus driver cruised to a rolling stop alongside the highway.

After Michael fought his way forward through the packed aisle, the driver left him in a cloud of diesel and dust in what was a fair approximation of farmland. The ludicrous spires of development now far behind him, Michael continued up the highway a few paces before hitting a crossroads where a blacktop road wound up a grassy hill. This was not what Michael had expected of China. Kansas maybe, but not the busiest manufacturing center on the planet. And yet, here it was, a golden field with a lonely road winding through it like something right out of middle America. If not for the salty ocean air, Michael could have sworn he was in the heartland. He imagined that the sea breeze had to be blowing in from the Pearl River Estuary, which was represented by a wide bay on his wrist-top LCD. Feeling that there might be another set of eyes watching, Michael scanned the periphery to see if he was being followed. Except for the trickle of traffic on the highway, however, the rolling hills appeared largely deserted. Hiking a few paces up the road, he found a hidden spot behind a knoll and took a quick moment to do some housekeeping.

Michael pulled his backpack off his shoulders and opened the drawstring to its main compartment. The pack itself was relatively low volume, small enough for him to always carry with him, yet big enough for the essentials. And though Michael had little experience with the Backpacker Circuit, he had spent enough time traipsing through the Cascades to know what those essentials were. He carried a change of clothes: a fleece jersey and a pair of cargo pants, underwear and socks; nothing fancy but warm enough for a cool night. Next up was a space blanket, the kind with a reflective coating on one side designed to preserve body heat in emergency situations. Michael had spent the night under just such a blanket, caught on the north face of Mount Rainer in a blizzard, and as far as he was concerned, he would never go anywhere without one again. In fact, as he fished through his pack, he took the moment to slip the space blanket into the pocket of his cargo shorts. In the unlikely event that he got separated from his pack, it would be there.

With that thought, Michael instinctively felt for the Swiss Army knife he carried in his pocket. After getting off the plane, the first thing he had done was pull it from his backpack. In general, Michael felt better about items he could keep on his person and to that end, his

GPS-capable watch, and a high-resolution smartphone were a perfect complement to the trip. His cash and identification were further contained in a special pocket he had sewn to an inner panel of his shorts. As long as he kept his pants on, Michael reasoned, he'd remain in good stead.

Still, the reason he had the pack was that though you could try, you couldn't possibly carry everything you needed to travel for months on end in a single pair of cargo shorts. For that reason, the backpack also contained amongst other essentials: a *Lonely Planet* guidebook of the region, a Gore-Tex rain shell, a self-filtering canteen that made the dirtiest of water safe to drink, and a Petzl headlamp, all of which he pushed aside in his effort to find what he was looking for. After dropping the pack thirty feet to the concrete below the previous evening, he hoped they were still intact. Luckily he had packed them within the folds of his down sleeping bag and with a final hook of the wrist he was able to extract what he was after—a compact pair of binoculars.

Michael had debated bringing the binoculars, but decided in the end that they were so lightweight, they wouldn't hurt. At least not physically. But after all these years, they still packed an emotional punch. Michael had been seventeen, staring through a pair of binoculars just like these ones, when it had happened. One minute he was a happy hiker and the next he was a hostage. It was without a doubt the single most horrific experience of his life.

Truthfully, the whole thing had started out great. His dad had invited him on one of his business trips. He was scoping out a new production facility for his company in Peru and Michael had jumped at the chance to go with him. Once they were done with business in Lima, they headed up to the Sacred Valley of the Incas near Machu Pichu. And that's when their little excursion went seriously off the rails. It was unclear whether the kidnappers had targeted them in Lima or not, but they knew what they were doing. They waited until Michael and his father were apart and they sprung. Michael had climbed a few hundred feet above to scope out the area with the binoculars while his father set up camp near the stream below. Michael was consumed by the lush mountain scenery, simply drinking it all in, when he felt a sharp tap on his shoulder. He was startled, but not scared. He figured it was just his dad. Even though Peru was home to hundreds of kidnappings a year, he had given little thought to the phenomena. Besides, Michael was seventeen. He was invincible.

Or so he thought. The first smack of the pistol dissuaded him of his invincibility pretty quickly and once the other two kidnappers trained their machine guns on him, it was all downhill from there. Michael tried his best to act brave, to look brave, to be brave, but he was scared and it must have shown. His attackers asked him at gunpoint where his father was and when Michael refused to answer, they pistol whipped him again. And that's when he got really frightened. Because, Michael thought, if his father wasn't here, where was he? Did he even know what was happening?

The lead gunman, his coarse black hair tucked behind his ears, ripped the binoculars savagely from Michael's grasp. The memory of it rocketed Michael back to the here and now. The abduction had happened nine years ago, but the thought of it still shook him. True, he was functioning again, and his nights of awakening in a cold sweat had become rarer, but they still occurred, reminding him of just how quickly anybody's life could be turned on end.

Focusing his mind on the task at hand, Michael slipped the binoculars into his now rather weighty pocket and tightened the drawstring on his pack. The top of the knoll lay twenty yards above and like any good boy scout, he wanted to take a look around before introducing himself. Michael scampered up the steep slope and laid down in the tall grass at the top of the knoll taking in what looked like a multi-story building across the meadow. If anything, the previous evening's events had reinforced that an abundance of caution was in order. This was no game he was playing. People had already died. And that meant he had to be careful, more careful than he'd ever been in his life.

Michael brought the binoculars to his eyes, gently spinning the focus wheel. About fifteen hundred yards ahead, approximately where he estimated the GPS coordinates to be, rose a six-story building, the road looping into a circular drive around the front of it. Flowers bloomed and ornamental trees blossomed in the surrounding gardens. The structure itself was constructed of decaying concrete with large warehouse-style windows, but the setting was so pretty, the building's generic form seemed almost incongruous. A second, more industrial building with a tin roof obviously served as some kind of garage facility, vehicles parked in front. Still, for all the evidence of human habitation, there wasn't a soul in sight. An elaborate metal sign mounted high on the west side of the main building identified the enterprise as Chohow Industries.

That these were the approximate coordinates indicated by his father's message was certain. What was less clear was what he was going to do next. Obviously he needed to get closer, but he wanted to do so in such a way that his approach didn't raise any alarm bells. Still, Michael reasoned, the most direct route might also be the least suspicious. He was, after all, a backpacker, and what did backpackers do but lope around seeing the sights? Granted an industrial building in the middle of nowhere wasn't likely to make any Condé Nast top ten lists, but who was he to judge? Maybe the structures were shining examples of post-communist Chinese architecture.

Michael picked himself up off the ground and hiked up the winding road. Within a few minutes he had reached the circular drive. His GPS told him that the coordinates his father had left him were somewhere within the larger of the two buildings. Slipping off his backpack and depositing it at the base of what looked like a banyan tree, Michael casually walked the final few feet into the open doors of the deserted reception area.

The first thing he noted was that he'd have to come up with another excuse for being there. The building wasn't a shining example of anything. The bare concrete floor and walls looked old, but Michael guessed that they were probably new and simply decaying before their time due to a combination of improperly mixed concrete and Shenzhen's high humidity. There was an unoccupied metal desk in the dark corner of the open lobby and a ten-foot-wide switchback staircase leading up through the floors. With no one to stop him, Michael kept right on walking, mounting the first flight of stairs.

He was struck by the quiet. The building appeared utterly vacant, and on each level he was met by a locked, green metal door, paint peeling off its face. Though the coordinates his father had left him accurately indicated a longitude and latitude, there was no indication of a precise elevation, so Michael knew that even if he stood exactly upon the spot indicated, he'd still be guessing. Now that he was in the building he was pretty much on his own. Except, he thought, if his dad had gone through the trouble of leaving him the coordinates, he wouldn't leave the floor of the building to chance. No, he would have provided that information. And with that Michael remembered the coordinates' final digit. The five. Initially Michael had thought it to be a fraction, but that was unlikely. GPS coordinates were routinely expressed to four decimal places. No, the final digit wasn't a fraction, it was a floor. Redoubling his step, Michael now knew his destination lay two floors above.

He also knew he was no longer alone. Rounding the fourth floor landing, chatter emanated from the hallway above. Michael mounted another two steps and listened. Unlike the green steel doors on the other floors, the fifth floor door was propped open by a plastic chair, women's voices audible from within. Michael considered rehearsing his cover story, but nixed the idea when he considered that it was unlikely anybody would speak a word of English anyway. He was in China after all, not Chattanooga. He needed to adjust his expectations accordingly. Mounting the final steps he stuck his head in the door expecting to find, at most, a couple of chatty secretaries. Instead he found a full-fledged assembly line.

Row upon row of young female workers sat in blue smocks assembling some kind of small product, each adding their part in turn as whatever it was made its way down the line. Two older, matronly woman wearing green smocks strode up and down the line keeping tabs on the workers. If this was a Chinese factory, it certainly wasn't the hell hole Michael had been led to believe they were. It looked more like a sewing circle than anything; a large group of women, working on what appeared to be a plastic toy as it was passed down the table. The whole process couldn't have been less high tech, or strangely, Michael thought, watching the completed widgets get thrown into a bin at the end of the line, more efficient.

Large grime-streaked windows let the sunlight in, a dented freight elevator parked on the far wall of the open space. Glancing at his GPS, it was obvious to Michael that the coordinates were near the end of the assembly line. Michael could tell his presence didn't go unnoticed; there were furtive looks in his direction, but he wasn't actively acknowledged, not even by the supervisors in green smocks. The lack of attention suited his purposes just fine. He didn't hesitate. He simply walked right in. The first few steps were fine. No one paid him much heed. Unfortunately, when he was about halfway down the assembly line a loud buzzing alarm sounded. Michael braced himself. But instead of security taking him down, the young female workers rose in perfect order, a few giggling at him as they filed out the door, leaving the factory floor. Glancing at the clock on the wall, Michael realized that he had just witnessed a shift change. They had literally left him alone in the room without a word. Before he could fully consider why his presence had generated so little interest, his GPS beeped plaintively. Aware that the unit was accurate to at best seven feet, Michael glanced around to find what he might be looking for. Eight feet away, he saw it.

Walking the final few steps to the end of the line, Michael reached into a large open cardboard box and withdrew one of the hundreds of identical objects the morning shift had produced. The object was a Lucite sphere, perhaps four and a half inches in diameter. It sat on a black plastic base and if Michael's initial perception was correct, it was a snow globe. A snow globe which in turn contained a globe of the earth suspended in whatever solution they put in these things. The interesting thing was that when Michael picked it up, green LEDs began to light up all over the tiny enclosed globe-like phosphorescence in a frothing sea. As far as Michael could tell the LEDs glowed on every continent but Antarctica. It looked like a lot of work had gone into the object's creation. What it didn't look like was anything worth losing a father over.

The globe was unpackaged, but the next table over was stacked with elaborate boxing material that Michael briefly imagined ending up in a landfill. The globe gave Michael pause as he considered what it was his father was trying to say to him. Sending him a set of coordinates made sense. But coordinates to what? A toxic child's toy? Michael tucked the globe into his pocket before glancing around the factory floor to ensure he wasn't missing anything. He tried to find some kind of message or sign, something that would hint that he had found what he was looking for. Instead, he felt the kiss of cold steel to his throat.

8

THE SECOND THING *Michael's father taught him about was fear. Michael was six years old. There was a gully behind their house. The gully was deep and rocky and a kid had been mauled there by a mountain lion not a year before. It was a scary place. That was why the neighborhood kids dared each other to go down there. Everyday after school the bigger kids would dare the smaller ones to climb down the rock gully, close their eyes, and count to twenty. Everybody did it. Then it was Michael's turn. His mom had told him not to go down there. His dad had told him not to go down there. But the kids wanted him to go. So he climbed down the rocky trail.*

Michael closed his eyes and started to count. And he felt the fear. Because he heard something in the undergrowth. Something scary. And it was getting closer. Michael couldn't take it anymore. He opened his eyes and he started to run. But whatever it was kept right at him, charging through the undergrowth. Michael ran as fast as he could, but it wasn't fast enough. The thing caught his leg, bringing him down. Michael screamed, and when he looked back at what had captured him, he saw his father. His father didn't look mad. But he looked worried. He asked Michael if he was afraid. Michael said yes. And his father said that was a good thing. It wasn't a good thing that he had come down into the gully alone, but it was good to be afraid. Because we all got afraid, the difference was what we did with it. Some people ignored fear and those people were foolish. Because you had to respect fear. Fear gave you an edge. Fear could keep you alive.

THE MEN WORE no shoes. **The bus looked** That explained why Michael hadn't heard them coming, but not where they had come from. It also didn't excuse the fact that despite his intentions to the contrary, he had been careless. Careless and stupid. He had become so absorbed in the snow globe that he forgot to keep one eye out for trouble. There were three of them. Short sturdy Chinese men in blue jumpsuits, but Michael really couldn't determine much more than that because they held him from behind. He did note that they seemed to have little interest in harming him. At least not immediately. They seemed more interested in transport. Knife still at his throat, they hauled him to the freight elevator on the far factory wall. After a dozen grinding seconds, the elevator descended several floors down to what Michael guessed was the ground level.

The elevator doors opened and Michael immediately noted that it was much noisier in here than he had expected. For whatever reason, the equipment must have been idle when he had come in. A series of machines were at work injecting plastic into hot molds that resembled industrial-strength waffle irons. Two male workers stood over each machine, one monitoring the flow of the plastic pellets that were poured inside while another trimmed the excess plastic as the product was stamped out. His captors brought him to a standstill in front of one of the machines and Michael recognized the plastic pieces being created as the two halves of the model Earth which sat inside the snow globe he held in his pocket. Whatever they were making here, they certainly weren't trying to hide it from him. Not yet anyway.

"Good afternoon," a heavily inflected voice said from behind him. "My name is Mr. Chen."

Michael had to admit that things were looking up. Not only were they talking to him, but the blade of the knife had left his throat. At this rate they'd be sipping monkey tea and chewing chicken feet in no time.

The man who identified himself as Chen stepped into view. Chen, who looked to be about forty, wore a well-pressed suit, his carefully coiffed jet black hair glistening under the overhanging bulbs. Michael sensed nothing malevolent or otherwise frightening about the man. And the bonus was he spoke English. Michael had been caught in enough places he wasn't supposed to be to know that talking would be the best way out of the situation. It always was. But then, Chen smiled, revealing a row of crooked teeth, black with decay, and for no rational reason, a little bit of the hope Michael had felt just a moment earlier began to drain out of him.

"Who are you?" Chen asked.

"I'm a backpacker," Michael said.

"Nice to meet you, *Backpacker*."

In the next instant Michael felt his head smashed down to the deck of the injection molding machine. What had been a knife to his Adam's apple was replaced by a cold metal bar. Michael was beginning to reconsider his tactics. Perhaps a reasoned response wasn't the way to deal with these guys. But he wasn't an idiot. A break for it now would likely result in a snapped neck, so he breathed the best he could through his constricted throat, waiting for an advantage. His cheek to the metal press of the molding machine, he looked up to see the other half of the mold on its hydraulic piston. The only positive thing about the situation was that the machine wasn't turned on. That advantage was quickly stripped from him with Chen's depression of the industrial-grade switch.

"What are you doing here?"

Michael tried to respond, but found his tongue didn't work very well with his face flattened on top of the steel mold. What he got out was a mumble, barely discernible even to him.

"I said, why are you here?"

"Traveling," Michael managed to grunt out.

"Whom do you work for?"

"Nobody."

"Do you think I am a fool?"

Chen signaled his goons and they powered the metal bar down farther across Michael's throat. Michael knew that it would take only a hint more pressure to collapse his trachea; he just hoped that his aggressors knew it too. After all, if they wanted information, killing him wasn't the way to go. Of course neither was molding his face into a cheery half-globe of the Earth, but given the sudden hiss of the hydraulics above, Michael couldn't dismiss that the latter might be exactly what they had in mind.

"I said nobody, I don't work for anybody."

The hydraulic press began its descent toward Michael's face.

"Why are you here?"

"I was curious."

Chen filled Michael's entire field of vision now, his thin nose and coal black eyes boring into him from above.

"Me too," Chen said. "I am curious."

As the hydraulic press lowered, Michael's cheek suddenly stung as a drop of molten plastic hit it from above. It was now readily apparent that regardless of whether Michael could move or not, he'd have to do something if he wanted out of there alive. It didn't matter that they'd break his neck if he moved; they'd mash his head with a hydraulic press if he didn't.

"I came here," Michael said, "to find my father."

"Your father?" Chen said, leaning closer.

"What about him?"

"You tell me, American."

And Michael stole his moment. Kicking out with his outer leg despite the pressure on his throat, he arced his right leg around in a solid rotation, knowing that if he didn't drop Chen he was done for. He felt the top of his foot connect with Chen's calf and was able to follow through, sweeping him to the concrete below. Michael heard a scream and he knew the sweep had achieved what he'd hoped. Most people don't know how to fall. The natural inclination is to put your hand out to break the fall, but the inclination is wrong. If you take the full force of your body weight on your hand instead of rolling and spreading the force across your entire body, you're more than likely to break your wrist, which given Chen's scream, Michael assumed had happened. But it wasn't over yet.

He'd need to get Chen firmly under control if he was going to have any leverage with the two thugs holding him down. Fortunately, Chen fell right into the sweet spot. And even though the thugs were now hammering down on the bar hard, Michael was able to pin Chen's neck between his foot and the floor in an improvised hold.

"Let me go or I'll snap his neck."

The hydraulic press continued its slow descent, Michael increasing the pressure on Chen's neck.

"Do it. Now."

One of the goons hit the stop button on the press, and the hydraulic piston came to a standstill, the mold an inch above Michael's ear. But the bar was still there, holding him in place. Michael leaned down harder on Chen's throat, Chen finally letting out a wheezing gasp.

"Off."

The two goons warily removed the bar, allowing Michael to pull his head off the molding machine.

"Now, move over there," Michael commanded.

The goons backed away.

"Not so fast."

Michael wasn't sure where the voice had come from, but he knew it wasn't Chen's. It didn't come from the blue-suited goons either, whose arms were now extended out at either side as if to demonstrate that they were unarmed. No, the voice belonged to someone else entirely. Kate.

"Let him go, Michael."

Kate's words were steady, her semi-automatic pistol squarely covering the five of them. Chen moaned and Michael increased the pressure on his throat reflexively.

"The bastard tried to kill me."

"I said let him go."

Eyeing Kate's weapon warily, Michael eased up on his foot, relieving the pressure on Chen's windpipe. All was quiet for a long moment, Kate breathing coolly, expertly controlling the situation. Then, she aimed the pistol squarely between Michael's eyes and twisted the corners of her mouth up into an ironic smile.

"It's time you and I had a talk," she said.

9

KATE HELD THE gun to the small of Michael's back, just below the Cordura bottom of his climbing pack. She had held it there while she locked Chen and his men on the factory floor, and she held it there for the long silent cab ride back to the city. Being held at gunpoint wasn't a feeling you got used to, Michael thought, but he didn't feel as hopeless as he had as a seventeen-year-old boy back in Peru. Michael felt somehow more in control of the situation. Stronger. He reasoned that if Kate intended to shoot him, she would have done it already. No, she was after something more.

The cab pulled off the street and Kate led him into a busy back alley. The narrow corridor was lined twelve feet high with bamboo cages housing live animals of all descriptions. There were turtles and monkeys and pigs and snakes and it smelled, Michael thought, like a low rent pet store, except these animals were more likely to end up on a plate than as somebody's beloved companion. Kate prodded Michael forward past the woman slicing a bulbous, strong-smelling yellow fruit on a cart, past the man gutting a meaty corpse, and past the entrails strewn across the stained concrete. Air conditioners moaned, dripping their condensation from the high windows above, laundry fluttering on bowed lines. Kate gave no indication of where they were going or when they would get there. She didn't speak at all. She merely prodded Michael ever farther up the narrow alley until it dead ended at a weathered wooden gate.

Behind the gate was a temple. Not a monument to capitalism like the theme parks and skyscrapers Michael had encountered so far. But a genuine Buddhist temple, its traditional wooden frame and graceful curving tiled roof a reminder of life in a simpler time. Entering its high wooden door, incense hung thick in the dark air, smoky gold leaf covering the walls. The temple looked very old, but in this city there was no way to be sure. It didn't matter, though, because something about Kate's stride told Michael they weren't there for the architecture. She led him past a wall of deities where the faithful wafted their sticks of burning scent into a narrow hallway. Kate bowed her head to a young man with a shaved head and they entered a door on the left.

Once inside the room, Kate didn't stop. She continued to the rear wall where a table and a set of chairs sat. There was a microwave here and a teapot as well. The room obviously served as an informal cafeteria for the temple staff. On the wall was a glossy poster of frigid Northern land, snow glistening on pine branches. Beside it was a large white refrigerator. Pistol still firmly planted in Michael's spine, she rolled the refrigerator forward with her right hand revealing a litter of dust bunnies congregated around the base of a narrow wooden door not more than four feet high.

"Get in," Kate said.

They were the first words she'd spoken for over an hour. Michael would have preferred she'd said something else and he definitely would have preferred that she'd taken the pistol out of his back, but regardless, he still didn't think she was going to use it. No, Michael believed her when she'd said they needed to talk. He just wasn't certain he wanted to bet his life on it.

"You sure you wouldn't rather go out for a beer?"

Kate opened the narrow door. "I'm sure."

Her answer didn't really matter, because the next thing Michael knew he felt Kate's foot planted on his ass and he was tumbling forward down a steep set of stairs. He was able to roll through most of it and luckily the floor at the bottom was packed dirt, not concrete, but he was beginning to question his assessment of Kate. Maybe she was going to use the gun. Maybe she was just looking for the right place to do it.

"Get up."

Kate aimed the gun squarely down at him as she descended the stairs. Some light bled in down here, enough to let Michael know that he was in a rock-walled chamber maybe twelve feet long and half as wide. The mortar was cracking around the larger rocks, moisture seeping in and making the hard dirt floor wet. Kate flipped on a bare bulb and Michael saw that the walls were no more than head high. The chamber had been cut into the earth and around it on all sides was the raised foundation of the temple. An old apothecary chest, covered in heavy dust, sat at the far end of the tiny subterranean room, a black folding metal chair open in front of it. Other than that there was nothing. Just rock and dirt. Michael pulled off his pack.

"Sit," Kate said.

Pistol trained between his eyes, Michael sat on the cold metal chair, feeling its legs sink into the soil.

"Who are you?"

"Chase. Michael Chase."

She cocked the gun, pulling back the integrated safety trigger. Michael noted that it was a Glock. Probably a twenty-six. Definitely a problem.

"I said who are you?"

"And I told you."

"What are you doing here?"

"Like I told you the first time, I've come to find my father."

"Who's your father?"

"Alex Chase."

"How do you know Alex Chase?"

"He's my dad."

Kate looked unconvinced.

"Don't believe me? Look at me." Michael reached for the pocket of his cargo pants. "Look at this."

Kate pointed her gun. "Careful."

Michael raised one hand and slowly reached into his pocket withdrawing his wallet. He opened it up, revealing a photo of himself and his dad. It had obviously been taken several years previously. The two of them were in shorts and t-shirts, grease everywhere, arms around each other's shoulders in front of a partially disassembled Volkswagen dune buggy. They called the dune buggy the Yellow Bomber and there was no denying that they were happy, just as there was no denying the family resemblance. It was in the blue eyes, the nose, and the chin, even the way they held themselves. Michael was his father's son all over.

"Fine. Let's say you're his son. Do you know who your father was?"

"Dad? The guy who changed my diapers? The guy who brought me to the ball game? What do you want me to say?"

"You don't know, do you?"

"Look. You helped me out last night and for that I'm grateful. But the way I see it, this isn't about me, or my dad, it's about you."

"Wrong. Open the chest."

"Why?"

"Four in, third drawer down. Open it."

Michael looked at the apothecary chest. It was so covered in foundation dust, it didn't look like anybody had opened anything for a very long time. Michael counted four drawers in and three down. He pulled the wooden drawer open. It was empty.

"There's a catch inside the drawer on the top panel. Pull it."

Michael felt inside the drawer. The wood was rougher in here, unpainted, but his fingers hit something that felt like a metal spring. He pulled it and heard a click.

"Now reach around the back of the chest."

Michael did as he was instructed. He felt it immediately. A metal box had popped out of the back panel. Placing a hand on either side of the box, Michael was able to remove it, bringing it into the light. The box was dented black metal. About three inches in depth and a little longer than it was wide, it was about the size of a standard Fed Ex parcel.

"Open it."

The lid was hinged. Michael struggled to undo the hasp, but it was sticky. He had to apply some force, and then, unexpectedly, the hinged side of the lid came open, depositing the box's contents onto the ground. The first thing Michael saw was a number of passports: Swiss, Canadian, German, British, and at least three others, though Michael couldn't make out the nationalities from where he stood. There was also currency, a lot of it: bank-wrapped packets of euros, pounds, renminbi, dollars. There were what looked like some cosmetic products, some hair dye, contact lenses. And there was a gun. A Browning semi-automatic by the looks of it, its muzzle dug into the dirt.

Kate kicked the Browning aside, hunching down to collect the passports. She opened the British one up first, displaying a photo of Michael's father. He had black hair and a goatee in the shot, but there was no disputing it was him. She read the name under the photo. "Randal Harris."

She tossed the passport to Michael, and opened up the next one. It was Swiss. Here Michael's dad had a shaven head and appeared to be wearing green colored contacts. She read the name under the photo. "Jacob Stringer." She tossed Michael the Swiss passport and opened the German one. This time Michael's dad wore a blonde crew cut with a bushy mustache. "Helmuth Heimler." She tossed the final passport to Michael without opening it.

"You want to play?"

Michael stared down at the passports he now held in his hand. There was no denying that the documents were disconcerting, but he wasn't going to let Kate have the upper hand. Not if he could help it.

"Your father wasn't the man you thought he was, Michael."

"There are explanations for this."

"Name one."

"He traveled."

"With a gun?"

"Why not?"

"Unlikely your average foreign shoe salesman would risk bringing a firearm to China."

"So he picked it up here. For self-defense."

"This isn't Texas."

"No shit."

Kate shook her head. "Let me guess. He needed a few fake passports too, right? For self-defense." Kate turned her glance down to the hard-packed floor. "Remember your kidnapping back in Peru? Remember the men who did it?"

Michael stiffened. "How do you know about that?"

"Didn't you find it strange that you were a target?"

"It was opportunistic. They followed us there. For money."

"You don't think it had anything to do with who he was?"

Michael felt his blood run cold. "What do you want, lady? Answers? What about you? Who are you? Why do you care about my father?"

Kate lowered her gun, tucking the weapon behind her back. "Your father worked for the CIA. He was an intelligence operative. A spy."

Michael just laughed. "And how would you know that?"

"Because I was his partner," she said.

10

PASADENA, CALIFORNIA

Mobi Stearn loved chicken. He loved fried chicken, he loved teriyaki chicken, he loved chicken kabob, but most of all he loved Zankou chicken. Zankou was the name of a river in Lebanon, somebody's dog, and most importantly, six or seven fast food restaurants dishing out the tastiest, tangiest Lebanese-style rotisserie chicken in all of Los Angeles County. The chicken was served with Lebanese pickles, tomatoes, hummus, and a tasty garlic paste, all of which Mobi was trying his best to wrap inside an undersized pita when the call came in.

Mobi dropped his whole pita upon the shrill chirp of the phone in fear that one of his supervisors had caught him violating the "no lunch in the lab" policy again. Mobi was a communications engineer in Pasadena, California, a mid-sized city about fifteen miles northeast of Los Angeles. And though Pasadena was best known for the Rose Bowl, the Rose Parade, and associated Rose events, it was also home to NASA's Jet Propulsion Laboratory, the world leader in the robotic exploration of space.

Operated as a civilian space research facility in conjunction with the California Institute of Technology, the Jet Propulsion Laboratory, or JPL as it was known, was both a cutting edge research facility and Mobi Stearn's nine to five. Mobi enjoyed the fact that referring to his work as a nine to five was an entirely accurate description providing one heeded the caveat that he actually worked the graveyard shift between the hours of nine p.m. and five a.m. Mobi's title was Deputy to the Deputy Director of Operations. He had ground his way through the grueling PhD program at Caltech to win the job, but the reality was that most of his duties were deathly dull. His work on the current mission, as all of JPL's space flights were labeled, was to monitor unmanned spacecraft Polo's orbit of Jupiter's moon Io. At a distance of three hundred seventy-two million miles, radio communications from Polo took about fifty-two minutes to reach Earth, so Mobi was fairly certain that another half second spent wiping the grease from his hands wouldn't add up to any major damage before he answered the phone.

"Stearn," Mobi said through a mostly empty mouth.

"Mobi? I need you up here right away."

Mobi immediately recognized the voice on the other end of the line as belonging to his boss, Deputy Director Allison Alvarez. "Is this about the chicken? Because if it's about the chicken—"

"It's not about the chicken. Hurry up."

The line went dead, which Mobi considered odd for the Deputy Director Alvarez who, while ever busy, was always polite. The other thing Mobi considered odd was the fact that she was still at work at this late hour. Sure she was known to pull overtime during critical missions, but Alvarez had a family to get back to and as far as he knew JPL's current missions were running well within operational parameters, all of which led Mobi to believe that something had come up. Something that would relieve him from the boredom he too often felt in his evening vigils. And so, his curiosity piqued, Mobi picked up his square frame, wiped the tahini from his chin, and headed upstairs for what he sensed was about to become a very interesting night.

11

WHEN MICHAEL TURNED *eight his father taught him how to lie. His real birthday party wasn't until the next day, but Michael's grandmother was coming over that night for a pre-birthday dinner. Michael would have to wear the blue suit she had given him. But Michael didn't like wearing the suit. It made him look like an old man. So when his mom told him to go put it on, Michael procrastinated. He looked at his comic books. Then he played with his Star Wars stuff. And then he found a book of matches. Michael knew he wasn't supposed to play with matches, but he lit one just the same. Then he lit another one. And somewhere between the fourth and fifth match, his new Fantastic Four began to burn.*

Michael didn't even notice it at first because he was too busy pulling the suit off its hanger. But when he did see the fire, flames licking toward the curtains, he knew what he had to do. He threw his suit jacket onto the pile of comics, smothering the flame. Luckily it went out, but by that time there was a lot of smoke in the room. And his suit was ruined.

After the inevitable relief that he was okay, his parents were upset. His dad told him that he was going to learn a lesson that night. But it wasn't the lesson about not playing with fire. Instead, his dad told Michael that he was going to learn how to lie. Telling the truth was always the first choice. But it wasn't always the best choice. Because some people couldn't hear the truth. And one of those people was his grandmother. He said it would upset her very much if she found out about the fire and what had happened to the suit. If she asked Michael where it was, Michael's father asked him to say that it was at the dry cleaners. To not mention the fire. It would only worry her. Michael did as he was told. It was the first time he had lied and from what he could tell, he wasn't bad at it. He wondered if he would ever have to lie again.

"You're a spy, he's a spy, I'm a spy too," Michael said, holding his father's many passports in hand.

"Give it a rest, Michael," Kate said.

"No really, you were right the first time. I'm a spy. Went to spy school. Learned some spy stuff. We even had a spy dance. We called it the spy prom. I brought Mata Hari, super spy leader and all round hottie."

"What I'm saying is serious."

Michael met Kate's eyes. They had softened since the cab ride. Since bringing him here. "And I'm not?"

"Your dad's job," Kate said. "The way he spent so much time away from home. Did you think that was normal?"

"He traveled for work."

"But did you ever really ask your dad what exactly he did?"

"We didn't talk about that stuff."

"It's because he didn't want to lie to you. Not if he didn't have to."

"He was a businessman," Michael said. "He sold sneakers."

"That was his cover. That's all it was."

"So what are you saying then? That the man I knew, that the man who raised me wasn't who he pretended to be? That he was a spy? That the both of you worked for the Central Intelligence Agency?"

"No. He was CIA. I'm MI6," Kate said quietly.

"This just keeps getting better. Now you're telling me you were my dad's Bond girl?"

"I wouldn't put it quite like that. I'm a field operative. Your father and I were teamed up on a joint intelligence project."

"The CIA and MI6. Working together? Back at the Academy we had a name for that kind of thing."

"Michael!" Kate lowered her voice. "Enough with the bullshit, alright? The CIA and MI6 have collaborated in the past and no doubt will again in the future. It was a loose affiliation. Your father and I traveled in different circles. But we met and updated each other regularly. Shared progress reports."

"Doesn't explain your teeth."

"What about them?" Kate said, running her tongue along them for any sign of stray food.

"They're too good to be British."

"I'll take that as a compliment. I'm half British. On my mom's side. Born in London, raised outside of Chicago. Libertyville. They have dentists there."

"Where do the Cubs play?"

"Wrigley Field."

"Where do you go for drinks after the game?"

"I don't know. Murphy's? They card at Cubby Bear. At least they did when I was there."

Michael relented. He hadn't spent much time in Chicago, but he had been to a game or two and as far as he remembered it, she was right. They did card at Cubby Bear. "Okay, suppose I bite. You're a spy and he's a spy. But I'm not him. What do you want with me?"

"Pay attention," Kate said. "This is where things get interesting."

• • •

SEVERAL THOUSAND MILES away, across the Sea of Japan, a sleek black phone rang. A powerfully built Japanese man studied the caller display. His name was Hayakawa and he knew the call was not a good sign. Calls from China were never good news and as such, they could not be ignored. Hayakawa picked up the receiver.

"Hayakawa," he said gruffly.

The person on the other end of the line took a moment to respond. When he opened his mouth Hayakawa knew it was Chen.

"We had an unwelcome visitor today."

Hayakawa had expected as much. Already what had started as a pet project had gotten out of hand. He stretched out his five-foot-six frame and stared out the floor to ceiling window of the towering glass building. It was raining in Tokyo, the pedestrians lost in a sea of umbrellas on the street below. Bad tidings often accompanied the rain in Hayakawa's experience, bad tidings and a whole lot of water. Hayakawa fingered a stray strand of his longish black hair, putting it back into place behind his ear.

"Who?" he asked.

"A man. A Western man. I think it was him."

"Where is he now?"

"I do not know."

"Can you find him?"

"I will try."

There was a long moment of dead air.

"Hayakawa-san, please be patient. I will find him."

Hayakawa eyed his reflection in the window, straightening the jacket of his impeccably tailored suit. As he had suspected, the news was bad, worse in fact than he would have thought. But that was only part of the problem. The other part, he could hear in Chen's voice. The man was losing confidence. He was becoming a liability Hayakawa could not afford.

"Thank you," Hayakawa said. "We will discuss this more thoroughly at another time."

Hayakawa terminated the connection without another word. He then entered a second number he knew from memory. He let it ring once, then sat the phone back down in the cradle and waited. He only hoped that he had not already waited too long.

• • •

MICHAEL WATCHED WITH interest as Kate pulled an iPhone out of her pocket and jacked it into an Ethernet port that hung loosely from one of the floor joists above. Her Glock was safely re-holstered and she made no attempt to gather the Browning off the dirt floor. Michael couldn't tell if she was trying to foster trust in him, or if she knew the gun wasn't loaded. It didn't matter. He had come this far. He was going to listen to what she had to say.

"The head monk let your dad use the space down here. This Ethernet port is hardwired into the T4 that runs the internet café across the street. In this part of the world, it makes this connection as close to anonymous as you can get." Kate hunched down on the floor and pulled out her pistol. "As you probably figured out, the backpacker thing is a cover."

Removing the clip from her Glock, she emptied the bullets into her lap. She reached for the final bullet to fall and held it between her fingers. It was a 9mm hollow point. Standard issue. Or at least it seemed to be until Kate proceeded to unscrew its base revealing a tiny USB plug. Michael watched with interest as she plugged it into a second port on what was obviously a highly modified iPhone. A photo of a daisy came up on the iPhone's screen.

"Pretty flower," Michael said.

"You have no idea," Kate said, tapping the screen. After a few seconds, the image of the daisy began to resolve itself into the finer lines of a blueprint. "Your dad and I were here in China looking for a very specific piece of machinery. A piece of machinery dating all the way back to the Second World War."

"I'm listening."

"There's more to this than just your dad's whereabouts. If we can find your father, I hope to God he'll lead us to this."

Kate turned the iPhone's glossy screen to Michael. The image on the screen could be described simply enough.

It was an airplane. A bat-winged airplane that looked more like a modern stealth bomber than a Messerschmitt, but an airplane nonetheless. It had a wingspan of twenty meters which Michael calculated would be about sixty-five feet. What looked like jet engines were integrated into both the leading edge of the wings and vertically mounted under them, the cockpit forming a low bulb where the two wings met. The blueprint was monochromatic, and there was only the single page, no section, no schematics, but just in case there was any doubt as to who built it, each wing was adorned by a single Nazi swastika.

"You've heard of the Horten 2-29?"

"German plane, right? Didn't *National Geographic* run some kind of documentary on it?"

"The Horten 2-29 was a Nazi stealth bomber. It never went into production, but the folks over at Northrop Grumman were recently able to build a mock up of it from a surviving prototype."

"Okay. Pretty plane, but who cares?"

"This is the Horten 21. Big brother to the 2-29."

"Again. Not following."

"Hitler's people were supposed to have built as many as fourteen working Horten 21s sometime during the last years of World War II. Like the 2-29, the 21 was an experimental stealth jet. Unlike the 2-29, it was designed to be capable of speeds in excess of Mach 1 and perfect vertical takeoff and landing. They wanted to use it to drop the bomb on New York."

"The bomb?"

"Yeah. The atomic bomb."

"Brutal."

"True, but that's not what makes it interesting. The Nazis were having a hell of a time with their jet engine design. To get around this problem and still generate the thrust for vertical takeoff, the Horten 21 was equipped with two propulsion systems. Both a conventional auxiliary and a primary system that was entirely unique."

"So it was a Nazi hybrid?"

"Basically."

"Let me guess, they ran it off breakfast cereal. Soy milk and Franken Berry."

"Close. Cold fusion."

"Cold what?"

"Fusion. The Nazis were said to have pioneered a working cold fusion reactor to power their plane. Something that to this day hasn't been done in the lab, let alone in an airplane."

"Do you really want me to believe that this thing is from World War II and no advances have been made since then?"

"Believe it, don't believe it, I'm just laying it out. The Nazis were somehow able to engineer a cold fusion reactor. They figured out a way to fuse hydrogen atoms at near room temperature releasing an enormous amount of energy. The basics are that a very cool gas was introduced into a very hot reactor and the super heated gas was shot out a nozzle creating lift. How they were able to create a reliable working fusion reactor we have no idea. Nobody anywhere has been able to do anything similar since. And not for lack of trying."

"So what are you saying? The Nazis were smarter than everyone else?"

"Look. The way my people explained it to me is that a part of science, maybe not the biggest part, but a part, is luck. Who knows? Maybe the Germans got lucky. What we do know is that they incorporated the cold fusion reactor into their aircraft. The record shows two full-size, fully functional Horten 21 bombers were shipped from Nazi occupied Königsberg to their Japanese allies in Tokyo in the spring of 1945. Our guess is that they wanted the Japanese to take the war to the Pacific Coast. Knock out Los Angeles. But at that point the Japanese war effort was already on shaky ground. For whatever reason, probably because Tokyo was about to be bombed back to the Stone Age, the decision was made to hide the Horten 21 somewhere in occupied China. Long story short, your father and I have been working together for the last two years trying to find it. I'm sure the fact that he's gone missing is connected to our work, Michael. I'm breaking every rule in the book in telling you this because I think we can help each other. You knew your father and I knew what he was looking for. Together we might stand a chance."

Michael turned his attention from the screen and just stared into Kate's wide almond eyes. Finally he said, "It's crazy."

"No, Michael, it's real."

"Trust me. It's crazy."

"Why?"

"Because now I have to figure out what your long lost airplane has to do with this."

Michael reached into the pocket of his cargo shorts and withdrew the Lucite sphere he had taken from the factory. He watched Kate's eyes widen as she took hold of the clear sphere, staring intently as cosmic snow fell on the globe of the Earth within, tiny green LEDs twinkling in harmony with its rotation. In that brief moment, Michael actually felt a chill run down his spine as he watched the world he thought he knew dissolve into nothing, to be replaced by something as yet unseen.

12

THOUGH KATE HAD little idea what the snow globe might represent, they had at least reached a truce, which allowed them to pursue the one commonality in their quest so far—Chen. It didn't take a genius to see that all roads led back to him. A quick internet search cross-referencing him against Chohow Industries revealed the man's place of residence and that he was in fact president of the aforementioned company. After that, all it took was a phone call to his secretary to learn that he was unavailable because he would be at a business dinner all evening. From there it was a short cab ride to the garish, gated Mediterranean-style condominium complex Michael now found himself outside of.

The complex, located in Shenzhen's outlying farmlands, consisted of maybe fifteen five-story buildings, each containing what looked like forty units. Kate's plan was simple. Since the gate guard had a closed-circuit view of the entire compound, she needed a diversion and Michael was it. He was to show up at the front gate with his backpack and a guide book asking directions to the nearest bus station. If Michael could win her fifteen seconds away from the prying eyes of the guard, Kate could hop the wall on the highway side of the compound and put in a call for assistance from one of the outdoor security telephones that were staggered between the buildings. The guard leaving his post would give Michael an opportunity to sneak in through the front gate. The guard would then see that the call had been an error and Michael and Kate would be free to go about the business of breaking into Chen's townhouse in peace.

That was the theory. In practice Michael discovered that either guards at gated communities didn't go for backpackers or else they were extremely lonely because, upon startling the guard with a tap at the window, he immediately got on the phone. Within moments a second guard had pulled alongside Michael on a motorcycle. Michael now had two guards to contend with. But it didn't stop there. Two more guards arrived by car, then another on a bicycle. They were coming out of the woodwork and as it turned out, they weren't angry, just eager to offer him a ride to the bus station. This wouldn't happen at home, but Michael had to remind himself, he wasn't at home. He was in China. And apparently the sight of a backpacker out here in the far flung suburbs was still unique enough to cause a spectacle.

Fortunately, Kate's call on the internal security phone soon came in and all five of the guards were off to the races, checking on what might be the matter. Michael snuck into the parking lot behind them. He skirted the far wall, meeting Kate on the south side of the complex as planned.

"What took you so long?"

"Made some new friends."

Kate ignored him. "As far as I can tell Chen's condo is the one nearest to the perimeter wall, there," she said, pointing at a dark building.

"No lights, no answer on the phone, we good to go?" Michael asked.

"As good as it's going to get."

"I was kind of hoping for some spook talk. Maybe you could tell me SAT RECON is in, subject identified, target acquired, that kind of thing. Like I told you, we spies expect that kind of thing."

"This isn't a game, Michael."

"I wasn't playing."

• • •

THE TRUTH REGARDING the "sat recon," which Kate hadn't shared with Michael, was that she had attempted to contact the MI6 sub-station in Hong Kong to get precisely this information. Her highly modified iPhone contained the latest in secure satellite technology. It was a marvelous piece of personal communication equipment, equipped with such an array of electronic shielding and countermeasures that interception of its signal was thought to be impossible. Unfortunately, on attempting to dial out, Kate had been greeted with dead air, no dial tone, no static, nothing. She had assumed that sunspot activity was interfering with her transmission, but as is often the case with such things, the real explanation was more sinister.

The Chinese Bureau of Scientific Affairs had for years been working on a special project code named 411 whose stated purpose was the interception and decryption of enemy satellite communications. To date, decryption was still a complicated affair requiring both the brute force of supercomputers and the time to let them work, but interception had proven to be a solvable problem. In addition to accurately intercepting satellite transmissions, the Chinese had discovered something else. If they had a particular region under surveillance, they were able to acquire the location of the transmission, something that the users of encrypted satellite phones, unlike their common cell brethren, believed they were immune to.

It was in such a way that Chinese Ministry of State Security Captain Zu Huang caught his break. Earlier in the day Captain Huang had been tasked with ferreting out an American spy. He had been given surveillance photos taken by a security camera at Chek Lap Kok airport and a purported agenda, but little else. Huang didn't need to be told that his homeland was an enormous country and that without actionable intelligence he'd been set up to fail. It was well known that all agents were set up to fail. The system was designed to ensure that only the strong survived.

Fortunately, in addition to being strong, Huang was a very thorough man. An earlier request to monitor the Greater Shenzhen Special Economic Zone for encoded satellite transmissions had resulted in two hits. One came from a known MI6 safe house in the Lo Wu border area, but the other, which Huang had just received word of, appeared to originate from a residential development far from the center of town. It was this transmission which interested Huang because to date there was no record of the use of such a device at that locale. And though Huang had no hard proof that the American was behind the transmission, absent any other leads, he was well aware that he'd be foolish to ignore the matter. And so, without further ado, Huang hurried into his Ministry issued sedan, commanding his subordinates to follow.

• • •

An elevator carried Kate and Michael up to Chen's fifth-story apartment. Upon reaching the top floor, Kate led Michael past two doors to apartment 534. Kate knocked at the door, but as expected there was no answer. There appeared to be no peepholes in the doors, so there was little chance of being seen by a neighbor. Still, she covered her hand with her sleeve and reached up to loosen the light bulb in the wall-mounted sconce. The darkness afforded her the privacy to pull out a simple lock pick which she held between her teeth. She then handed Michael a pair of latex gloves which he stared at for a moment before pulling on. Kate followed suit, pulling on her own gloves before going to work with the lock pick, the only real sound the noise of traffic on the expressway behind them. Less than five seconds later, they were in.

It was darker inside than out. Glock in one hand, Maglite in the other, Kate immediately checked for a security system, but found none. The wall where such a keypad was generally mounted was bare. Kate then shut the door behind them leaving Michael to stare into the full height decorative mirror at the end of the corridor. Kate put a finger to her mouth and motioned with the Glock. Michael realized that she was about to clear the area and didn't presume to follow. Instead he stood at the ready, listening to Kate move through the rooms. There weren't many of them and it didn't take long.

By the time Michael had estimated that the apartment probably consisted of a galley style kitchen, living room, two bedrooms, and two baths, she was back.

"Nobody here."

"Probably why he has that big mirror. So he doesn't get lonely."

"It's a feng shui thing," Kate said. "The Chinese don't like dead ends. They trap Sha Chi."

"Sha who?"

"Sha Chi. Bad energy."

"From the vibe I'm getting the mirror didn't work."

Michael continued down the hall into the living room. Even in the shadows, everything about the place screamed bachelor pad. A shiny black leather couch did time alongside two jade end tables and a fake electric fire burning in the hearth. The walls were covered in gaudy prints, Chinese landscapes and the like, a set of beaded curtains covering what looked like a sliding glass door to the balcony. The curtains were printed in a tropical beach scene, a scantily clad woman bent longingly over a mai tai. The illustration was so evocative, Michael could have sworn that the woman was gyrating, the palms ruffling in the breeze above her. It took Michael a moment to realize that the woman actually was moving, a breeze blowing at the long strands of beads.

"I thought you checked the place."

"I did. The sliding door is locked."

"Then why's island girl hulaing?"

Kate put a finger to her lips and moved silently toward the sliding glass door, Glock at the ready. As she tried the door Michael could clearly see it was latched from the inside. Keeping her Maglite low, she flashed it outside onto the balcony, circumscribing an arc around the apartment before she stopped cold.

Kate mouthed a single word. "Window."

Michael followed the beam of light to the wall behind the couch. There was a window all right. And it was open. Michael hadn't seen it at first because it was hidden behind a printed pull down blind, but now with the breeze ruffling the blind, there was no mistaking it. It was small, probably two by two, with an oxidized aluminum frame and the screen popped out. Just the right size for a person to enter or exit the space. Michael stepped around the couch to get a closer look, but caught his toe on an obstacle in the darkness, lurching across the heavily padded floor before regaining his balance.

"Are you all right?"

Michael stared down at the floor for a long moment. "I'm fine," he finally said.

"Then what is it?"

Michael returned his gaze to the base of the couch where a familiar man lay on his side, a bullet hole in his forehead, blood draining from the exit wound onto the heavy carpeting.

"Chen," Michael said. "He's dead."

13

It wasn't the first time Michael had seen a dead man, and he was certain it wouldn't be the last, but the way Kate whipped through Chen's bedroom drawers disturbed him just the same. Chen had been a bad apple, that much was sure, but something about the situation still called out for a modicum of respect, or so Michael felt. Kate, however, was more practical in such matters. Emptying the final drawer, she moved onto the closet, sweeping the clothes within it away as if she already had an idea what she was looking for—something big.

"Did you search his pockets?"

Michael held up a car key. "No wallet, just this."

"Keep it," Kate said. "We may need it later."

"You want to tell me what it is you're looking for?"

"Your dad marked Chen as a player. The factory's coordinates confirm that. The question is why?"

Michael stepped back into the living room where the breeze continued to blow in from the open window, undulating the bead curtain girl under her plastic palm.

"Might as well be asking her," Michael said.

"Lot of good that will do."

But Kate must have thought there was something to Michael's suggestion because she opened the sliding glass door, continuing out onto the patio.

"Same as before. One slightly rusted garden set, floral table cloth, no umbrella."

Michael stepped onto the small balcony behind Kate. A metal railing enclosed the six-by-twelve-foot concrete deck. There was a gap of maybe four feet and immediately to the right sat Chen's neighbor's balcony, identical in every respect to Chen's except the end of the corridor running along the perimeter of the building sat adjacent to it. Michael peered down at the patio table. Like Kate had said, a long floral table cloth was draped over it, its legs reaching down to the concrete below, four dirty upholstered chairs pulled around. Michael turned back to the door. Then, something, he wasn't sure what, made him take a second look at the table. It was hard to see in the low light, but the surface of the table wasn't level, it was almost convex, sloping down from a higher center. Michael put his hand down on the table. He was right about the incline. You'd be hard pressed to balance a Margarita on it.

"What?" Kate said.

"Nothing," Michael replied, still staring at the table. And like that Michael lifted up, pulling the cloth up from the table like a magician revealing a cage of tigers. Only there wasn't a tiger in this cage. There was a top.

• • •

Tʜᴇ ᴏʙᴊᴇᴄᴛ sᴀᴛ cradled within the rusty patio furniture legs exactly where the table top should have been. It was a metallic capsule approximately four feet in diameter, turned out like an oversized version of the retro children's toy. The capsule had engraving around its perimeter, and a bulb at its base, again like a toy top. Except this top had obviously been exquisitely crafted out of some very expensive metal—platinum or the like. All in all, the thing sitting there between the cheap patio furniture legs was the equivalent of looking at a Ming vase in a dumpster. It just didn't fit.

"It matches the blueprint," Kate said.

"The blueprint was an airplane."

"Not all of it," Kate said.

Michael rapped the capsule lightly with his fist. It rang hollow. "Good. I'm glad that's settled. For awhile there I thought you were actually going to keep me in the loop."

Kate took a breath. "I'm not a hundred percent on this, but my best guess is it's an original scale model of the Horten's power plant—the cold fusion reactor your father and I were looking for."

"That some dead guy is using for patio furniture?"

"Like I said, I'm not a hundred percent. But I will be."

"How?"

Kate placed her fingers under the lip of the capsule and lifted. "Take an end," she said.

Uᴘᴏɴ ᴅᴇᴛᴇʀᴍɪɴɪɴɢ ᴛʜᴀᴛ the Shenzhen Riviera Condominiums were the source of the encrypted transmission, Captain Huang had had its residents run through the Ministry databases. As he suspected they had come back with a hit: a person of interest by the name Hao Chen. Huang had been an agent in China's state security agency for long enough to know that its person of interest designation could mean anything from Chen being a potential dissident to a successful capitalist to an outright spy. That information would be shared on a priority basis. Regardless, what was relevant now was that Chen was a reasonable starting point in his search for the American.

It was for this reason that Huang now stood silently outside Chen's unit. Construction drawings courtesy of Shenzhen's central planning department indicated that the only entrance and exit from Chen's inner top floor unit was the front door. To be safe, however, Huang had deployed a team to the underground garage and a team to the outdoor fire escape. He kept his two remaining men with him. Confident that the exits were covered, he now listened for any sign of movement inside the condominium. When none was found, Huang took the direct approach. He rang the bell.

MICHAEL FROZE AS the roar of an ocean wave rushed through the room. He reflected that either Chen's apartment was a lot closer to the beach than he thought or they had a problem. Following the synthesized roar to a doorbell mounted above the front door confirmed the second scenario. They now stood within a few feet of the front door, the capsule held between them. Kate lifted a hand, balancing the load which Michael estimated to be about sixty pounds on her thigh. She indicated that they should wait before proceeding forward. There was an interminable pause. And then the doorbell rang again.

Huang decided he was done announcing himself. He motioned to the two men behind him, one of whom was carrying a police issue close quarter battering ram. A single hit from the device would easily breach the exterior door. Huang's subordinate moved into position, but Huang took the compact battering ram from him. He wanted no mistakes and he trusted only himself not to make them. Huang stepped to the side of the door, preparing to throw his full eighty kilogram body weight behind the ram, his two sub-agents at the ready behind him. Then he silently counted down from three with his fingers. Huang's last finger came down, and he let loose with the ram, a loud crash echoing throughout the hall.

But Michael and Kate barely heard it. They had reversed course from the front door and were now passing the capsule over the gap to the neighboring balcony. Michael caught a glimpse of their pursuers' shadows through the beaded curtain, but had shuffled over the railing onto the next balcony before they got much closer. They shuffled over one more balcony wall and found themselves in the adjoining outer hall. Not a terribly secure way of designing a building, Michael thought, but it probably worked well for amorous couples in need of a quick escape. The outer hallway was clear and Michael found himself calculating the odds that the elevator was still on their floor. Fortunately, the math was with them and twenty seconds later they found themselves on the garage level, Kate jamming open the stainless steel face panel covering the elevator buttons with her Swiss knife.

"GET THE CAR," Kate said.

Michael hit Chen's key fob, a shiny blue and white Mini Cooper chirping back at him from the parking lot. Michael dropped his end of the capsule and strode a dozen steps, slipping into the driver's seat and cranking the engine. Chips of concrete began to explode around him before the motor even caught. It was automatic gunfire. A team of men had made it down into the garage and now held a bead on Michael from the opposite wall. Michael did the first thing that came to mind. He ducked down low in the Mini and threw it into reverse, motoring the little car backwards toward the open elevator. Michael hit the trunk release as he squealed backwards on the slickly polished concrete floor. Shots rang out, reverberating off the concrete walls one after another, but Michael refused to look up. Instead he stared straight back through the open hatch, pounding on the brakes just before impact with the elevator.

The Mini hit with a crash, buckling in the rear hatch, but Kate knew this was her moment and she took it. Stepping away from the elevator wall, she fired two carefully aimed shots, scattering Huang's men. She then picked up the metal capsule with one big hernia-inducing heave and shoved it into the rear of the Mini, diving in over it.

"Drive!"

Michael needed no further encouragement. Slamming the car into gear, he took advantage of the lull to screech around one pylon and then another and up the exit ramp. Sparks flew as the Mini's chassis bottomed out, hitting the rise to ground level at speed. There was an enormous bump, followed by the grating of metal on concrete, and like that they were out of the garage. But they weren't out of the woods. Because even as they raced past the guard gate, Michael saw their pursuers sprinting toward their vehicles. Whoever they were, they weren't giving up.

14

Michael plowed the beat-up Mini through the Chinese night with no idea where he was going, but every intention of getting there fast. Already he could see headlights gaining on them in his rearview mirror.

"Who are they?"

"By the looks of them, I'd say someone official, probably Ministry."

"Ministry of what?"

"State Security. China's CIA. Turn here."

Michael could barely see the turn off for the fields, but he responded to the cold confidence in Kate's voice with laser precision. The rear end of the Mini swung around and a second later they were flying along the rutted washboard gravel of the tiny service road. Kate didn't have to tell him to turn off the headlights. He did so instinctively, using the moon to guide him.

"Why are they after us?"

"You tell me, Sherlock. We just robbed a dead guy."

"They didn't know that."

"Look, I don't know how they found us or what they want, but it doesn't make any difference now," Kate said, staring down the road. "The airport is less than a mile north of here."

"So?"

"So punch it."

Michael hit the accelerator, actually getting air off the next rise in the dirt road. Glancing in the rearview mirror, he could see the headlights relentlessly following. Ahead, the lighted airport control tower came into view. He floored the Mini over another bump and as his head hit the roof he could just make out the blue lights of the taxiway. It looked like metal far ahead, metal glinting off the poles of a chain link fence.

They flew over another rise and now Michael was sure of it. The road dead ended in a meandering concrete drainage ditch bordered by a chain link fence, several feet of barbed wire rimming the top. On the left side of the road a gravel ramp extended to the east. It was clearly the beginning of a bridge over the drainage ditch but the forms were empty and the concrete had yet to be poured. Idle road making equipment sat in the shadows. To the right there was nothing, just the long expanse of fence and ditch, the groomed fields of the airport beyond. Michael glanced behind him. Their pursuers were still gaining. His seat belt was secured. He looked over at Kate and saw that hers was too.

"Is there a good reason we're going to that airport?"

"Staying alive is good, right?"

Michael didn't like where this was going. But he figured he'd like being perforated by bullet holes less.

So he made a choice. A choice that would have seemed insane just a short while ago. "Open your window, pull back your seat, and button up your Daisy Duke's."

"Michael," Kate said calmly. "I want you to stop the car and let me drive."

"It's not driving when your wheels leave the ground."

Michael stomped on it and the tiny blue car gave what little it had left. Michael knew that what he was about to do was not without risk. For one thing, the drainage ditch was no rut in the road. It was at least forty feet across. For another, the gravel ramp ran at a rough forty-five degree angle to the fence. It was pointing in the right direction to cross the bend in the ditch, but it was a stretch to think the little car would make it up the ramp and over the chain link. Plus, it wasn't like Evel Knievel was his uncle. Michael knew he could drive. But he had no idea if he could fly.

Short of surrendering, though, Michael didn't see a lot of options. So he hit it, hammering the gravel ramp at as oblique an angle as seemed prudent. The Mini's bumper hit first plowing through the gravel like an upended dustbin before the front wheels gained traction and dug into the dirt. It was all momentum from there. Michael would have liked to think it had something to do with skill, but at that point they were a projectile. A projectile in need of a target.

Michael wasn't sure exactly when they left the ramp behind them. He did notice that they had a good view of the airfield from up there. And then an eerie calm replaced the sound of rubber on gravel. They were airborne. But the weightless sensation didn't last long.

It was a second, maybe more, before Michael saw the glint of barbed wire in front of him. He thought they were going to clear it. He hoped that they were going to clear it. He prayed as much. But then he heard the tug of barbed wire on the grillwork as it took hold of the little car, pulling her back to Earth. And WHAM! A fraction of a second later they were plowing through the chain link as it levered downward like a too stiff shock absorber guiding them to terra firma.

The little Mini crumpled exactly where she was supposed to, front end flattening as they coughed over what was left of the fence. It was the airbags that were harder to deal with. Fortunately both he and Kate had pulled their seats way back, minimizing the impact. Michael glanced backward, but despite their brief flight there had been no discernible change in their circumstances. The headlights were still coming. Michael hit the gas, even though he could see nothing but the airbag, but the Mini's rear wheels seemed to be caught up in the mess of chain link and barbed wire. He glanced at Kate.

"You okay?"

"Never better." She tossed the hair from her face and pulled out a laser pointer which she fired at the runway in three short bursts. A hundred yards away in what had been blackness, a dim glow emanated from the cockpit of an aircraft which moved slowly toward them. "Now help me out with this thing."

Her door wouldn't open so Kate climbed out the Mini's broad open window, Michael following through his. They took hold of the capsule from the rear hatch. It appeared undamaged, but the airfield was already awash in yellow light, the racing engines of their pursuers reverberating off the plain. Fortunately, Michael now saw Kate's plan. The aircraft moving toward them was an extended frame Cessna 180, its large cargo door open. It was being towed by an air truck that disengaged its hitch as it approached. The Cessna's single prop started with a snort. Michael could hear the screeching of car brakes behind them.

"Halt!" a man cried out.

Michael might have been a novice in the world of espionage, but it was obvious that now was not the time to concede their escape. The taxiway was thirty feet off, the plane almost upon them. Michael instinctively ducked as a bullet flew past. They ran the last few strides, the capsule strung between them. As the Cessna crawled by, mere feet away, Michael and Kate heaved the capsule into the open door, diving onto the hard floor behind it.

• • •

Twenty-five feet away, Huang continued to fire his weapon at the American. The Cessna was picking up speed now, he and his men just barely over the breach in the fence. The American was getting away, but Huang was undaunted. The tow vehicle would do nicely for his purposes. As the tow vehicle turned about, fresh from releasing the small aircraft, Huang strode toward it, gun in hand. His men continued to fire at the plane, the driver of the tow vehicle stopping and raising his hands in surrender. Huang pushed the driver aside and took the wheel of the open vehicle, popping its tired clutch and aiming it for the Cessna as it turned onto the runway.

Huang clicked his seat belt on, recognizing that what he had to do wouldn't be pretty, but it would be effective. He only hoped his men had the sense to stop firing when they saw him coming. Speeding across the runway toward the Cessna, Huang zeroed in on the plane with the heavy tow vehicle. Certain that the only way to end things was to keep going, he broadsided the light plane squarely behind the wing. The blow was enough to send the plane cartwheeling up onto its far wing. The Cessna did one complete rotation, its propeller digging into the earth. It then continued around, vaulting upwards in a second cartwheel until finally, its kinetic energy spent, it hung there for a long moment, wing tip reaching for the sky, before crashing back down to Earth.

Huang jumped off the tow vehicle, his pistol at the ready. All was quiet now, the plane's engine silent as he advanced cautiously ahead. The left wing of the aircraft was twisted off at an unnatural angle. The American would be in rough shape, but he would be alive. Huang covered the area cautiously, his men picking up the cue and advancing behind him. Huang saw the pilot, unconscious, still strapped into his seat. Huang continued to sweep the aircraft with his pistol. He knew the American would be in the cargo area, possibly unconscious and most definitely injured. And he knew that an injured, cornered animal was the most dangerous of all. So when Huang finally swept his pistol into the open cargo area, he was prepared for a fight. What he wasn't prepared for was what he found—namely nothing at all. The fuselage was still essentially intact, but the American, his companion, and the object that they had been carrying were nowhere to be seen. Huang carefully examined the cargo bay, but wherever the American was, he wasn't there. He was gone.

15

JET PROPULSION LABORATORIES, CALIFORNIA

MOBI HADN'T KNOWN what to expect when he left his post in JPL's main control room to take the short flight of steps up to the Director's office—a reprimand maybe for clocking in late that evening, perhaps a complaint about the chicken, maybe even some gentle ribbing about his alma mater, Caltech, from Deputy Director Alvarez, a dyed-in-the-wool MIT grad. What he didn't expect was an audience with what appeared to be a highly decorated Air Force colonel. After all, JPL was a civilian institution. The closest Mobi had gotten to the military was a recruitment commercial, the kind with swooping jets and lots of talk about teamwork. The confusion must have been readily apparent in Mobi's eye because Alvarez quickly filled him in.

"Colonel Rand is the ranking official from Air Force Space Command. He's been sent here because he requires our help on a project."

"Good evening," Mobi searched for the correct salutation, "Colonel."

"Mr. Stearn."

Mobi looked like he was about to say something, but then stopped.

"Question?" Rand asked.

"It's nothing," Mobi said.

"I'd say it's something, or you wouldn't be standing there with your mouth half open."

"I have a good memory, sir, and I seem to remember you. Are you the same Colonel Rand who was detained by the Chinese government on Hainan Island after your spy plane was escorted down?"

"I was a major back then, but yes, that's me."

"Wow. Didn't they hold you for like five days?"

"Six if you include the night I got there."

"What was that like?"

"A major international incident," Rand said. "I really can't comment beyond that."

Mobi looked like he was about to say something else but stopped himself, instead staring at the silver eagle on Rand's uniform.

"You want to discuss fashion now?"

"No, sir."

"Spit it out."

"Not to fly my freak flag too high, Colonel, but we fly civilian missions here."

Alvarez took control of the situation. "So we do," she said. "But lest you forget, the lab also receives a significant portion of its funding from the Department of Defense, and as such we've always remained open to their needs, just as they've been open to ours." Alvarez was using her soft voice, and though she was in no way a hard-edged woman, Mobi knew that soft voice meant one thing: that there were outsiders in their midst and he'd better listen. "Colonel Rand, would you like to take it from here?"

Rand didn't mince his words. "Can I assume Mr. Stearn has security clearance?"

"Class Two Civilian," Alvarez said.

"Then let's get to it. Being in your line of work you no doubt know that the Germans had a number of unique aircraft in development during Word War II."

"Sure, the V2 rocket, the Heinkel He 178 jet, any number of the Horten brothers' designs," Mobi said.

"So you're aware that the V2 rocket was the predecessor to every ICBM on the planet. You know the Heinkel He 178 was the world's first jet aircraft. What do you know about the Hortens?"

"I'm a communication engineer, not an aircraft historian."

"I didn't ask you what you did for a living."

Mobi cast a glance at Alvarez. Her look told him to play nice. "The Horten Ho 2-29 was the world's first stealth aircraft. The Horten 18, a larger version of the 2-29, was a long range bomber. The Nazis probably would have won the war if they'd been able to get either one of them into production in time."

"Good. Now what you might not know is that the Germans are also said to have invented a number of lesser known technologies."

Mobi was quiet for a long moment. "You're talking about the 21."

"So you do know something."

"The Horten 21 was built on the 2-29's basic design. It was larger with an aluminum skin, but the big difference was the power source. It was supposed to contain a working low energy nuclear reactor—the holy grail of nuclear design—cold fusion."

"That's right. Cold fusion. Anything else you'd like to add, Mr. Stearn?"

"Yeah. Nobody's ever been able to confirm the existence of the 21. And not because they didn't try. Project Paperclip was launched by the OSS after the war to, among other things, get to the bottom of what exactly the Nazis might have done with the prototypes. They came up with nothing. Nada. As far as the official record stands, the Horten 21 was never built."

"It's a good analysis, but not quite accurate," Rand said.

"What did I miss?"

Rand's lips curled into a crooked smile. But there was nothing nice about it. It was a smile designed to prove a point. "You missed the little detail about one of these Nazi birds being found. Approximately five years ago, a heavily corroded Horten 21 was pulled from a Chinese rice paddy. By the time officials got to it, the locals had melted most of it down for scrap metal, but the reactor and communications systems were still intact."

Mobi let out a slow breath. "I knew it. You guys have got one, don't you? Where is it? Nellis? Edwards?"

"No. In spite of our best efforts, we don't have a 21, Mr. Stearn."

"Then what are you saying?"

"They have one. An unmanned Chinese satellite incorporating what our experts believe to be a working model of the Horten's cold fusion reactor was launched into orbit twenty-six hours ago."

Unable to contain himself, Mobi jumped up from his chair. "Awesome. What can I say? This is just awesome."

"It's not entirely awesome, Mr. Stearn."

"Which part? The part about cold fusion being the answer to the world's energy crisis? The part about not having to burn oil anymore? Or the part about no nasty radioactive waste like you get out of nuclear fission?" Mobi threw his hands into the air. "Which part of this equation could not possibly be awesome?"

"The part about the Chinese having lost control of their satellite," Alvarez said.

"Lost control?" Mobi asked, "As in dead in the air?"

This time Rand made no effort to disguise his smug superiority. "As in the Chinese bird is on a collision course with Earth. Unless we can do something about it, your totally awesome cold fusion reactor is about to blow a whole lot of people all the way to hell."

16

One day Michael got home from school early. He must have been in the fifth or sixth grade. His dad had just gotten back from one of his trips and he had a gift for him. It was a little woven bamboo tube called a Chinese Finger Puzzle. The trick was, you stuck a finger into either end of the little woven tube and you pulled. The tube grabbed your fingers and wouldn't let go. The more you pulled, the tighter it grabbed. The only way to get your fingers out was to go in the opposite direction. To push them together so that the little tube squished back down and widened, finally letting your fingers out. Michael played with the finger puzzle for weeks after that until finally it broke. It was fun while it lasted, though. And it taught Michael an important lesson. Sometimes to move forward, you needed to take a step back.

Michael wasn't accustomed to Houdini acts. But a Houdini act was apparently what Kate had planned for them from the start. From the moment their bodies hit the hard aluminum floor of the Cessna, Kate made it clear that

Michael shouldn't get too comfortable. As soon as the plane began its slow arc onto the runway, Kate pulled Michael back to his feet, beckoning him to lift his end of the capsule. Before Michael could ask why, a second shot had hit the cowling of the aircraft. Deciding he might live a longer life off the plane than on it, Michael picked up his end of the load and followed Kate out the far cargo door. Using the Cessna as cover, they made their way across two taxi ways to an ancient propeller-driven DC3 revving for takeoff.

A quick heave of the capsule later and they were through the DC3's open cargo door. It only took another moment for their pursuers to sideswipe the Cessna, but by that time the DC3's wheels had left the ground. Examining their current conveyance, Michael had to wonder if taking a bullet might not have been a better option. The old DC3's cabin was no more than a bare shell, hay swirling in the heavy breeze. There was a crate of pigs at the back and a hole in the fuselage where the cargo door should have been. A manufacturer's plate mounted above the hole indicated that the aircraft dated back to 1942. Michael was about to hazard a guess as to how often it had been serviced since then, when the logical half of his brain told him to stop. If the plane was good enough for the pigs, it would have to be good enough for him.

"Hand me the cargo net!" Kate shouted over the wind.

Michael looked up at the canvas cargo net he held with one hand. He released it from a tie bracket and handed it to Kate, careful to avoid the open door as they secured the capsule in place.

"Good. Now follow me."

Michael followed Kate toward the cockpit, moonlit clouds visible through the open door below. When they reached the cockpit Michael was surprised to discover that he could see the stars through an open escape hatch in the top of the fuselage. There was a single pilot at the controls. He was Chinese, maybe thirty years old and solidly built, and he seemed to know Kate.

"Almost didn't make it," he said in passable English.

Kate responded in Cantonese, then added, "I've brought a friend."

The pilot turned his head to Michael and smiled. Michael smiled back, but his grin faltered as his glance wandered over the pilot's muscular neck. There was a tattoo inked there: a disturbingly familiar image of a lone tiger wrestling a snake.

"Everything okay?" Kate asked.

Everything was all right, Michael thought. Everything was just fine other than the fact that he might be totally screwed. Because Michael had seen the pilot's tattoo before. It was the same tattooed tiger and snake worn by their attacker at Chungking Mansions. There was no mistaking it. Like Zebra before him, the pilot belonged to one of Hong Kong's oldest and most brutal Triads. He was a Tiger Snake Boy.

"Kate?"

"Yeah?"

"Can I see you for a second?"

Kate looked to Michael, then followed him out of the cockpit. Once they were out of earshot, Michael got to the point.

"That guy is Triad."

"I'm a quarter Welsh."

"The guy who murdered Larry was Triad."

Wind whipped at Kate's face through the open cargo door. "Look, I know how this looks."

"Do you?"

"It's like this. The pilot is a private contractor. Contracted by my government to provide a service. He no doubt doesn't know who we are, and I don't want to know who he is. It's cleaner that way."

"You're telling me you didn't know who he was?"

"I'm telling you all I did was put in a call for an extraction. I'm NOC. I'm operating under non official cover, get it? Six contracts out my support to the locals. This is Tiger Snake Boy territory. Of course they're going to get the gig."

Michael considered her words. He wanted to believe her. But he wanted to know the truth more. And with Kate, he sensed, there was one way to be sure. Physically. In one deft move Michael rotated his hips and swept Kate's legs out from under her. Unlike Chen, Kate knew how to roll. But she had to expose her back to Michael for a fraction of a second to do so. And that fraction of a second was all it took for Michael to disarm her. Michael had done take down weapons training in his martial arts days. Everybody had. But it was only after his abduction in Peru that he had taken it seriously. Michael regarded it as a personal failure that the kidnappers had been able to abduct him. It was the beginning of the most horrific experience in his life and after rescue had finally come, he had vowed never to allow something like it to happen again. Not ever.

Michael tossed Kate's Glock to the rear of the plane and followed through with an improvised head lock, holding her neck firmly between his forearm and the floor. It was more of a judo style move, but it made the point.

"Jesus Christ," Kate moaned. "How the hell did you learn how to do that?"

"My father. Same guy who taught me that the gun you were carrying is a Glock 26 with a five-and-a-half-pound trigger and a ten round magazine. Same guy who said if I'm in downtown Seattle and I see a guy with shiny shoes and a snake crawling down his neck, I should probably keep my distance. Same guy I came here to find."

Michael adjusted his position. His right forearm barred over her neck, her head in the crook of his left arm. He straddled her, a leg on either side of her torso. It was a submission hold from which she could not likely escape. Not if she wanted to keep her head attached to her neck. "Now I have some questions. Some simple questions and I need you to answer them truthfully."

Kate lay absolutely still. "Shoot."

"Why did you follow me?"

Michael looked Kate directly in the eye. Straddling her like that, feeling her heart beat below him, he was close, close enough to feel her breath on his face. And as much as this was all about business, he liked holding her tight. He liked it a lot.

"I told you. I was your father's partner. I want to find him as much as you."

"The pilot. You know him."

"He's done one other pick up for me before. That's it. Luck of the draw."

Michael thought about it. "Okay, fine." He adjusted his position bringing himself even closer, his forearm bearing down just a little harder. Hard enough to make her think about her next answer. "You want to find my father and the pilot thing is a fluke." Michael torqued Kate's head to the side with his left arm just enough to remind her that he was in control. He eyed the capsule. "What," he said, "is that? And don't give me any shit about you not being sure. I saw your eyes light up when I found it. You know exactly what it is."

Kate coughed. "The capsule is a marker," she said. "In addition to the two full-size Hortens hidden somewhere in China, two metal capsules were engraved with relevant information as to their whereabouts. We think the idea was that should the location of the Horten aircraft ever become lost due to the misplacement or destruction of documents, these capsules could fill the gap. Engravings of regional topography would lead the bearer to the Horten's hiding spot. Flash forward six decades. A badly damaged Horten was located by two Chinese farmers approximately five years ago. They found it with the help of a capsule marker like this one."

"So what you're saying is, this saucer thing is going to lead you to the second Horten. The one my father was supposedly looking for? The one they haven't found yet?"

"I certainly hope so."

"Makes sense," Michael said. "So why do you need me?"

"What do you want me to tell you? You're a resource, Michael. You know your father. You know how he thinks. With your help I'll have a better chance of getting this done. And like it or not, it works for you too. Finding the Horten is your best chance of finding your dad. I want your help to find the both of them."

Michael was quiet for a long time. The roar of wind in the fuselage seemed to have lessened, but more than likely he had simply grown inured to its pounding. He released his hold on Kate and got up, offering her his hand. Kate took it, cracking her neck as she did so. Then she rose, straightening her blouse before looking Michael in the eye.

"You owed me for that little shove I gave you back at the temple, so I guess we're even, but make no mistake. If you ever, and I mean ever, pull something like that again, I will not take it lying down. Understood?"

"Lie to me again and I won't be so friendly. Sound fair?"

"Perfectly."

Michael reached down and handed Kate back her gun. "Now, where in sweet China are we going?"

Kate smiled. "I'm so glad you asked."

17

SOMEWHERE IN RURAL GUANGXI PROVINCE

THE BLACK LIMOUSINE traveled swiftly through the night, its armor-plated panels designed to provide the ultimate in peace of mind to the occupant within. Yet despite the safety features of his executive transport, Li Tung felt a growing constriction in his chest, a constriction he hadn't felt in the entire length of his seventy-six-year criminal career. Li was concerned. One of his key men had just informed him that the pick up at the Shenzhen airfield had been successful, but barely so. The decoy pilot had been hospitalized and would surely be interrogated if he could not be pried from the Ministry's grasp. The MSS was close behind, closer than they had planned, and Li knew there was too much at stake for events not to unfold exactly as scheduled. But these thoughts would have to wait. The limo had slowed, turning onto a wide shoulder on the side of the road. As the car stopped, Li could just make out the dim outline of a single tractor-trailer in the moonlight. Li thought to himself that, regardless of the outcome, the mission was bigger than just him now. It had begun.

• • •

THE AIRFIELD WAS little more than a dirt strip beside a country road. There were a few old burnt out military planes and a couple slightly more modern private aircraft, but it was dark and difficult to see much else. Whatever the case, this was no Chek Lap Kok. Air traffic control was no more than a guard at a windsock. Absent a set of stairs, Michael and Kate leapt the few feet down from the open cargo hold to the dirt runway below. Pulling the capsule out behind them, they carried it several paces in silence without drawing any attention, not even from the lone guard.

"Where are we?"

"Guangxi Province. Four hundred miles northwest of Shenzhen."

Ahead was a ten by ten concrete block shed locked down by a beat-up metal roller door. An outdoor lamp buzzing with insects and the high hum of electricity provided the only illumination. There was a well-used payphone bolted to the side of the building, but little else; no people, no vehicles, not a single sign to remind Michael they were standing in the heart of the most populous country on Earth. A one-yuan coin in hand, Kate lifted the receiver of the phone.

"What are you doing?"

"Calling a cab."

Michael placed a finger on the phone, cutting off the line, the open dial tone just audible above the buzz.

"I need to make a call first," he said.

"Hold on," Kate said. "We call a cab, we can get out of here. We start calling across the country, it's going to attract attention."

"Like the attention you brought down on us?"

Kate was silent.

"No more lies, remember? They knew we were at Chen's."

"Okay. I put in a call to Six before we broke into his apartment. But my line was at least supposed to be secure. If that was the Ministry behind us, you don't think they've got fifteen supercomputers filtering for our voice prints right now?"

"I'll be quick," Michael said, dropping Kate's coin into the phone.

· · ·

TED FAIRFIELD WAS anxious. His evening the night before had been everything he had expected under the circumstances and more. The police had rounded up and questioned everyone at the restaurant keeping him at the Yau Ma Tei police station well into the next morning. Ted was surprised by both the speed and zeal of the police response given that the incident had occurred at Chungking, but when he learned that a fully vested Triad member was also a victim, their interest made sense. Their concern was no doubt part of an ongoing investigation into the gang's hierarchy rather than any sense of duty to maintain law and order in Chungking.

Ted's anxiety, however, was not a manifestation of the previous evening's events. He was worried about Michael. Prior to Michael's arrival in Hong Kong, they had made a clear plan to meet at 9:00 p.m. the next night at the Forum hotel in Shenzhen. Besides being a favorite of Ted's, it would allow Michael a gentle introduction to the People's Republic. Ted was well aware that Michael had experienced adversity in the past. His experience had changed him, hardened him to the point that Ted was fairly certain that Michael was quite capable of looking after himself wherever he was. But Ted also knew that this was China. And China presented its own set of challenges.

So far, however, Michael hadn't shown up and as things stood it didn't look like he was going to. Ted's rendezvous with Michael had been very specific. If he couldn't make the meeting, he was to place a call to the payphone outside the barbershop adjacent to the hotel. That the barbershop was really a brothel disguising its trade with a cheap façade and a striped pole made little difference. It was nearly five hours later and there had still been no call. Ted was about to give up when the brothel's wizened Madame, with whom he had been sharing the payphone, handed him the line.

"Where have you been?" Ted said.

"Seven-seven-seven," Michael replied.

"Are you sure?"

"Seven-seven-seven."

And the line went dead. Ted cursed to himself and handed the phone back to the tired Madame.

"Thank you," he said in flawless Cantonese.

Seven-seven-seven. Screw the budget, Ted thought. Screw the backpackers too. He'd been seated ramrod straight in a cracked plastic chair listening to tired prostitutes squeal about how cheap their johns were for the last five hours. All things being equal, he intended to spend what was left of the night dead to the world on a clean firm mattress. Ted dragged his weary bones into the expansive lobby of the Forum hotel and within five minutes he was headed up the glass elevator to his room. He couldn't be happier to be done for the evening.

• • •

COOL BREEZE IN his hair, cab speeding through the night, Michael had to admit that life, for the moment at least, was good. They had been traveling along the same rutted road for over an hour now and though the taxi driver was short on conversation, he apparently had a limitless supply of ice cold Tsingtao Lager. And though perhaps problematic in the way of safety, the beer was such a balm to Michael's parched throat that he chose not to over think the matter. Outside, bicycle rickshaws pulled their massive loads, men played cards under lantern light, and whole families gathered around cooking fires, dark mountains looming in the distance above. Even the air out here in the country smelled sweeter, somehow more primal than Michael remembered it being just a few hours earlier.

"Pull?" Michael asked, offering Kate the tall bottle.

"Seven-seven-seven?"

Michael passed Kate the beer as he pulled the *Lonely Planet Guide* from the top flap of his backpack. He turned to page 777, reading from the page, "Yangshuo, ninety minutes south of Guilin. That's where we're headed, right?"

"Right."

"So Ted kind of feels responsible for me over here. I promised I'd keep him in the loop."

"Is that it?"

"That's it."

"Good."

Less than ten minutes later, the cab turned in front of a group of structures built at an intersection in the road. A few hundred yards more and they came to a stop before a timber frame building identifying itself as the Whispering Bamboo Backpacker's Hostel.

• • •

FOUR TIME ZONES away, Hayakawa stared down from his walnut-paneled boardroom into the early morning streets of Tokyo's Shinjuku district below. A second phone call had arrived. It indicated that a Chinese cargo plane had deviated from its prescribed flight path, landing in Guangxi Province. The deviation was recorded and per procedure, the MSS was notified. Twenty-six minutes later two individuals meeting the profile boarded a taxi bound for Yangshuo. Hayakawa had not thanked the caller. He had simply replaced the phone in its cradle and considered the content of the call.

This time, Hayakawa thought, there was a real chance that the object would be found. And that was not something he could allow to happen. Not now that they were so close to their goal. Hayakawa exhaled slowly, reminding himself that he was more than simply the CEO of one of Japan's leading heavy industries. He was the leader of an even older consortium. His father before him had also been leader of this consortium. And his ancestors before that had been samurai. And so, like all good samurai, Hayakawa reflected that rising stakes served only to make the victory sweeter. Preparations had been made. The course had been set. All that was left now was to follow through.

18

YANGSHUO

SOFT MORNING SUNLIGHT filtered in through the slatted window, but Michael's mind was on his aching back. His bed for the night had been about as comfortable as a wood pile. On the plus side the spartan room was clean, but it wasn't much consolation for his sore spine. He gazed across the gap to the second single bed. It was empty, indicating that Kate had already gotten up. Time to rise. Michael pulled his legs out of his sleeping bag and threw them over the side of the bed.

"Ow!" Kate moaned as he stepped on her sleeping bag-shrouded form.

"What are you doing on the floor?"

"It's more comfortable than that bed. What time is it?"

Michael glanced at the watch on his wrist to discover that he hadn't reset it since leaving Seattle.

"I'm thinking breakfast time."

"Sounds like a plan."

• • •

Michael's body was sore but his spirit was rested, and after throwing a sheet over the capsule and securing the door of the room with a padlock, they stumbled down the chipped stone steps and into the new day. A few early rising backpackers were already out and about and one thing was clear to Michael: he had stepped into a new world, a world he could have scarcely imagined existed if he wasn't standing smack dab in the middle of it. What had been shadows in the dark night, had now, under the magic light of day been transformed into mountainous green hills. But they weren't ordinary hills. They were jutting vertical towers that popped out of the landscape in all directions like a gang of angry gum drops; soaring dollops of vegetation-encrusted earth that would look more at home in middle earth than modern day China. And at the end of the street, a magnificent river glistened jade green in the morning light, the same crazy hills rising from its loamy banks, fishing boats crowded around a tiny pier. It was a scene right out of Wonderland.

"Like the landscape?" Kate asked.

"Yeah, it's so—"

"Surreal?" Kate said.

"Sugarcoated. The mountains look like, I don't know, emerald-green cotton candy."

"They call them karsts. But, yeah, this place has that effect on people."

Michael soon discovered that in addition to its spectacular limestone karsts, Yangshuo was known for a second attribute, its food. Or to put it more specifically:

the best Western food east of Bangkok. Teahouse after teahouse advertised banana pancakes, Western omelets and grilled cheese sandwiches, all to be consumed under the mellowing influence of Bob Marley, the Eagles and a hundred other old-school acts. Michael and Kate wasted no time stepping onto the veranda of a tea house named Yangshuo Bob's and sinking into its richly padded bamboo furniture. Almost immediately a young Chinese hostess appeared with two hand-drawn menus. Kate didn't need to look at hers.

"Tell Bob I'll go for the muesli. And a large milk coffee." Kate looked to Michael. "The banana pancakes are famous in forty countries."

"And a banana pancake," Michael said. "And another coffee."

Michael felt briefly self-conscious of the fact that he had been in China for thirty-six hours and had yet to eat a meal of actual Chinese food, but he let it go. If there was one thing Michael knew, it was that the most expeditious route between two points didn't always involve a straight line. More often than not you had to roll with what came. The hostess smiled and returned a few moments later with two steaming mugs of coffee and Kate's muesli. Apparently the banana pancake was going to take a few more minutes, but Michael didn't care. His attention was focused on the street outside where vendors had set up their carts selling everything from vegetables to Hollywood movies. Alongside them backpackers of every ilk, some worn from travel, others spiffy clean in their Gore-Tex caps and Northface cargo shorts, crawled out of their guest houses to life. Like a slow wave, the teahouses up and down the street filled with them, a displaced expatriate community who had found a common home, at least for the moment, in this storybook corner of China.

"You look confused," Kate said.

"Let's go with curious."

"Curious then."

"It's nothing, it's just that, when you said this place was on the Circuit, I didn't expect it to be so..." Michael struggled to find the right word, "...*on the Circuit.*"

"They come from everywhere. The year before college. The year after college. The year before grad school. In between jobs. In the UK they call it a gap year. I forget what you guys call it."

"Slacking off?" Michael said. "And believe me, I know. Since college I've done two tours of duty at Starbucks with a stab at Internet entrepreneurship wedged between mystery shopper gigs. When it comes to the art of the slack, I'm a master."

"So would you prefer people laze about locally? Contribute to their hometown angst instead of traipsing off to the far corners of the Earth?"

"No. Nothing like that. Don't get me wrong. I've got no problem with seeing the world. I just didn't realize the whole world was doing it."

Michael's banana pancake arrived, succulent pieces of fried banana poking their heads out of the lightly fried batter, a swirl of whip cream with blueberries on the top. Michael wasted no time digging in, pausing long enough between mouthfuls to say, "Damn that's good." What he didn't expect was a heavily accented reply in return.

"Yes, they are very tasty."

Michael looked up from his pancake at an attractive young Chinese woman with a friendly face, a wide-brimmed straw hat covering her head. She wore sandals and stained blue trousers, a man's white shirt covering her torso and a devil may care glimmer in her eye.

"My name is Ester," the woman continued. "May I be your guide today?"

19

Ester turned out to be a college student studying in nearby Guilin who worked as a guide in her native Yangshuo on break. After some quiet back and forth, Michael had agreed with Kate that a local might just be of some help, especially if they were looking for a particular peak as the engravings on the rim of the capsule suggested. So, after finishing their breakfast, Michael and Kate returned to the hostel where they examined the inscriptions. Looking at the capsule now, Michael admired the finely cut beauty of its craftsmanship. Though it appeared to be no more than a shell, the karst-shaped engravings had obviously been etched by the hand of a master metal worker.

After carefully photographing the engravings, they took the precaution of hiding the capsule. After a few minutes searching, a spot was found under the cowling of a disconnected metal swamp fan on the building's roof. The metal enclosure had a rusty hasp which Kate then secured with another padlock. It wouldn't stop anyone who actually knew where to look, but Michael thought it was about as good a hiding place as they would find under the circumstances. From there they joined Ester at a bicycle stall in the street below. She had already arranged for the rental of a pair of well-used mountain bikes and within moments they were pedaling after her up West Street and into the countryside beyond.

Green limestone karsts towered above them as they followed Ester's squeaky bicycle down the narrow dirt berm between rice paddies. Here, in the country, people practiced agriculture as generations had before them. The rice, green in flooded mud flats, was still planted seedling by seedling, and it still needed to be tended by men and women standing up to their thighs in muddy ooze. There was the odd nod to modern contrivance here and there: one man rode what looked like a paddlewheel equipped tricycle in the mud; another wore a "Nirvana" t-shirt, Kurt Cobain's mug peering up from the rice shoots, but all in all, this pocket of paradise offered no hint of the modernity that lay just beyond its dew drop gates. It was a timeless China, a place of such serene bucolic wonder that it almost seemed self-evident that the weight of the world had never touched it and never would. Michael silently reminded himself that every place, no matter how beautiful, had its secrets, and it was the pursuit of those secrets that had led him here.

With this in mind, Michael forced his mind back to the inscriptions rimming the capsule. Though varied in shape and appearance, they consistently returned to the motif of what looked like a broken horn, or in the lexicon of the regional topography: a crooked limestone karst. Of the sixteen engravings, the image of the crooked karst was repeated four times and for that reason, both Michael and Kate had agreed it was as good a place to start looking as any. Kate had shown Ester a digital photo of one of the engravings and Ester had vowed to take them there. It had been that simple.

Regardless, even with a one-stop destination, Ester apparently had too much of the tour guide in her system to completely shirk her duties. She happily pointed out the sights along the way. There was the Moon Hill, a karst with a perfectly round opening naturally occurring at its peak. Not far beyond it was an ancient carved wooden bridge where the villagers were said to catch magical fish. Then came a cave spawning a tale of a hidden jade Buddha, followed by a bend in the stream that was once home to a nesting dragon right out of the Chinese Brothers Grimm. Michael was convinced that the next sight would involve three Panda bears, porridge, and a hungry girl with long golden hair lost in the forest. Instead, Ester simply dismounted her bicycle.

Ester said, "This is the place."

Michael immediately looked up. He saw it right away. They had stopped in a shadow at the base of what looked to be a crooked karst. It wasn't a perfect match to the inscription, but it wasn't unlike it either and Michael reasoned that the next thing to do would be to thoroughly search the area. He thought Kate could accompany him and perhaps Ester could watch the bikes, but before he could articulate his plan, Ester began to speak.

"I knew this crooked mountain from long ago. This is the place my mother lived."

It was then that Michael noticed several grave stones marking the sight, a tiny entrance to what appeared to be a limestone cave, visible through the thick foliage. A small brook ran close to the path here and Michael noticed that the karst, covered in emerald-green trees, rose so steeply that standing in the shadow at its base as they were, the mountain was more like a skyscraper than any kind of natural formation. Once Michael had laid his bike in the grass, Ester continued.

"When my mother was a small girl the Japanese soldiers came to our village. The soldiers were not good men. They gathered the men from the village to work on the railroad. The women, they made to work in the lady's trade in Guilin. Do you know the lady's trade? How do you say it, the brothel?"

"Yes," Kate said. "The brothel."

"My grandfather and grandmother brought my mother here to hide from them. They hid here in the caves inside this mountain for many weeks. Grandfather fished from this river and Grandmother brought water from those stones. They all lived in a cave, but for my mother, life was good."

Kate smiled and Ester continued.

"Then the Japanese colonel came. He was relaxing, taking his vacation in our Yangshuo mountains and he saw my grandfather catching fish. He knew that all the men were brought to Guilin, so he knew my grandfather could not be here. This made the Japanese colonel very angry. He threatened to shoot my grandfather with his pistol. Then he saw my grandmother."

Ester looked away.

"My grandmother had told my mother to stay very still in the cave. But the inside of the cave had many tunnels. My mother climbed to the top of this mountain to see why my grandmother had gone outside." Ester pointed to a crag up the hill, an opening just visible in the cliff above. "She did not hear what my grandmother said to the colonel, but the next moment there was a loud bang and my grandfather fell backwards into the stream. The colonel took my grandmother by her long hair and led her away. My mother never saw her again."

Kate moved in and hugged Ester warmly, even as Michael stood inert, caught in the awkward zone between empathy for Ester's plight and intimacy with a total stranger. Michael was, after all, no stranger to pain. He had lost, or at least he had thought he'd lost a father. Now he wasn't so sure, but it didn't mean he didn't know Ester's suffering. He may well have known it better than Kate. But that was beside the point. They had found what appeared to be the crooked karst. It was time to dig deeper.

20

Mobi's excitement at the launch of the Chinese spacecraft had quickly morphed into something more closely approximating terror. Because the sky was falling. Literally. For reasons known only to the Chinese, the satellite had been launched into geosynchronous orbit above the continental USA. And that orbit was degrading. Rapidly. Alvarez told him that within hours after the launch it had become evident that the Chinese had lost control of their bird. There was chatter amongst the usual sources. There was a conspicuous silence on the diplomatic front. And perhaps most importantly, there was evidence, hard evidence from the Goldstone deep space antennae array, that the object was slowly but surely moving closer to Earth. At its current rate of orbital decay it would violently reenter the atmosphere within forty-six hours. How the cold fusion reactor would behave under the stresses of reentry was anybody's guess. It might go pop or it might incinerate a city.

To compound the problem, it wasn't just the cold fusion issue that had Mobi concerned. The Chinese satellite was also believed to contain a secondary power source consisting of an isothermal coil and one hundred thirteen kilograms of enriched plutonium. True, these were only the Department of Defense's estimates of what the satellite had onboard, but if they were even close to correct, an uncontrolled reentry into the Earth's atmosphere would magnify the disaster.

The icing on the cake as far as Mobi was concerned was that it had been made very clear to him that he was to tell no one and do nothing until he received further instruction. And that's where Mobi drew the line. As far as he was concerned, Rand and Alvarez were the ones who had brought him into the loop. If they'd wanted someone to do nothing, they should have gotten another engineer.

Given Mobi's familiarity with the system, it didn't take him long to find a backdoor into JPL's Horten file. What shocked him was what he found when he got there. Instead of thirty-year-old notes on a historical oddity, Mobi was dumbfounded to discover that the file contained current engineering plans for a modern-day reactor. The Horten cold fusion project which was, according to everything he'd ever read, mothballed in the eighties, was here, rendered in living color, the latest materials technology incorporated into its design. Whatever else it was, the Horten was an active project.

What this meant was that neither Deputy Director Alvarez nor Rand had been straight with him. From Rand he expected it; Mobi doubted you got to be an Air Force colonel without keeping secrets, especially an Air Force colonel who suffered a brutal five-day interrogation at the hands of the Chinese. But from Alvarez it was something else. She was a scientist, not a soldier. If she knew about the project she should have told him. After all, this wasn't the kind of secret that didn't have consequences. Lives were at stake. If the information in the Horten file was even indirectly applicable to the Chinese satellite, then Mobi might just have the tools he needed to avert a disaster. He decided that he'd deal with assigning blame later. All that mattered now was that he scour the data for some clue as to how to keep that bird in the sky.

21

ESTER'S EMERALD-GREEN KARST turned out to be a dead end. Though it was similar to the engraving on the capsule, when the engraving was superimposed over a photo of the real thing on Kate's iPhone, it became apparent that the crooks in their peaks didn't match up. In addition, the base of the real karst was wider. Regardless, they had entered the narrow opening of the cave on their hands and knees to be sure. There were a few charred animal bones and a fire pit on the damp dirt floor, but other than the narrow tunnel to the rock outcropping above, not much else. It was readily apparent that though what had happened here was tragic, it wasn't what they were looking for.

After looping back to Yangshuo on their bicycles, Michael had to admit that in spite of their failure, he'd had an invigorating day. It was true, Ester's story had been sad, but Yangshuo's siren-song landscape had been perfect, too perfect to merely shrug off. Under less pressing circumstances, Michael could imagine nothing better than a hot burger, a cold beer, and a long night's sleep to end the day. As it was, however, there was still work to be done and after parting ways with Ester he found himself seated beside Kate at a busy café, reexamining the contents of Larry's mobile phone. The video message was exactly as he had remembered it—his father standing in a cell halfway between a gray metal table and a tubular chair reciting a number which they now knew to be a waypoint. As before, a battered metal door was visible in one corner, but that was it. Kate checked it again, but other than the single video clip, the phone was empty. No agenda, no to-do list. Nothing.

"I had Six's tech team run the last incoming call. It went to a Kowloon cell tower before bouncing across forty-four different servers on six continents. They're working on it, but it looks like another dead end."

"It doesn't matter," Michael said. "We have the engraving. That's what we need to be looking at."

Kate was quiet as their waitress arrived, gently placing a glass bottle of Coke and a fruit smoothie on the teak table. A green karst rose above them, West Street just beginning to buzz with the evening dinner crowd, the first stars visible in the twilight.

"It's not enough."

"Not enough? You ever hear of Google Earth? It's the twenty-first century. Your people don't have topographical maps, satellite images we can compare this to?"

"If it were only that simple."

"It is that simple. Pull out your iPhone."

"Did you forget the last time I pulled out my iPhone?" Kate said. "Unless there's no alternative, we need to use hardwired ISPs. Besides, we've already tasked satellites over the area. What we need is ground-based photography.

It's all in the angles. We need a profile of the very top of the karst. The crook."

"So search databases. It's not like this area hasn't been photographed before. A photo of exactly what we're looking for has to exist. We just need to find it."

"And we will," Kate said. "Six is running through all known photographs of the region as we speak. But it takes time."

Michael cast his glance toward the jade green Li River where the cormorant fishermen were plying their trade. It was the most ingenious way of catching a fish that Michael had ever seen. They made the birds do the work. Literally. The fishermen sat on bamboo rafts shining lanterns into the river. They each held a cormorant tethered by a thin rope with a brass ring around its neck. When the fish showed up in the river, attracted by the light, the cormorant would dive in and catch it, happily giving up its catch for its master. Michael had to wonder whether the birds ever got to eat, but he admired the fishermen's ingenuity just the same.

"See those guys down there with the birds?"

"The cormorant fishermen? They've been doing it that way forever. They say one guy with one good bird can feed his whole family."

"So maybe we should take a page from their book."

"You want to go fishing?"

Michael took a pull on his Coke, the old glass bottle worn from being refilled a thousand times. "I want to work smart," Michael said. "Those fishermen, they probably couldn't catch a fish on their own if their life depended on it. But the bird, the bird knows how. If the Horten is hidden in these hills, it's been here for a long time, but someone's got to know about it. Maybe not Ester, but someone. Let your people work their satellite maps; we need to find someone who remembers where this thing is. We've got to find our bird."

Michael thought the analogy was apt, but more importantly, he believed it. As lovely as Yangshuo was, he had come here to find his father. They had a job to do and he wasn't going to blow any more time wandering around without a well-reasoned strategy. They needed to find somebody who knew, a living memory to the location of the Horten. Michael reasoned that if he and Kate put their heads together, they could generate some idea as to where to find this person. But instead of an idea, they got an invasion.

"Hi Ho, Mates!"

Michael peered up from his drink to see Crust and crew fly in on rollerblades and broomsticks.

"Was hoping we'd find you here," Crust shouted as he did a pirouette around the table and plunked down in a free chair, Song and the Frenchman in tow. "We did Yangshuo on skates and tubes."

"Skates and what?" Michael asked, certain that tubes was some kind of backpacker vernacular for smoking the local weed.

"Skates and tubes," Song chimed in. She tossed her broomstick through the air like a spear, watching it land on the other side of the street, dead in the middle of a pile of inflated inner tubes. "We rode the current halfway down the river. You poke the broomsticks to keep clear of the buffalo."

"You're kidding, right?"

"The river's full of them," Crust said, "always swimming from this side to that. How you doing, Kate?"

The Frenchman smirked. "Kate, I think, is good."

Kate smiled. "I'm all right."

"Glad to hear it," Crust said. "The thing is, I'm feeling bloody marvelous."

"Are you now?"

Crust leaned back in his chair, and started unlacing his blades, Song and the Frenchman following his lead. Kate had a sly look on her face as though she knew what would be coming next.

"I thought you guys weren't into the whole Guilin Circuit?" Michael said.

"Not into the Guilin Circuit? My God, my American friend. Life itself is the nectar we poor pilgrims pull from the Guilin Circuit." Crust stood up on his chair, taking a step above it onto the rough-hewn teak table, thrusting his arms into the twilight like a burly messiah. "I have come to Guilin and learned to live."

On cue, Song and the Frenchman bent down on the ground on one knee like Knights Templar serving their one true king. Michael wasn't quite sure how to react to the spectacle before him, but from the looks of Kate's even response, she'd seen it all before.

"A tad short on coin, Mr. Crust?"

Crust immediately got down from the table, seating himself respectfully before them, his knights following suit.

"A smidge. Johnny Dole's caught in the post again."

Michael raised an eyebrow, but Kate seemed to know exactly what Crust was saying.

"Are you two waiting on Johnny as well?"

"We are, my lady," Song and the Frenchman said in unison.

A moment passed, just long enough for Crust's broad smile to quiver, before Kate uttered the magic words. "Then let's eat."

DINNER WAS A kaleidoscopic dream. Michael began the meal anxious to get back to work, but somewhere between a fettuccini Alfredo, several more Tsingtao lagers, and a sampling of desserts, his anxiety morphed into a sense of general well-being. The atmosphere at the table combined with all manner of folk parading up and down West Street, the soft warm air, and the simple fact that Jimmy Buffett was crooning away, *in China,* seemed to catch up with him all at once. Unwilling to fight the sensation, Michael simply sat back and listened to Crust's raspy voice drone on.

"Now I've ridden some fine beasts in my time, some exemplary beasts, but none compare to the Bactrian humpback."

"You mean a whale?" Song asked.

"A camel, of course, my good Madame. Depending where you are, you might be tempted to consider a dromedary, but don't do it. It's the Bactrian you want. The Bactrian pulls out all the stops."

"Is that the one with one hump or two?" Kate asked.

"One big one. But it's got nothing to do with the humps. When you're talking camels it's all personality. A Bactrian will go to the wall for you. He'll let you ride him as long as you see fit and give you a lick of the tongue when you're done. But a dromedary, those buggers are a mean lot. And stubborn. They'd just as soon spend the day sniffing shit as walking anywhere with you between their humps. Of course, when they decide to go, they can really move, but all the hemming and hawing in the interim; it's not worth the stress."

"So do you do that a lot?" Michael said. "Transcontinental camel travel?"

"When time and geography permit," Crust said, taking another pull on his beer. "What you've really got to watch is that the big fellow doesn't lick your knickers. You go home with camel slobber on your private parts and there'll be hell to pay with the wife."

Kate snorted, trying to contain her laughter. "Please, Crust. You with a wife?"

"It remains a possibility. When I settle down and make something of my life."

"You'll never settle down."

"You mean I'll never make something of my life."

"That too."

"You're too kind. But say I did?"

"I tell you what," Kate said, glancing at the check and carefully laying four bills on the table. "If you settle down and make something of your life, I'll marry you myself."

"I'm maid of honor," Song screamed.

"And me, I will be the man," the Frenchman said.

"You mean the *best* man?" Michael said.

"Yes, the man."

"Sounds fabulous," Kate said. "Until then, I'm off to bed. Michael?" Crust and his clan smiled dumbly as Kate took Michael by the hand. "We'll catch you lot later."

Within moments they were lost in the crowd.

"Sorry for the quick exit," Kate said. "Had to nip it in the bud. Sometimes those evenings can go on forever."

Michael was just able to make Kate's fine features out in the lantern light emanating from a clothing vendor's cart. Standing there, staring at her like that, Michael felt it again, that same spark that wouldn't die. He didn't like that he felt it, not given the circumstances, but there was no denying it was there and he thought that maybe the weariness he had felt earlier in the evening was fleeting, that maybe, just maybe, the night was young.

"Michael?"

"Sorry," he said, snapping out of his reverie. "Where to?"

"Where would you like to go?" she said.

"Somewhere quiet," he said. "Somewhere we can talk."

"Follow me."

22

MOBI'S UNAUTHORIZED HACK had allowed him to study the Horten project's schematics, but despite his efforts, only two things were obvious: A—the blueprints were without a doubt based on the old Nazi cold fusion reactor design; and B—what communications data existed on the project was woefully incomplete. These facts not withstanding, it was obvious to Mobi that if the Chinese had indeed lost control of their bird, there would be a way to reestablish communication with it. The question was how?

From Mobi's calculations, at its current rate of orbital decay, an uncontrolled reentry would be inevitable within thirty-eight hours. As luck would have it, it looked as though the crash would take place within the geographic limits of California. Nevada was a possibility, as was the Pacific Ocean, but if Mobi had to guess, the bloody thing was going to burn in directly above Palmdale, about twenty miles as the crow flies from where he currently sat. It was almost as if the Chinese were aiming it at him.

Mobi needed to take a leak. Logging off of his terminal, he headed down the hall for the restroom. He knew that even if he figured out how to recommunicate with the satellite, he wouldn't be able to do anything without some very specialized hardware. He entered the restroom through the swinging door and stood at the old porcelain urinal. It boggled the mind how many great minds had worked here at JPL and its sister institution, Caltech, just down the street. Hell, Einstein himself had no doubt once stood before this same old calcified urinal. Mobi found comfort in the idea. Not so much in the fact that the great man had once been here, letting it all hang out so to speak, but on the more human level that even the most brilliant of us still needed to take a leak. And for a brief moment, Mobi let his mind wander free, content in the notion that whoever we were, whatever we said, we were all just jumbles of protoplasmic goo, circling around our tiny sun on satellite Earth, here today, gone tomorrow. He was still lost in the thought when his free arm was pulled abruptly behind his back.

"Mobi Stearn?" a gruff voice said.

"Huh?"

"You're under arrest for violation of Title Eighteen of the United States Espionage Laws."

"I'm what?"

"Shut up and follow me."

23

WHEN HE WAS *eleven, Michael's father taught him how to fight. Not karate. Not a martial art with niceties and rules. But how to brawl. How to survive when the other guy wanted you down. It wasn't because he was getting beat up at school. He wasn't. But Michael's dad wanted him to learn anyway and he said it was important that he paid attention. Michael had been going to karate since he was seven and the first move in karate was always defensive. It was a good strategy. A noble strategy. But it wasn't always the best strategy. Because sometimes you had to hit first and hit hard if you wanted to be the last man standing. He said that for all the moves Michael learned in the dojo, one thing they couldn't teach him was the will to survive. Nobody could teach him that.*

He had to listen to the voice deep within him to learn it. And the will to survive was at the heart of the fight. It didn't matter how good you were, it didn't matter how much you practiced, without that will, without that raw determination to put the other guy down, none of it was worth anything. Michael's dad made him promise that he

*would choose his battles wisely, but if it came time to fight,
he would listen to the voice deep within him and fight like
his very life depended on it. Because it did.*

MICHAEL AND KATE stepped off West Street and onto an
ancient stone bridge gracefully arched over the dark water
of a canal. Yangshuo was an old town, rich in history,
but Michael's attention was more squarely focused on
Kate than the surroundings. Part of it was just good
common sense. He still didn't know the woman and he
wasn't ready to trust her. But the bigger part was that
latent energy he felt growing between them. He had felt
it as he held her down on the cold metal floor of the
airplane and he felt it here in the South China night.
It was a dangerous energy, a force that if not properly
harnessed, might just kill him.

It was this sobering thought that grounded Michael.
Kate looked up at him as if she sensed the change in
his mood. They were nearly halfway across the bridge
now, the newly risen yellow moon reflecting off the
swift moving water below. Five men pushing two large
vegetable carts approached from the other end of the
bridge. They wore wide-brimmed straw farmer's hats
on their heads and worn flip-flops on their feet. The
bulbous yellow fruit in their carts emitted a sweet nearly
overpowering odor that Michael recognized from his trip
through the Shenzhen market the day before. Durian.
According to his guidebook, the Chinese called it the god
of all fruit. What caught Michael's attention, however,
was not the pungence of their cargo, nor the wear of
their shoes, but a glint off the ear of one of the farmers.

Michael wasn't sure if it was the cart or the farmer that moved first, but whichever it was, several hundred pounds of freshly harvested fruit headed down the bridge straight for them. Michael instantly pushed Kate out of the cart's way to the side of the bridge, the first of the men brandishing a sickle blade. Time seemed to slow in that moment. Michael recognized the arced blade as being about thirteen inches long, similar to what he had seen the farmers use in the fields, but unlike those, this one shone with a finely honed razor edge. The blade brought Michael back nine long years to the mountain mine in Peru where his abductors had held him.

The kidnappers hadn't said what they wanted. But when they took out the blade and the video camera, it soon became apparent that it wasn't him. No, Michael was the leverage, not the prize. Even he could see that. They drew blood that day. Not enough to kill him, but enough to make a point on camera. Then they gave him a rag for a bandage and told him to clean up. But where was his father? When was his dad going to save the day?

The very thought of his father rocketed Michael back to the here and now. He involuntarily touched the lone raised scar his kidnappers had left him behind his ear. He was no longer seventeen and he was well aware that if anybody was going to save the day, it was going to have to be him. But he was also aware that a close-quarter knife fight involved a serious risk of being cut, something he didn't want and couldn't afford, even if it meant subduing his attacker. No, what he needed was an exit strategy because a quick glance from left to right informed him that all five men were closing in fast.

The first cart hit the stone balustrade just below them, while the second impacted above. The intended effect seemed to be to box them in and it worked like a charm. It was fight or flight time and Kate was ready to fight. Michael could see it in her eyes. What worried him now was her gun. Michael knew she could probably get several shots off before their sickle-wielding attacker got any closer, but it wouldn't do either of them any good if at the end of the day they were left with a bridge full of bloody men, a handful of witnesses, and the local cops investigating the crime.

The farmer with the sickle slashed. Michael pivoted to the side and sucked in his abdomen, handily escaping the blade, but the largest of the farmers now blocked all exit. The big farmer reached out with a single straight arm, drilling Michael squarely between the shoulder blades. A third assailant pawed at Michael's pockets causing an avalanche of coins to bounce off the bridge at his feet. Michael instinctively shielded Kate with his body while looking for an opening. The farmer with the blade came in for a second jab. Michael sidestepped away, but there was still nowhere to go; the carts blocked their escape from either side.

In the time it took the farmer to ready himself for another slash, Michael faked with a front kick then let go with a roundhouse to the man's solar plexus. The fake served to put the farmer off guard and Michael's second kick connected with an audible crack. So far so good. Instantly, he pulled back to deliver a swift sidekick to the man's kneecaps. Once his attacker buckled, he would follow it up by a jab to the throat which would give him the requisite millisecond to take hold of his wrist and disarm

him. Then he could move on to the others, providing Kate
hadn't already shot them, of course. Except something
was off. His assailant wasn't looking at him anymore. He
was staring vacantly down the bridge.

"Michael!" Kate called out.

And Michael saw what all the fuss was about. A
vehicle raced toward them. It was moving so quickly
that all five of their assailants had already leapt away.
True, it was traveling without its headlights, nearly
invisible in the blackness, but the whine of its engine
was now so loud Michael had no idea how he could
have missed it. Adrenalin, he thought. Adrenalin and
the task at hand.

In that instant Michael and Kate leapt up onto the stone
balustrade. A split second later they were both caught in
the sudden glare of a single headlight as the fruit carts flew,
durian cascading down like rotten rain. Michael noted
that their assailants had disappeared into the darkness.
Instead of looking into the eyes of five angry farmers, he
was now facing down the speeding vehicle which had
caused the crash. It was a compact, three-wheeled truck,
a Chinese cross between a pickup and a motorized tricycle
and its snout-like front end was thoroughly flattened by
the impact, radiator belching steam into the blackness.
Michael looked to Kate who seemed more shaken by
this turn of events than she had been by the melee which
preceded it. He noted that she had chosen this juncture to
draw her Glock, aiming it squarely through the smashed
driver's side window.

"Seven-seven-seven my ass," a disgruntled voice said
from within the vehicle.

Kate kept her finger steady on the trigger.

"It was seven-seven-four and I had to dig through three editions to get that."

The man in the truck poked his head past the deployed airbag and out the window, revealing his gray ponytail. It was Ted at the wheel. Kate shot Michael a glance.

"Ted," Michael said.

"Always happy to serve."

"How did you find us?"

"You called me, remember?"

"No. Here," Michael said. "How did you find us here?"

"A thanks would suffice. But since you ask, I spotted you on West Street and followed you up through the crowd. Looks like you're lucky I did too."

"Looks can be deceiving," Kate said, lowering her weapon to her side.

"You're telling me," Ted said. "Now holster that thing and let's get the hell out of here."

• • •

Four hundred yards away, safely ensconced in his makeshift command post, MSS Captain Zu Huang expressed his displeasure with a sharp look toward his subordinates. Though the farmer peasant cover had worked well, the violence, in Huang's opinion, had been overplayed. A simple threat, accompanied by a hip check, or a bump to the shoulder would have been more than ample to plant the device. After all, they had found the American. Their objective now wasn't to scare him away, it was simply to follow. To wait and follow and let the People's Republic's superior technology sing.

24

TED STRODE UP West Street, Michael and Kate following him through the crowd. They were safely anonymous, at least for the time being, and Michael felt his composure return. Still, he was embarrassed that he had lost his focus, even momentarily back on the bridge. What had happened so long ago on the mountainside in Peru had happened. Nothing could change that. But he couldn't let the past interfere with what he had to do now.

"Those guys on the bridge were MSS," Ted said. "Ministry of State Security."

"How do you know?" Michael asked.

"My gut. My gut and the fact that I think I saw an ear piece on one them. Your typical farmer doesn't wear earpieces. Earrings maybe, or ear plugs, but not earpieces."

Ted was walking quickly now, Michael and Kate struggling to keep up. "Suddenly you're an expert on Chinese Intelligence Services?" Michael said.

"I never said that."

"Kate's been telling me things, Ted. Stuff about my dad. Stuff you'd never mentioned."

"Like what?"

"Like the fact that he was CIA for starters," Michael looked to Kate before adding the next part. "The fact that she's MI6. That they spent a couple of years partnered together looking for an old Nazi airplane. That maybe the reason he's gone missing is because of it."

Ted clicked his tongue and redoubled his pace up the street.

"Is that all you have to say? You were his best friend. Are you going to tell me you didn't know about any of this?"

Ted ignored Michael, instead leading the way toward an establishment that was about as different from the ramshackle guest houses lining West Street as you could get. Its expansive gardens and reflecting pools made it look more like a palace than anything else. Kate seemed to know the place.

"The Yangshuo Hotel?" Kate said.

"I'm getting too old for the backpacking thing."

"And?"

"And it's time to read the writing on the wall."

THE WALL IN this case was to be found in the resort's gracious glass-paneled lobby. Outside, the landscaping was lush, waterfalls and exotic plantings covering the inner courtyard. Inside, the floor to ceiling windows were broken up by traditional bearing walls at fifteen-foot intervals. A polished marble floor separated them from the empty reception desk at the far end of the lobby.

Other than the bellhop outside the swinging glass doors, they were alone.

"Check out the artwork," Ted said. "See anyone you know?"

Michael noted that the walls between the glass panels were covered in framed photographs. He turned his attention to the nearest one—a framed photo of what looked like some Japanese tourists in front of the hotel. Strike that, they were Japanese dignitaries; their suits were formal. Michael turned to the next picture and saw a similarly laid out photo of the British Royal Family. Continuing along the wall, the next shot was of President Nixon standing with a cadre of Secret Service; the next showed President Carter with his Secret Service; then President Clinton alongside his protection detail; then George W. Bush.

"So this place is popular with Royals and ex-presidents?"

"Presidents," Ted said. "They were in office when they visited."

Michael's eyes skipped across the glass panels overlooking the courtyard to the solid wall behind the reception desk. There was a bell on the desk and on the wall behind it were more of the same photos, each sporting an identical layout to the last. There were dignitaries from Africa, India, South America, the list went on.

"So what do you think?" Ted asked. "Why so many official visitors?"

"The banana pancakes?"

Ted ignored Michael's quip. "What if I told you I have firsthand knowledge as to why one of these guys was here, flawless intelligence on two more, and a lot better than a guess on the rest of them?"

"I'd say, start talking."

Ted eyed the front desk. Even though there was nobody there, he beckoned Michael and Kate to follow him outside just the same. Once they were clear of the bellhop, he spoke quietly.

"All those presidential visits from Nixon on up amounted to one thing." Ted quietly surveyed the area as they walked to ensure nobody was within earshot. "They were official cover to get a CIA team into Red China under the auspices of a Secret Service Security Operation."

"How do you know any of this?" Michael asked.

"Kate didn't tell you?"

"Tell him what?"

"I was on the CIA team," Ted said to Michael. "So was your dad."

Michael bit down on his tongue as a group of Japanese tourists shuffled past on their way back to the hotel.

Kate said, "I had no idea, Michael. I swear."

"Calm down, nothing to get uppity about," Ted said. "I just assumed you knew. Nixon on his trip to China in seventy-one. I was a new agent. Your father and I had just finished the basic operative training course at Camp Peary. Everybody calls it The Farm now. Both of us were pretty psyched when we got the assignment."

"You're saying my dad was here all the way back in nineteen seventy-one?"

"Michael, your father ran one mission for more or less his entire career—the recovery of the Horten 21. Everything else, every single other thing he did for the CIA, was filler."

"Yeah, but you're saying he was looking for this thing for decades?"

"That's what I'm saying. It was our first assignment together. He just never let go. Back when we started, half our classmates were stuck in embassies somewhere and we were out here on the front lines posing as Nixon's security detail. You've got to remember, back in the Nixon era coming here was big news. His was the first US presidential visit ever and the Chinese wanted to impress him. They even built a bloody highway for him. They call it the Nixon Road, from the airport to the city, and they did that just to make Tricky Dick feel welcome. You can imagine how they'd feel if they knew a big old chunk of the reason for his trip to this part of the country revolved around a CIA plan to find the Horten."

"Let me make sure I got this," Michael said. "You're basically telling me Nixon came to China in seventy-one to look for a Nazi airplane?"

"Look, I can't speculate as to every reason Nixon had for his presidential trip to China. I can't even tell you how much he knew about the Company's plan to locate the Horten. But I can tell you this. Posing as his security detail provided us with about as good a cover as we were going to get back then. We traveled up and down these hills doing bogus security reconnaissance in anticipation of his visit. Chinese Intelligence followed us the whole time but we still managed to cover a lot of ground." Ted paused. "In the end it didn't matter much, though. We didn't find a thing."

"And Carter and Clinton? Bush?"

"Same deal. Though I was out of the Agency by the time Bush came around. Word has it that the British did the same thing with their security teams. And the Japanese. Everybody wanted a piece of that lost Nazi tech."

They reached the main road. Locals still sat on bicycles, backpackers wandering up and down the street.

"Your dad stayed with the project and became something of an expert on the Horten. The way I hear it, he even kept the search for it alive when nobody else seemed to think it was worth finding. Your father realized that the Horten was more than a plane. It was the holy grail of the energy crisis. Its reactor could solve the planet's energy needs and redraw the world map in the process. If the word passion wasn't as played out as a Thai hooker, I'd say he had a passion for it—a passion to find that technology. He managed to get himself reassigned to the project multiple times that I know of. It looks like this last time, with Kate here, he just didn't come back."

Michael slowed to a standstill, crickets singing in the sweet night air. He took a long moment, breathing it all in before finally speaking. "So let me make sure I've got this," Michael said. "She's MI6, he's CIA, now you're CIA too? Did any of you ever consider the private sector? You make better money and you're less likely to get shot."

"No job security," Ted said. "But you're right about the getting shot part. That's why I took early retirement. I'm a part-time lecturer for the Royal Asiatic Society now. With the exception of what happened to your father, I haven't looked back since."

"So is there a reason you didn't tell me any of this back in Hong Kong?"

"Yeah. You were better off not knowing."

Michael shot a glance at Kate, but her expression was hard to read. There was no doubt she wanted to hear more, but her body language seemed to suggest that the discussion was between Michael and Ted and that she should be left out of it. It didn't matter. Michael could conduct this conversation on his own.

"Okay, I'll bite. Why do I need to know now?"

"Because I can see now there's no keeping you out of it." Ted lowered his voice. "When I first brought you into this, I was thinking closure. I thought the whole mess would end with Larry. That he'd cop to what he knew and you could go to the police with it and put the whole thing behind you. With everything you've been through, both before and now, I knew that would be important to you."

"And now?"

"Now I can see you're in way deeper than that. Nothing I say or don't say is going to make a difference. And if that's the case, you might as well know it all."

"That's it?"

"Pretty much." Ted turned back toward the lobby. "Now get some rest. I'll meet up with you two in the morning."

Watching him go, Michael finally opened his mouth. "Ted?"

"Yeah?"

"Thanks."

"No problem, kid." Ted grinned in the moonlight and continued on his way.

25

Mobi was escorted out of the restroom and down a waiting elevator by two men who were about as far removed from the prototypical laid back JPL employee as you could get. They wore buzz cuts and plain gray suits, and even though they weren't in uniform per se, it wasn't much of a stretch to see that they were military, most likely Air Force like Rand. The men silently escorted him to a secure lower level of the laboratory that Mobi had never been to. Though this lower level of the facility was officially designated as storage, it was rumored to be much more: a covert laboratory for projects requiring many times the normal civilian security clearance. So despite the pain from the handcuffs on his wrists and the foreboding in the pit of his stomach, Mobi's eyes were wide as his escorts led him down the worn corridor. A moment later, a key card was swiped through a cipher lock and Mobi found himself inside a mid-sized room.

The space was closer to a broker's office than the torture chamber Mobi had been expecting. An Ultrasuede sofa sat in one corner, a Mission Revival desk in the other. One of the military types removed Mobi's cuffs while the other entered some kind of code into a Blackberry. Then, without another word, they both exited the room, the steel-reinforced, wood-paneled door clicking shut behind them. Less than five seconds later, an automatic panel slid open on the far wall and Deputy Director Alvarez entered the space.

"I see you made it past security," Alvarez said, handing Mobi a cup of coffee. "I'd have spared you the escort, but that's how they run this section of the lab."

"Exactly which section are we talking about?" Mobi asked.

"The fun one."

Alvarez beckoned Mobi to follow her out the open panel in the wall. He was right to think of the preceding area as some kind of waiting room, because the corridor he found himself in was all business, though significantly more sterile business than Mobi was used to. The original structures at JPL dated back to the nineteen forties and even though there had been substantial construction since then, the buildings, for the most part, had a tired feel to them. This underground corridor, however, was different. The walls were sheathed in white polycarbonate panels that bore no sign of wear, while an illuminated yellow line embedded in the floor indicated direction of travel. It was weird. Even though Mobi realized that the corridor was probably designed in this way to minimize airborne contaminants, he still felt like he was treading the corridors of the Death Star. If R2D2 had reared his head, Mobi had no doubt he would have chirped right back at him and taken another slug on his java.

Alvarez led Mobi past several closed doors into a marginally wider section of corridor overlooking a massive clean room. Mobi now realized that his hypothesis as to why the walls were coated in the polymer panels was correct. It would be a means of keeping the particulate count in the air low, given that this corridor no doubt provided entry and egress to the clean room, a room that unequivocally had to stay sterile. There was a reason for that, of course; it was because they assembled spacecraft there. And looking down through the transparent polymer panels of the observation corridor, Mobi laid eyes on a team of scientists in bunny suits tending to the most unusual spacecraft he'd ever seen.

"The JPL Horten Project," Alvarez said.

Mobi took a moment. He had seen the blueprints. He knew what the Horten was supposed to look like and this wasn't it. Not even close. The object in question was roughly the shape of a shallow bowl, about fifteen feet in diameter, and composed of what looked like a molybdenum skeleton covered with a titanium skin. Inside the bowl were a series of outtake valves and tubes that clearly constituted an engine or propulsion device of some kind. It was only partially assembled. Mobi could see that. But he was having difficulty imagining what he saw as part of a larger machine. Still, Alvarez was a serious woman. If she said this was the JPL Horten Project, this was the JPL Horten Project.

"Not impressed?" Alvarez asked.

"No, it's not that."

"Is it that in the last however many minutes you've been arrested, brought to a level of the lab that isn't supposed to exist, and shown a secret project that doesn't look anything like you thought it would?"

"That about sums it up," Mobi said.

"Then you're really going to like what comes next."

Alvarez opened a door in the corridor revealing an office. It was a sterile cube, about fifteen by fifteen with a polished steel desk and three chairs. There was a window overlooking the corridor and a multi-line telephone on the desk, but other than that the space was bare. She led him inside, closing the door behind her.

"Look, we don't have a lot of time here. I was lucky to get you away from Rand's guys at all so I'm going to get straight to the point. You're on a level of the lab that as far as the rest of world is concerned, isn't here. Why it's here I'll save for another time, but for now, just know that Rand had you arrested because we traced your hack. He figures you're more bother than you're worth. I know better. That's why I'm bringing you into the fold."

"So am I under arrest or not?"

"If Rand gets his way, probably. There's no gray area with him. As far as he's concerned, you became a security breach the minute you broke protocol and hacked into the system. His job is to plug the hole."

"Did he remember bringing me into the loop? Did he not expect me to be curious?"

"I get it, Mobi. We'll deal with Rand later. What you need to know now is that we've been engaged in a space race of sorts with the Chinese for a number of years now. That prototype below? That's our interpretation of the Horten—not the plane itself, but the cold fusion reactor it contained. It looks a little different because we had to make modifications to the original plans, but that's largely irrelevant now. What is relevant is what you already know—that the Chinese version of the Horten reactor, complete with a secondary plutonium coil, is on a crash course with LA County."

"What can we do?"

"Listen carefully." Alvarez eyed the hallway outside her office to ensure they were alone. "Rand is here because he thinks he knows how to deal with the problem. He wants to use one of the DOD's orbital anti-satellite weapons' platforms to blow the Chinese bird out of the sky."

"Which would be a good plan if it worked," Mobi said. "Except word is the last time they deployed one of their ASAT platforms, it couldn't hit the broad side of the moon. And I mean that literally."

Alvarez lowered her voice. "That's why you're here. Look, from what we know, the Chinese haven't so much built a new reactor as reverse engineered what was left of the Horten found in that rice paddy. As far as we know, they don't entirely understand what they've done. Our sources tell us that they haven't changed much about the project. They weren't able to isolate the original communications system from the reactor control, for instance. Instead they just built a new shell, added a few processors, and stuck the whole damn thing on the end of a rocket. Call me crazy, but I'm betting that if we can establish communication with its onboard mainframe, we can keep it in the sky."

Mobi considered Alvarez's words. He tended to smile when he was nervous and what Alvarez had said put a grin on his face.

"Why are you laughing?"

"I wouldn't call it a laugh."

"Spill it, Mobi."

"You're telling me you want me to establish communication with their satellite."

"Yes."

"But you're also telling me that this thing's communications system dates back to World War II."

"Like I said, yes."

Mobi shook his head. "You know the Chinese are cautious. Who knows what kind of encryption protocols are in place? If it's an analog system, and given its age I don't see how it isn't, we're talking about infinite variations. To break that kind of encryption I need a strand, a thread, something to start parsing their code. What possible resource can you offer me to do that?"

"This is where you listen very carefully."

"I'm hearing you."

"Quiann," Alvarez said.

"What?" Mobi asked incredulous.

"I can offer you Doctor Jie Quiann."

DOCTOR JIE QUIANN was a legend. He was infamous in the halls of JPL, and Mobi knew the man's career path by rote. A brilliant young mathematician who had been born in China, but claimed refugee status in the USA just after the Second World War, Quiann had soon found his way to California and Caltech where he began his career as a Doctoral Candidate in Applied Physics. From there, Quiann's career trajectory had been straight up and he soon became one of the world's preeminent rocket scientists. That, however, was a long time ago. Because before Mobi was even born, Dr. Quiann had defected back to China where he had single handedly founded his mother country's space program. Nobody knew what spawned his defection; if he had been a plant from his first arrival on US soil, or if he had simply longed for the county which he had left behind, but whatever the case, Quiann went on to become a bona fide hero to the Chinese people.

As such, even if little known amongst average Americans, he was an embarrassment to the US government and the alma mater which trained him. What made the sting of Quiann's defection particularly acerbic, however, was not the general technical know-how that he had brought back with him years ago. Any number of rocket scientists could have taken those secrets to China. It was the project Quiann was chosen to lead—the Horten Cold Fusion Project—and all that entailed. Many considered cold fusion technology to be key to the long term exploration of space and when Quiann defected in the late-nineteen fifties, a whole lot of research was said to have left with him; potentially dangerous research that many people feared he had yet to share with his colleagues.

From that point, Mobi's knowledge of Quiann was sketchy at best, which is what made Alvarez's mention of him seem odder still. It wasn't like Mobi had a relationship with him, or knew him beyond the lore. In Mobi's mind Quiann was an infamous footnote, a piece of JPL history that had been all but forgotten to this moment. What could Alvarez possibly expect to achieve by means of illicit communication with a known traitor? But Mobi didn't have long to think about it, because before he could even fire the question back at Alvarez, Rand and his men had marched into the room.

26

THERE WERE SOME *things Michael's dad didn't bother telling him much about at all. Like sex. Michael's dad never talked to Michael about sex. He never told him about the birds and the bees, or what he should expect his first time, or what he should do not to get a girl pregnant. Michael knew that the other kids' fathers had had this talk with them and he wondered why his dad hadn't. Finally, Michael didn't want to wait any longer. So he asked his dad. Not about sex. But about why his father hadn't told him about sex. When Michael's dad asked him what he wanted to know, Michael said nothing in particular, he just wanted to know why they hadn't had the talk.*

Michael's dad was very clear. He said that sex was one of those things that if you had to ask about, you probably weren't ready to hear. It was a cruel irony. But a lot of life was like that. And understanding the irony was far more important than any father-son chat about the birds and the bees. Because Michael could learn everything he needed to know about sex on his own in about five minutes flat. But life's ironies took a lifetime to comprehend. And it was only through conversations like this one that his dad would be able to point the way.

Michael was exhausted. They'd made it back to their room at the Whispering Bamboo, but he doubted he'd be able to sleep. He was beyond that. Beyond anything really.

"What are you doing?"

Kate, who had entered the room a step ahead of him, had stripped the mattress off her bed and now held it folded like an accordion between her arms.

"What does it look like?" she said, plopping the mattress down on top of Michael's. "I'm doubling up the mattress."

"For who?"

"For who do you think, Michael? Don't be such a prude. We've each got a sleeping bag. Maybe this way we can actually get some sleep." Kate unrolled her sleeping bag and lay down atop the double mattress staring at the ceiling. "Much better." She rolled onto her side so she could face Michael. "What do you think about Ted?"

"What about him?"

"Showing up on the bridge the way he did. Saving our asses. His timing was a little too perfect."

"I don't know if I'd be throwing stones, Kate. You're telling me you had no idea Ted used to be Agency?"

"Agency. Listen to you now. You're talking the talk." Michael shot her a look and Kate relented. "I met him for the first time the other night at Chungking. Crust invited him. I swear."

"Well he seemed to know all about you. He didn't blink when I told him what you did for a living."

"Your father must have said something."

"And that's it?"

"Yeah, that's it. Stop deflecting the issue. Your dad revealed a confidence. Case closed. It doesn't change my concerns about Ted."

Michael looked to Kate. The bare bulb in the sconce was flickering now as if the connection was loose. "Whatever you're suggesting, one thing I know is, I've known Ted for a long time. He might not have been straight with me until tonight about him and my dad, but I know I can trust him. I always have. Okay?"

Michael got up and turned the flickering bulb off. The only light in the room now bled in through the wooden shutters leaving striations across the bed.

"Okay."

"Really? That's it? You're satisfied? No skulking around to find out what he's really up to? No spy stuff? Because I like to keep in practice you know. Espionage is a 24-7 game. You got to keep your groove on."

"You do that. I'm flossing my teeth. After that I'm brushing. Then I'm going to bed."

MICHAEL DID ONE better than brush his teeth and took a shower, luxuriating under the mercifully hot water as it washed away the past days' sweat and grime. He hadn't had an opportunity to bathe since Seattle and he was pretty sure it showed. Michael's mind was on more than hygiene, though. It was on Kate. She was an attractive woman. There was no denying it. Still, he didn't know her. He didn't know who she was or what she was capable of; he didn't really know anything about her at all. And he knew that what he didn't know was dangerous. It could get him killed. But the thing was, it also excited him. It excited him to the point that he was willing to take the risk.

The hot water cleansed what was left of the soapy lather on his skin. He'd have a long day tomorrow. It was time to turn in. Michael reached for the rough copper valve when he noticed something unusual. His towel. Through the gap in the shower curtain he could see it hanging there but something was off. It was on the wrong hook. It had been moved, he was sure of it. Now the bathroom wasn't secure, Michael knew that. There was no more than a push button on the door. You could pop it with a credit card. But if someone was in there with him, they had also been quiet. Silent like a thief in the night. Like a professional. Then the wooden floor creaked. He heard that. A shadow was cast across the room.

Michael looked around. He was wet and naked with little more than a travel-sized shampoo bottle in way of weapon. A shampoo bottle and a shower rod. The miniature bottle was useless. The shower rod might offer some utility, but it was bolted to the wall. He couldn't risk not being able to get it out. No, this situation called for the direct approach. There was a lack of information and as such Michael knew that his only play was to own the element of surprise. Michael moved his hands toward the copper valve as if he was about to shut off the stream of water. But he didn't shut it off. Instead he turned his body tight against the valve and reached powerfully through the crack in the shower curtain, taking hold of his assailant with his left hand. Michael immediately found purchase on a firm upper arm and blindly wrenched his attacker into the shower stall.

His next move would be a choke hold and Michael twisted back with his grappling arm and raised his right arm in preparation to subdue the intruder. But then he stopped. Because there was no intruder. There was only Kate looking shocked and more than a little frightened in a terry cloth robe. Michael released her.

"Don't you knock?" Michael shouted.

"Don't you listen?" The hot water was raining down on both of them now, Michael's pulse slowing. "I knocked ten times. When I got nothing I carded the lock. The other bathroom is full."

"Why'd you move my towel?"

"Because it was getting soaked."

Kate, too, was wet now, her robe dripping wet under the shower's steady stream. Hot water ran down her long auburn hair, her eyes moist in the steam. Michael felt his pulse quicken again. But it wasn't danger doing it this time. It was desire. He was close. Close enough to feel Kate's firm breasts pressing against him from under her robe. She turned away from him and Michael's heart sank. He knew that leaving it alone was the right thing to do, the prudent thing. He didn't know this woman. He did know that getting involved with her would complicate what was already a messy situation. And that was on the good end of things. If things worked out differently it could be worse. Much worse. Besides, they had to work together. It was better to keep it simple. Michael reached for the faucet, shutting off the stream of hot water. Then he reached for his towel. It would end here, now. Any awkwardness they could discuss in the morning.

Or they could have, if Kate hadn't dropped her robe.

She stood there, her back to him, water running down the nape of her neck and Michael knew in the pit of his gut that this was not the way the night was supposed to go. But when she turned to him, tight to his body in the confined space of the shower stall, it didn't matter. Nothing mattered now but the moment. Michael pulled her close and in that instant her lips found his. Kate opened her mouth, her tongue darting out to meet him. He kissed her. Slowly at first, then deeper and harder. She tasted salty, like the Pacific, and Michael liked it. He liked it a lot. He could feel her heart beating close to his own as he ran his hand down her perfectly contoured back. Kate purred softly, her response gentle but immediate. She took his hand in hers and continued to guide it up her soft skin until Michael's palm found her firm round breast. His hands slid down lower and he pulled her tighter, his hungry mouth finding her breasts, followed by her neck, then back to her lips.

As he kissed her, harder still, Kate reached for him, her body sliding ever closer until he was locked in her warm embrace. Michael lifted her toward him, Kate's feet arched against the walls of the shower stall. He could feel the pressure building inside of him and he knew it was building in her, too, as she pulsed against him. Kate must have sensed when the anticipation was too much to bear because she reached for him, guiding him urgently inside of her. In that instant Michael knew that whatever concerns he had about Kate, about

China, about anything, would have to wait. Nothing mattered now but the moment. He pulled her tight to him and all that was left was the rhythmic motion of their bodies in the night.

27

Sunlight dancing over his sleeping bag, Michael awoke with a smile. He didn't want to say it out loud, but he could admit it to himself. Lying there, Kate's long auburn hair draped across his chest, he felt like a real Backpacker Bond. A Backpacker Bond on a mission for his Majesty's Secret Service. Granted, Michael was American. And his idea of a vodka martini included a shot of Red Bull. But for the moment at least, he was a secret agent and he had to admit, it felt good. Bond or not, though, he knew that they had too big a day ahead of them to be simply lounging in bed. It couldn't be past six a.m., but the sounds of early morning sweeping were already rising from the street below. Time to get up. Michael shifted his weight carefully, not wanting to wake Kate before he was dressed, but she stirred almost immediately.

"Modest?"

"Just eager."

"Me too," she said, pulling him back toward her.

"Not for that," he said kissing her deeply. "Not right now anyway."

"For what then?" Kate asked as Michael hastily threw on his pants.

"A second look."

"A SECOND LOOK" in Michael-speak meant reexamining the capsule. He had been mulling over it for some time now and it seemed to Michael that the saucer-shaped shell had to be more than it seemed. Otherwise why build it? A marker to the location of the Horten could be left in far simpler ways. After carefully ensuring that they were alone atop the roof of the hostel, Michael bent low to remove the padlock from the hinged cowling covering the swamp fan. Kate hunched down beside him as he lifted the sheet metal with a grating squeak. The capsule was there, exactly as they had left it, glimmering in the morning light. Michael ran his fingers along the circumference of the metal disc looking for a catch or an indentation, anything really that would either open it up, or set his suspicions to rest, but nothing did. The four-foot-diameter capsule was exactly as it had been the night before—the perfect enigma. Or was it?

"Did you see that?" Michael said.

"See what?"

Michael placed his palm under the capsule and tilted it away from the direct sunlight.

"Squint a little and hold your head at an angle."

Kate craned her neck to the side, staring across the diameter of the capsule. A hairline indentation was just visible on the capsule's smooth surface.

"That wasn't there yesterday."

"Not under a forty watt bulb anyway," Michael said, excited now, following the barely visible hairline groove with the tip of his finger as it radiated out from the center point along the diameter of the capsule. Michael checked over either shoulder to ensure that they were the only ones on the roof. He then lifted the capsule entirely out of the cowling and set it on end between his knees as he crouched, putting the full weight of his upper body into torquing it around.

Nothing happened.

Michael took a breath and grunted, the muscles in his arms and back straining as he tried to twist the capsule in half for a second time. Still nothing happened. If it was going to give, it had no intention of doing so gracefully. But Michael had no intention of giving up either. Eclipsing his previous attempts with the sheer force in his grip, Michael grasped the capsule between his knees and twisted for a third time, this time putting his hips and legs into the action. Like the previous attempts, at first there was nothing, but then, a low groan emanated from the core of the capsule itself. It wasn't music, but it certainly sounded like it as Michael continued to twist, the low torque of metal moving on metal filling the morning air until the seal gave away with a neat pop. After that, the top half of the capsule spun off as easily as the lid on a pickle jar. Within moments Michael had laid the now separated halves of the capsule down on the tar roof revealing a cavity within. He turned the lower half of the capsule on its side and a second later a metallic green box tumbled out of the cavity into his waiting hand.

"Gotcha," Michael said, pausing to regain his breath. His eyes met Kate's. It didn't take a genius to see that she knew what it was.

"Purple Sky."

"Purple what?"

Kate turned the anodized green box over, exposing the sheath of color-coded wires that hung loose behind it.

"If I'm right, it's a communications device circa 1942. Its code name was Purple Sky."

"It's green."

"I'd call it more of a chartreuse, but yeah, it's green. The name referred to what the device did, not what it looked like."

"Which was?"

"Rock the Allies' world."

Michael watched as Kate located what must have been a recessed catch on the metal box's lower edge because she pressed in with her fingernail and the box's cover opened revealing an old-style mechanical keyboard. But it wasn't a typewriter. It looked more like the kind of machine that a court reporter would use. At the rear of it, behind the paper roller, were a series of vertically aligned spindles. Michael counted eleven of them as Kate carefully placed the machine down on the tar roof.

"This machine, Purple Sky, is a second-generation version of the Japanese Purple Encoding Machine."

"You're going to have to give me more than that," Michael said.

"During World War II the Germans made use of an encoding machine called Enigma to keep their radio communications secret. Both sender and receiver of the message needed an Enigma machine to decode whatever message was sent. This was a big problem for the Allies because they had no idea what the Germans were going to do next. As a result, German U-boats were sinking Allied ships all over the place. Then a guy named Alan Turing came along, and with the help of a captured Enigma machine, broke the Enigma code."

"Didn't they make a submarine movie about that?"

"More than one. The point is, breaking the code was a turning point in World War II. This green box here, if it is what I think it is, is a second-generation encoding machine based on the Japanese variant of the German equipment."

"Time out. The Japanese had one too?"

"The Germans and the Japanese were on the same side, remember? Part of that alliance was based on the trade of technology. The Japanese took the Enigma technology and refined it further. Like I said before, they called their machine Purple. When the Germans heard about this, they decided to go one better. They designed a next-generation variant of the Japanese equipment specifically for the Horten 21. Each Horten would be equipped with one, enabling secret communication between the planes just like the U-boats. Without one of these machines, there would be no way to amend or decipher the Horten's aerial transmissions. Hence the name, Purple Sky."

Kate pressed a key which in turn rotated a spindle on the back of the machine.

"Like with Enigma and Purple, you typed your message in here. The rotors that fit onto these spindles would mechanically transpose your message into something completely unreadable which was then broadcast by way of high frequency radio waves. This unit relies on analog technology. Infinite variations remember, not just ones and zeros. My guess is that the code it produces would be effectively unbreakable, even today."

"May I?"

Kate handed Michael the device. It looked about the same as it felt. Cold, metallic and unwieldy. The spindles turned freely on their rods, the keys on the unit still taut.

"So a rotor that creates a unique code fits on the end of each of these spindles?"

"That's the idea."

"So where are they?"

"It's been years. They could be anywhere."

Michael turned the unit over and stared through the lattice of metal keys into the sunlight. One thing was clear, whatever Purple Sky was, German engineering had ensured that it was built to last. The underside of each key lever was oiled slightly like an old typewriter, dust clinging to its surface. Michael began to turn the unit right side up when the flicker of a shadow caught his eye.

"Michael, let's save the archeology for the professionals. We need to get word to my people."

"There's a piece of wire hanging from the hasp of the swamp fan. Could you hand it to me?"

"The MSS is out there," Kate said. "Given what we've just found, I'm getting awfully uncomfortable about sitting on this roof."

Michael reached over and removed the short bit of wire from the hasp himself. Holding the encoding unit up to the light with one hand, he passed the length of wire gently through the keys, snagging what looked like a small lump from the case's metal bottom. Carefully prodding the lump up and out through the maze of levers, it took shape in the light of day.

"What is it?" Kate asked.

Michael put the machine down with one hand as he carefully took hold of the lump between his fingers. He uncrumpled it slowly revealing a very old, very tired sheet of carbon paper. Holding the dark purple carbon paper up to the sunlight, bright-white script now shone through where its ink had been deposited on a long-forgotten document. The first of the characters were obviously Chinese, but below them was an English translation. Michael read it aloud.

"Yangkok. Whoever last used this machine typed the word *Yangkok*."

28

A QUICK GLANCE at Michael's wrist-top GPS revealed Yangkok to be a remote village about fifteen miles into the mountains. There was little detail of the area on the LCD map underscoring the fact that Yangkok was known more for its complete lack of interest to the outside world than anything else. It was of interest now, however, that much was certain. First things first. Both Michael and Kate agreed that the encoding machine was too valuable to leave on the rooftop. Fortunately, it fit nicely in Michael's daypack. After reassembling the capsule and returning it to its hiding place, the next order of business was to contact Ted. Kate was indifferent to the idea, but at Michael's insistence they stopped by the Yangshuo Hotel to find him. Ted, however, was nowhere to be found. Agreeing to put Ted aside for the moment, they concentrated on getting to Yangkok.

A survey of the local buses confirmed that there was no road connecting Yangshuo with the isolated village. That meant they'd have to walk, or potentially take a bicycle, but both those options would be slow.

Still, if the paths they had traveled the day before were any indication of terrain, there wasn't much room for anything else. Michael looked up and down the block where West Street met the main road. The teashops and auto-repair shanties alongside the highway were just coming to life and Michael noticed something he'd missed a moment earlier—a row of men lined up farther down the hill.

What caught Michael's interest wasn't the men per se, but what they held in their hands. Helmets. Michael quickened his pace down the grade to see that each of the men was seated on a mid-sized motorcycle, a yellow placard embossed with a number sticking up from their front fenders. The placards gave it away. These men were motorcycle cabbies awaiting their fares. And as with any cabbie, all that was left was the negotiation.

Michael's proposal was simple. Instead of a ride about town, he wanted to rent one of their motorcycles for the day. If Michael was to be honest, he had to admit that the idea was crazy. Go to Manhattan and try to rent a yellow cab for the day. But Michael knew they needed the extra flexibility that their own transportation would provide. So, with Kate's help translating, he tried his luck. As it was, after the predictable laughter followed by stunned silence, there was a motorcycle cabbie who looked like he might just need the money enough to be convinced. It was in this way that after a circuitous driving test, followed by several hundred yuan notes and a thousand assurances that they would be back before sunset, Michael and Kate found themselves the proud lessees of a beat-up 250cc motorcycle.

The morning had progressed and leaving Yangshuo turned out to be busier than Michael anticipated. They were forced to share the road with diesel-belching trucks and tractors, but once they turned onto a secondary road a few miles from town, things quieted down dramatically. While Michael was busy demonstrating his safe driving skills to the cabbies, Kate had been able to augment the meager detail on the GPS map with halfway decent directions to Yangkok. After a few miles of gravel road they would find a walking trail which would take them to a still narrower path along the base of the mountains. Ultimately they would follow this winding path for nine or ten miles, finally crossing a bridge over a stream which would lead them directly to the village.

So far the directions had been accurate. The karsts sprouted out of the earth like magic mushrooms growing closer and closer together until the rough road petered out entirely and was replaced by the narrow walking path. Michael felt Kate grasp him tightly as he twisted the throttle in an effort to keep them upright on the rough, rolling trail. He liked having her there, feeling her closeness. And he wanted to trust her. But he just didn't. There were still too many unanswered questions.

Continuing on, they soon found themselves in a meadow, the trail an ocher line stretching like a ribbon across the green grass. A small river was now visible in the distance, winding between the karsts where the meadow turned to water-filled rice paddies. Michael marveled at the place as he piloted the bike forward, careful to avoid dropping it on the path, which was soon reduced to a low berm between paddies, green rice shoots poking their heads out of the flooded fields.

Water buffalo lolled in muddy ponds and footprints dotted the berm, but there wasn't a human being in sight. After some time, Michael slowed the bike to a standstill, shutting down the engine in an effort to get his bearings. A gentle breeze could be heard rustling the trees growing up from the rocky soil of the karsts, a rooster crowing somewhere in the distance.

"There," Kate said, pointing to the other side of the far off river, where a wisp of smoke curled its way off the valley floor and up the side of a bent mountain. "Look familiar?"

Michael nodded. "I think we found our crooked karst."

• • •

A MILE AWAY the all-seeing eye of the MSS watched with detached scrutiny. The tracking device was working as specified, but truth be known, for the moment Huang was more interested in the landscape. He remembered fields like this from his time as a boy in rural Guangdong Province. Huang was still in the prime of his life, but he recognized that by and large, those times had passed. Nowadays he was more likely to rest his eyes on the never-ending array of newly constructed skyscrapers than to happen upon an empty field. Regardless, it didn't much matter. Huang had a job to do and he was getting close. The American was near his goal and he was near the American. Even without the assistance of their spies in the American camp, Huang believed his mission would soon be complete.

"Captain Huang," a junior agent interrupted.

"Yes?"

"The target is moving."

Huang snapped back to attention, focusing his gaze on the moving icon on the LCD screen. He reminded himself that now was not the moment to let his mind wander. There would be time for those reminiscences later. Now was the time for hunting.

• • •

As promised, after crossing the stream on a narrow crumbling foot bridge, they reached their destination. A studied look at Kate's iPhone confirmed that the crooked karst matched the engraving on the side of the capsule. This time, there was no disputing the angles. But why here? What made this place special? The village was quiet, almost eerily so, a ribbon of dirt running right through the center of it, stone huts on either side of the path. Michael and Kate continued to tool along slowly on the motorcycle until they passed a boy guiding a lone goat off the path and into a pen. Michael brought the motorcycle to a stop in the middle of the path where Kate got off to address the boy. The boy replied with a single syllable and a smile.

"What did you say?"

"I asked him if this was Yangkok."

"And?"

"He asked me, where else would it be?"

Michael kicked the bike onto its stand and they walked past several more vacant doorways, Michael finally poking his head inside one of the huts that seemed to promise more life than the others. There was what looked like a raw cotton mattress in the corner with some hay and a clay cooking oven in which the embers were still smoldering. The floor was unfinished stone and mud like the walls. As Michael's eyes adjusted to the dim light he was able to make out a short-haired pig sleeping in the corner. There was a blackened wok, and a set of chipped, recently washed plates. Not exactly a manse, but it would keep the rain out.

There were no signs of the hut's inhabitant and Michael was about to move on when he heard an enormous squawk behind him. He turned to find himself facing the boy whose path they had already crossed. He now held a live chicken which he carried upside down by its feet.

"Ask him where everybody is."

"You mean like, take me to your leader?"

"Just ask," Michael said.

Kate addressed the boy in a few simple Mandarin words, and the boy responded. "He said the green creatures came. They inserted probes into the children. Then they beamed the village elders into their golden space ship."

Michael just looked at Kate.

"I'm kidding," she smiled. "He said most people left the village when the government told them this land would be flooded in a hydroelectric project. Only his grandparents and a few of the older people have stayed behind."

The boy then said something else.

"He asks if we are friends with the American man who came here many months ago."

Michael felt a jolt of pure electricity run up his spine. If there were Americans way out here, he knew he wanted to hear about them. The boy continued to speak, Kate translating.

"He says there was a man that looked something like you, only older, with gray hair, but the eyes, the blue eyes were the same. The man came here and asked a lot of questions."

"What kind of questions?"

Kate translated. "He says he doesn't know. He says he only saw the man speaking with his grandfather. He couldn't hear well."

"When did he come?"

Again Kate translated. "He thinks about three months ago."

Michael felt something that he hadn't felt for some time, something that felt like hope.

"Where is his grandfather? I want to speak with him."

The boy didn't seem to require a translator. He simply looked to Kate and uttered three short syllables.

"He says to follow him."

THE BOY LED them past several more open doors, to another hut, in many ways identical to the ones they had passed. The difference was that this hut showed activity both inside and out. An old woman, her silver gray hair shorn, swept off the dusty stones in front of the door. The fresh scent of stir-fried vegetables hung in the air, a steady chopping sound echoing out from within. The woman smiled at the boy before straightening her tired back in the presence of the strangers. Despite her smile, Michael guessed that she was less than pleased with the intrusion. She called inside the hut and the chopping ceased, Kate taking over in Mandarin.

"Hello. We met your grandson on the path." Both Michael and Kate smiled as the old woman eyed them warily. "He said an American that looked a lot like this one," Kate pointed to Michael, "came here many months ago."

If the old woman looked disinclined to help before, she was positively tight lipped now. Michael observed what seemed to be the particularly Chinese habit of smiling under duress. Whatever this woman knew, he doubted very much she'd be sharing it with them, and by the looks of that smile, he suspected the kid would get a few whacks with the end of her broom as well. Michael spoke to Kate without turning to her.

"No way she's talking."

"Not a chance."

"So what now?"

Kate smiled back at the old woman and stepped past her, poking her head into the open doorway. Michael appreciated Kate's initiative, but wished there was another way. It was after all this woman's home she was entering uninvited. As fate would have it, though, Kate did little more than bob her head into the shadowy interior before she bobbed right back out again, staring into the face of a man who looked older than time itself. The man carried a worn pocket knife in one hand, a long green onion in the other. Michael wasn't sure if the old man intended to whip Kate with the onion or cut her eyes out with the knife, but he did neither. Instead, he simply stepped into the sunlight and appraised his visitors. The old woman was quiet, the boy observing silently from the path. Even the chicken stopped squawking.

Kate opened her mouth and began to say something in Mandarin, but the old man put a finger to his lips. Kate was silent and the old man, who looked like he had been crying, rubbed his tired fingers over his sweaty brow and up through his long strands of greasy hair. The action revealed a keloid scar which started near the middle of his forehead and looked as though it kept on going right over the top of his skull. The scar was clearly old and had obviously been sewn up with little concern for the finesse of modern plastic surgery. From the steely stare in his wizened eyes, though, Michael could tell that aesthetics of the wound were long forgotten, even if its cause had not been. The old man uttered a word, flicking the wet green onions like a switch as he did.

"What did he say?" Michael quietly asked Kate.

"He said, go."

"Ask him about the American."

Kate began to translate, but this time the old man's answer wasn't a word, but a gruff scream. "He says to go, now."

Michael looked to the old lady, then back at the man with the scar. It was most likely her husband, possibly her father, but it was hard to tell. Either way, it didn't matter. The chicken squawked behind them, Michael fairly certain that they would learn no more. Not under these circumstances. Not on this visit.

"Then let's go," Michael said, and as he turned, he cast a second glance at the pocket knife the old man held between his thumb and fingers. The rust-colored blade was extended, its tip broken off, no doubt from hard use. But what caught Michael's eye wasn't the blade, or the way the old man held it. It was the insignia embossed on the piano-black handle exactly where the Swiss Cross would have been be located had it been a Swiss Army knife. Except, Michael noted, it wasn't a Swiss Army knife. It was a German Army knife. And it wasn't embossed with a Swiss Cross. It was engraved with a silver swastika. The Nazi emblem glinted in the midday sun, still shiny after all these years.

29

When he was *eighteen, Michael's father taught him about honor. Michael's grandfather had just died and Michael was due at the funeral. The problem was, Michael was away at college. There was no way to go to the funeral without missing his final exams. Michael had been reasonably close to his grandfather and he knew that he wouldn't want him missing his finals. Not for his funeral. Not when he was already dead. But not going would look bad. Michael knew it would. It would look bad to his aunt and uncle, his cousins, and everybody else. Michael asked his dad what he thought he should do and his dad told him to do what Grandpa would. So Michael thought about it. Then he drank a Black and Tan and hit the books. Michael skipped the funeral. And he knew his grandfather was smiling in his grave. Because honor isn't about doing what's popular. It's about doing what's right. And Michael's dad gave him the permission to do that.*

Less than ten minutes had passed, but Michael knew that the image of the Nazi pocket knife had been seared into his brain for an eternity. He sat with Kate, straddling the motorcycle at the base of the crooked karst, staring down the path to the village of Yangkok below. They needed to think, they needed to regroup, but most importantly they needed to find a means of getting the old man to share what he so obviously knew.

"There you are talking about how we have to work smart. How we need a bird to catch our fish for us. Well we got our bird, Michael. That was him down there with a scar the size of Cuba running down his forehead. What are we doing here?"

"We weren't going to get anywhere. Not like that."

"Like what then? Look at it. The mountain we're sitting on is a match to the engraving. The old man had the knife. The knife is a direct link to the Nazis and the Horten and whatever else went on here during World War II. An American that looked a lot like you went through there three months ago. Three months would have been February. Everything, and I mean everything, adds up. Hell, if we can get that old man to talk it might just be a road map directly to your father."

"You think I don't know all this?"

"Then what?" Kate got off the bike, addressing Michael head on. "It's time we pushed. Maybe the old man won't say anything. But the woman might. Or the kid. We just need to be persuasive."

"And the best way to do that," Michael said, "is to learn more. They made it clear they don't want us asking questions. If we're going to get anywhere with these people, we need to know who they are and what they want. We need an in before we try again."

"If we even have time to try again."

Michael looked directly at Kate. "What does that mean?"

Kate pulled the stray strands of hair away from her face. It was a habit Michael had made note of. She did it when she was nervous or anxious. Michael guessed that she also did it when she was about to come clean.

"Last night, while you were sleeping, I made a call."

"Please tell me you used a payphone."

Kate nodded. "I talked to my handler in London. He only spoke a few words before getting off the line, but it was enough."

"What did he say?"

"The bird's gone south."

Michael was silent.

"Like everything else, the Chinese are looking for supremacy in space. Three days ago they launched a satellite incorporating a new version of the Horten's cold fusion reactor as its power source. About fourteen hours after that they lost communication with that satellite. Subsequently its orbit began to degrade. If its orbit continues to degrade at its current rate, its most likely reentry point is somewhere above Southern California. Exactly what will happen when it reenters the atmosphere is unknown. What we do know is that a breach of the reactor core will result in an explosion on an order of magnitude the world has seldom seen. And even if by some miracle the breach from the primary reactor isn't catastrophic, prevailing winds will ensure that the radioactive fallout from its secondary coil will be worldwide." Kate met Michael's eyes. "If this thing comes down a whole lot of people are going to die, Michael."

"Why didn't you tell me about this before?"

"You're a civilian. I didn't want you to have a complete meltdown."

"I wouldn't exactly call myself a civilian." The truth was Michael hadn't considered himself a civilian since he was seventeen. Not since that fateful day when his kidnappers had given up. Despite holding him for three days, his father had not come. That meant that Michael was no longer of any use. They said they would kill him. But they weren't that kind. Instead of killing him, they locked him in a narrow mine shaft—no food, no water, and no way out. Michael didn't know how long he had waited there before help came. But he knew he was no longer a civilian. After that he'd never be a civilian again.

"What would you call yourself then?" Kate said.

"A realist."

"Good. Then understand this. That satellite is the equivalent of a very large bomb. To make that bomb the Chinese reverse engineered their reactor design including all of its communications protocols from the damaged Horten they found. If we can locate the second Horten and plug it into that green box we found, if the boys in tech can find a clear-code that will reboot its systems, there's a chance we can keep that bomb from blowing."

"Just a chance?"

"A chance is the best we've got."

Michael stared down at the low clouds hanging over the valley. Regardless of the belated manner in which Kate had shared this information, he knew in the pit of his gut that she was right. The stakes were too high to beat around the bush. They needed to talk to the old man. But something material had to change. They needed a reason for him to trust them. Instead they got a clap of thunder. A gunshot echoed up from the valley below. It sounded like a twelve gauge, but Michael guessed it could have come from any large caliber weapon. It was followed quickly by a second shot, this one seemingly louder than the first and in that moment, Michael knew that the luxury of decision was no longer his. The second shot still reverberating through the hills, he kicked the bike to life, Kate hopping on behind him.

They heard the screaming before Michael even killed the engine. The boy stood wailing in the middle of the path, tears streaming down his face. The old woman then stepped out of the hut and one look at her told Michael that the man with the knife had been her husband and he was dead. She ignored Michael and hunched over on the ground, knees in the dirt. Others appeared, hurrying down hidden trails onto the main footpath of the village, and soon the wailing was everywhere. One of their own had fallen.

Michael dropped the bike in the soft dirt and headed into the hut where the old man had been cooking. He only needed to poke his head in the doorway for a second before looking away. It wasn't like an automobile accident seen from afar, it was more visceral than that. And despite everything Michael thought he knew about being born from the earth and going right back to it, he felt an overpowering urge to sink to his hands and knees and vomit. The old man's head, or what was left of it, was slumped to the side of his neck at an unnatural angle. A second shot had taken out most of his face, reducing what had been a person to what looked like a bloody rump roast hanging from a stump of flesh. Michael grasped his gut and dry heaved. Kate, who had entered the hut cautiously behind Michael, looked momentarily stunned, a faraway look in her eye. Michael left the hut.

"Who did this?" Michael asked two of the villagers. "Who did this?"

The villagers ignored him. Michael's only response was the low moan of the old woman, the boy now seated against the stone wall of a nearby hut dropping a pebble repeatedly into the mud as though caught in an infinite loop of disbelief.

Kate echoed Michael's question in Mandarin. The stray villagers who had come down from the hillside looked up at her, but quickly redirected their attention to the old woman. Kate, undeterred, continued forward, repeating the question. The villagers only shook their heads. Looking at them, still breathing hard from their run from the fields, it was unlikely that there would have been any witnesses except for the kid and the old woman. No, it was obvious to Michael that if he wanted answers he was going to have to go straight to the source. But Kate beat him to it. She knelt down in the dirt before the old woman, taking her by the hands.

Kate spoke in soft Mandarin, but the woman didn't reply to her. She just looked directly through Kate as though whatever these foreigners might do or say from this moment on didn't matter. Her husband was after all sitting not ten feet away, dead as Mao, his head hanging off his neck like so many pounds of raw meat. But Michael was now convinced there would be more death if they didn't press on.

"Your husband. He had a knife."

The old woman looked up at Michael and wailed the long, low moan of the emotionally dead. The moan didn't end, it just went on and on echoing through the hills until finally Michael stood, taking Kate by the shoulder. Even if this was the only way forward, Michael reasoned they had to give it time, if only a little. But then, as Michael raised Kate to her feet, the old woman looked up from the dirt and met Michael's eye. She held the look for a long moment. Then she muttered something, barely audible at first. To Michael's unpracticed ear it sounded like a single syllable, maybe two.

Kate addressed the woman softly in Mandarin. "What was that? I didn't hear."

This time the old woman screamed in forceful Mandarin, slapping her open hand against her skull.

"What is it? What's she saying?"

Kate struggled to understand, the old woman still screaming. "It's in his head," Kate said. "She says it's in his head."

30

THE OLD WOMAN moaned down at the earth, arms clutched against the side of her skull.

"What? What's in his head?"

Michael did his best to reach out to the woman, placing his hands on her shoulders to calm her, but she pulled away, slapping her skull, still screaming.

"Tell me what's she saying."

"The same thing. It's in his head."

Michael turned toward the villagers who had gathered from the surrounding hills. "Ask them if they know what she's talking about."

Kate addressed the villagers. They responded, but one look at Kate's face told Michael she didn't understand what they were getting at. "They say the old woman talked a lot. About the war."

"Which war?"

Kate translated as the villager went on. "He says the war that happened long ago. The war with many doctors."

"What kind of doctors?"

Kate translated. "He says, Japan. Japanese doctors."

Michael thought about it. "The Imperial Japanese Army was a Nazi ally here. They had a whole lot of guns, but not many doctors, at least not out here. Not in the sticks." Michael paused for a moment. "Oh, Jesus."

"What?"

"I read some of the history of the area before I left home. There were hospitals in Guilin. They were known for certain procedures."

"Procedures?"

"Keep the woman outside," Michael said, already halfway back to the hut.

MICHAEL KNEW WHAT needed to be done, he just wasn't certain he wanted do it. What he hadn't made clear to Kate were the type of activities the Japanese Imperial Army had become famous for: namely the medical experimentation upon and vivisection of conquered peoples. Michael recalled that the experiments ranged from testing vaccines to the clinical administration of torture, right on through to genetic manipulation and vivisection. But staring down at the old man lying there in a spray of arterial blood, his head half blown off, Michael was less concerned with what the experiments were comprised of than with what came next.

Steeling his nerve, Michael looked away from the old man's corpse to the clay oven in the corner of the hut. On top of the newly washed dishes sat a pair of yellow rubber gloves. Michael put them on, noting that the old man's fingers were still wrapped around his pocket knife, rigor mortis setting in. Michael had no desire to make this process anymore invasive than it had to be, so he reached into his own pocket for his newly purchased Swiss Army knife. He opened up the main blade thinking that this was probably not what the manufacturer had intended. The old man's face was gone, disintegrated in a flurry of shot, and Michael knew that his first task was to cut away the skin so that he could get to the skull. Holding the head steady in one hand, Michael exhaled and made his first cut, sinking the blade into the flesh laterally along the pulpy scalp. Though this was definitely a first for him, he thought that all those years of carving jack-o'-lanterns could finally be put to good use.

"Michael?" Kate said, poking her head in the doorway unable to keep the look of what had to be horror from spreading across her face.

"Just keep the woman and the kid away."

Michael carefully sliced the bloody skin back from the skull. He continued cutting slowly but firmly with the knife, slicing the skin down toward the left eye.

"What are you doing?"

"You heard her. It's in his head."

"It's an expression. Like, I've got a song in my head. It doesn't mean I literally have a song in my head."

"Here I think it does."

Michael doubled back and continued his incision down toward the right eye. Holding the head steady in one hand, he took hold of the flap of skin between thumb and forefinger and peeled the flesh down the skull like the skin of a grape.

"Do you have to?" Kate asked, covering her mouth and looking away.

Michael's medical training was limited to basic first-aid, but with the skin gone and the bone of the skull exposed beneath, he saw exactly what he had thought he might: a discoloration in the skull. The discoloration was darker than the rest of the area, round, and about two inches in diameter. It's hue was a yellowish black, but when Michael rubbed it with his glove, the fatty substance rubbed away revealing a perfectly round metal plate inset in the old man's skull like an all-knowing third eye. Michael reached back toward the sink grasping a pitcher of water. Quickly rinsing the plate, the small recessed screws holding it anchored firmly into the skull became visible, their tiny Phillips heads shining out at him like stars. The four screws were encrusted with calcium deposits after being in the old man's skull for decades, but with the help of his Swiss Army knife, Michael was able to scrape them off and twist them two turns each. After this he inserted the blade of his knife into the edge of the skull around the perimeter of the plate. One smooth lever motion and the plate popped out, nearly hitting the floor before Michael caught it in his yellow-gloved hand.

Though it was hard to tell in the low light if the plate was nickel or platinum, one thing was clear: it had been cast to resemble a full moon. Japanese Kanji were inscribed around its circumference, a stylized relief of a double-peaked karst etched in the foreground. Twin peaks rising before a full moon, the pointed mountain looked strangely familiar yet like nothing Michael had ever seen before. It looked, Michael thought, like the devil's pitchfork.

31

Rand laid into Mobi like there was no tomorrow. He threatened prison. He threatened a lively physical interrogation before Mobi made it to prison. And he threatened an active sex life for the duration of Mobi's stay in prison. Then, after several wasted hours during which Mobi was forced to sit in the corner like a new improved Buddha, Rand decided he needed him. He conscripted Mobi to assist his men in the installation of their equipment in JPL's main tracking station. Apparently, the ASAT orbital platforms Alvarez had referenced could be controlled from just about anywhere, provided there was a set of eyes to monitor their progress and a large enough antenna to provide secure communication. Through its Goldstone Deep Space Antenna Array and trained technicians, JPL provided both.

Alvarez clicked her tongue, clearly done with the long wait. "It looks like you've got all the angles covered, Colonel."

"Nice try, but you and your engineer are sitting in on this one. I don't want to encounter any resistance up here and the best way to ensure that is to keep you two on tap."

"Respectfully, I have eleven active missions that I need to keep flying today. I'm sure NASA would prefer that you let us do our jobs."

"I couldn't give my sorry-ass pension what NASA prefers," Rand said. "That stunt your engineer pulled, hacking beyond his pay grade, proves he isn't to be trusted. If there's a problem with the uplink, I want him here where I can see him."

"Which is where he's going to be," Alvarez said, pointing across the large room. "Right behind that door, watching space traffic in Secondary Ops while you get the prime real estate here in Mission Control."

Rand considered. He might still need Alvarez. No need to piss the lady off for nothing. "If I need him," he said, "I want him stat."

"You'll have him."

Rand eyed his two operations engineers, both comfortably ensconced in front of their terminals. "How long until we're in range?"

"If the current orbital degradation holds?"

"Ballpark," Rand said.

"Thirty-nine, forty minutes."

Rand looked to Alvarez and said, "Keep him close."

Mobi immediately understood he was being offered a reprieve and stepped across the room, moving to pull the door to Secondary Ops open. But as he laid his fingers on it, Alvarez's hand touched his, opening the door for him. Mobi's eyes met Alvarez's for a split second as he felt her fingers on his palm, but he quickly looked away. Once in Secondary Ops, Mobi kept right on walking out the door on the other side, buoyed by the keycard he felt hidden in the palm of his hand.

Mobi knew what the keycard meant. Thankfully, the rigorous biometric security protocols of JPL's secure level entrance were behind him. He swiped his way back down to the lower lab and within a couple of minutes he was inside Alvarez's office. Alvarez had a pair of louvered blinds on the glass window to the corridor which he promptly closed. He checked the multi-line phone on the desk. It had an internal configuration. Then he examined the keycard. Alvarez had scrawled an eighteen-digit number on the back of it which Mobi guessed included a contact number for Quiann. But Mobi knew he wouldn't be able to make a call out without going through the JPL operator. Not the best plan under the circumstances. He tried the desk drawers, but found little of note: a few pencils and pens, a ream of paper, and a pack of batteries. Mobi began to question his assumptions. Was her office where Alvarez had intended he come? With the exception of her long mohair coat sitting rumpled in the corner, the place was empty.

Mobi rifled through the pockets of the coat finding nothing but a half-empty box of Tic-Tacs. He was about to eat one when he noticed something else—a bright-green foot poking out from under the coat. Mobi could immediately tell that the foot wasn't human, or even real for that matter. It belonged to a green alien balloon— the kind you could buy for five bucks from a vendor in Griffith Park. Lifting the coat off the floor revealed that the alien had the typical Roswell look. It wasn't the first time Mobi had seen this particular toy. This alien was something of an unofficial mascot at JPL and more than one employee had one strung up in their office. What Mobi found strange, however, was the fact that Alvarez would have one in an office completely devoid of any other personal touch. Alvarez must dig her X-files, Mobi thought, or else....

Mobi examined the alien balloon carefully, noting that it was a little heavier in one foot than the other, not much, but a little. The green-tinted PVC plastic was transparent under the right light, and holding the little bugger up to the fluorescent tube, Mobi was able to see what looked like a black plastic wafer in its left foot. Feeling a surge of excitement now, Mobi placed his thumb on the sole of the inflatable foot and his fingers on the heel, pressing down on the black wafer inside. No sooner did Mobi feel a bubble switch in the plastic wafer click down, than a hum emanated from the rear of the office. Turning around, Mobi watched Alvarez's entire rear wall slide open behind her desk.

"Nice," Mobi muttered quietly to himself. Then, clutching the inflatable alien at his side, Mobi silently entered Alvarez's inner sanctum.

32

By the time Michael and Kate got back to Yangshuo, the sun had already set, casting long shadows across West Street. The same thought had been cycling through Michael's head for the entire ride back. Another damn karst, he thought, picturing the engraving on the platinum disc. The same karsts that covered the landscape were apparently the solution to his problem. After all, a Japanese surgical team had chosen to implant one in a man's head. That wasn't the kind of thing you did without a very good reason. No, both the pitchfork-karst engraving and the Kanji around the disc's rim were significant. He just needed to figure out why.

Michael and Kate returned the rented motorcycle to its much relieved owner and climbed the Whispering Bamboo's wooden stairs roofward. If there was a solution to their problem, it was here, in the inscriptions on the capsule. Kate latched the wooden door behind them to ensure they wouldn't be disturbed, but it took only a moment to discover that they had a much bigger problem.

"Shit," Michael said.

The capsule was gone.

There was no other way to put it. The cowling of the swamp fan stood open and the lock was snapped off, but the capsule was nowhere to be seen. All that was left were boot prints, lots of them, covering the tar and gravel surface of the roof. Michael crouched down and ran the gravel through his fingers, the rough crush warm to the touch. Then Michael's eyes widened in the fading light. There was something else. A pool of something dark and sticky. Blood.

"Kate?"

"I see it," she said, staring down at the blood.

"Not that."

Michael was halfway across the rooftop by the time the words had left his mouth. The form had been just a dark mass in the dusk, but now as Michael approached it became clear that it was a body. And not just any body. It was Ted, lying there, facedown on the roof. Michael locked his hand over Ted's shoulder, preparing for the worst. But he didn't get it. With a simple touch Michael could already tell that Ted was still breathing. He turned him onto his back to reveal the nasty gash on his friend's forehead.

"Ted?"

There was no response.

"We need to get him out of here."

Kate stood, but immediately froze, Michael followed her gaze. The wooden door to the stairs had begun to rattle on its hinges. Kate reached behind her back, withdrawing her Glock with the smooth grace of a seasoned professional. Crouching down on one knee, she extended her arms, holding the gun at ready. They were in a decent enough position on the corner of the roof, out of the immediate angle of sight. Michael studied Kate's hands. They were steady, her trigger finger icy calm.

Ted groaned. Now was not the time for him to come to, Michael thought. Then he groaned again and what happened next occurred very quickly. The door broke. It literally exploded off its hinges accompanied by a scream the likes of which Michael had never heard before. A dark figure burst through the door and rolled twice across the roof before taking cover behind the swamp fan. Kate tracked the figure with her weapon as an object, it looked like a box, or a bomb, came skidding across the gravel roof toward them. Both Kate and Michael dove behind the cover of a large water cistern. The rectangular object skidded to a stop, maybe twenty feet away from them. There was no way to get any farther away from it without literally leaping six stories off the roof to the concrete below. They waited a moment, then two, and in the dying light Michael thought he recognized a symbol on the object. Not a swastika this time, a cross. A red cross.

"Mates?" a voice said from behind the swamp fan.

Michael recognized the voice immediately. It took Kate a moment longer, but she got it too, lowering her weapon. It was Crust. He edged into view from behind the cowling, picking up the box with the cross on it, now clearly recognizable as a first aid kit.

"I heard voices up here and it got me worried." He indicated the first aid kit and said, "Thought the old man might need this."

Crust explained that he, too, had been looking for them. Instead he had found Ted unconscious on the rooftop, blood seeping from the nasty gash on his head. Fearful of moving him, Crust did the next best thing and went to get medical help. Unfortunately, the best he could come up with was the first aid kit.

"You nearly shot me, sister! What are you doing with a gun?"

"Defending myself from crazy Ninjas."

"People," Ted said groggily, "this is beside the point."

"He's right," Michael said. "Ted. Tell us what happened?"

"Let's just say I ran into a problem with your friends from the bridge."

"The thing I wanted to show you?" Michael said, careful not to give away specifics in front of Crust.

"Gone," Ted said, wiping the blood from his forehead. "Tell me you had more luck than I did."

Michael cast a glance at Crust and then thought to hell with it. He reached into his pocket and removed the platinum disc revealing the engraving of the double-peaked karst. Ted was silent for a long moment.

"Are you sure it's genuine?"

"I'm sure."

"Then we need to find out where it is."

"There are over ten thousand peaks in the immediate area," Kate said. "Just like with the first engraving, it's going to take time to narrow it down."

"I don't think so," Crust said.

Both Michael and Kate looked over their shoulders. "What do you mean?"

"All you need to do is float, brother."

"Float?"

"Snag yourself a tube, a kayak, a sheep's stomach if you prefer. Just float."

"Why?"

"Because mate," Crust said pointing at the platinum disc. "This gnarly mountain is about eight clicks down our lovely Li River."

• • •

HUANG AND HIS subordinates watched the LCD screen blip from their safe house. He and his men had easily taken the metal capsule from the rooftop. With the American tagged it had been simple enough to find it. But analysis would have to wait. What Huang hadn't expected was that after so many years of searching, events would progress so quickly. The American was once again on the move and needed to be followed. Huang reminded himself that this was a good thing. His sources told him that progress was being made with the errant satellite. If the American actually found what he was looking for here on the ground, they would capture both him and the Horten. If not, Huang knew he had already netted sufficient gains to impress his superiors. Either way, the American would lose and Huang would win.

• • •

AFTER A CHORUS of thank-yous and promises of yet another free meal, Crust, still a little leery of Kate and her sidearm, had gone happily on his way. Ted, however, insisted that he had recovered sufficiently from his concussion to continue on. As far as Ted was concerned, he may have been ambushed by the bad guys, but the game was far from over. After picking up several packs of equipment that he had procured after Michael had brought him up to speed the night before, they made their way down West Street to the Yangshuo river docks. The fishermen had already gone home for the evening so renting or bartering a vessel was out of the question. It was clear that if they wanted a boat, they'd simply have to take one.

Michael chose a blunt-nosed, flat-bottomed riverboat of about twenty-five feet in length with a small cabin abovedeck. As a rule Michael didn't like to steal, but given the circumstances, he didn't see the alternative. He managed to get the boat untied, and with Kate's help they quietly poled it into deeper water where the current quickly took hold. Michael had some experience with engines thanks to the Yellow Bomber dune buggy project with his dad, but it didn't take much to get the motor going. After manually connecting two wires to complete an ignition circuit with the battery, the engine fired after the fourth or fifth attempt. Though it seemed like the motor might be creating more racket than it was thrust, soon there was a tiny froth of water at the stern, and more importantly, he was now able to steer.

Looking behind them, Michael saw that they had already rounded the bend, any sign of civilization lost to the lush green karsts lording over the river. Ted poked his head out of the cabin and took a seat beside him.

"I take it we're clear?"

"So far."

"So what do you say we take another look at what you found out there?"

Michael cast a glance down at Kate belowdecks as he removed the engraved platinum plate from his pocket. He carefully dipped it in the river, rubbing it with his thumb to remove the dried blood from its surface.

"One condition," he said.

"Name it."

"You tell me the whole truth about my father."

33

THE SKY DARKENED quickly now, towering limestone peaks throwing black shadows over the landscape. The river was narrower here, maybe a hundred feet across, their tiny boat swallowed by the enormous gorge, the bases of the karsts themselves forming the walls of the winding waterway. The drone of the boat's engine reverberating off the rock walls accompanied them like an old friend, and though he tried to write the thought off as just another bad memory from high school, Michael felt like they were sailing into the heart of an immeasurable and immense darkness.

"The truth is your dad was a complicated man," Ted said, toying with the platinum plate between thumb and forefinger. "More than that, he was a driven one. He pushed the recovery of the Horten long after it had lost its luster with management." Ted looked directly to Kate. "He pushed it even after they took him off the mission."

"So you're saying he wasn't supposed to be looking for it?"

"He wasn't exactly off the reservation," Ted said. "The Company gave him some latitude, but yeah, they would have preferred if he'd left the Horten alone for a lot of those years. Until recently that is."

Michael held the tiller firmly in hand as the hulking karsts sailed slowly past like watchmen to the great beyond. He knew Ted would go on even if he didn't ask the next question. He asked it anyway.

"What changed?"

"People started dying, that's what." Ted took a breath as Kate took a seat a few feet nearer. She was clearly as interested as Michael, if not more so. "Management started to pick up independent reports of what your dad had been telling them all along: that the recovery of the Horten was about more than just finding an old Nazi airplane. That the Horten's cold fusion reactor was a source of clean energy that could make oil obsolete. That certain fringe groups were not only actively after the Horten, but they were willing to kill for it. And they weren't willing to kill just anybody. They were willing to kill Americans. The Uruguayan embassy bombing really put one group in particular on the map. They call themselves the Green Dragons. We think they're an offshoot of an earlier organization that came to prominence in wartime Japan."

"They're thought to be an evolution of the samurai groups," Kate said. "We've heard rumors that the group still engages in sword making and, on occasion, in the ritual seppuku suicide ceremony, but none of that really tells us much. Pretty well every social structure in Japan is traced to the samurai in one way or another."

Ted nodded. "She's right. Other than that we don't know a lot. Are the Green Dragons a terrorist organization? A quasi-religious order? Some type of multi-national investment group? We don't know. What the chatter out there does tell us is that through a series of shell companies they appear to have acquired massive energy interests across the globe. Hydroelectric, coal, oil, even nuclear. They've been active since World War II, but they really started to roll in the energy sphere in the eighties, back when Japan was flush with cash."

"Chen was making snow globes at the factory," Michael said. "Snow globes of the Earth marked by tiny lights. What do you think? Do the lights represent the Dragons' energy interests? Maybe their power plants?"

"They might. They might not. That's what's so frustrating about this group. We don't know enough about them to know what their endgame is. It may be just to make money. Or to control the political landscape. Or it may be more. We're not even sure about their interest in the Horten. The prevailing theory is that they have more of a negative interest in it than a positive one. That the Horten's cold fusion reactor would interfere with business as usual, so they want it to remain hidden. It would certainly explain why your father was such a thorn in their side."

"So my dad, how close was he to exposing them?"

"Really close if you were to ask him," Ted said. "And that's the other side of it. That's why the investigation into your dad's death ended so abruptly. Understand I haven't been active for years, but I have it on good authority that the Agency thought he was close too. They did everything in their power to maintain your father's cover by quelling any civilian investigation into his disappearance. The long and short of it is that your father had made some real progress and management didn't want to spook the Dragons with a local investigation. They wanted to give them the freedom to pop their heads out of the sand so they could come in and lop them off."

Michael thought it over. "This Green Dragon Group. The CIA with all its resources must have found more on them than what you've just told me."

"Well there is one other thing, but they didn't find it."

"Who did?"

"You." Ted pointed out the Japanese characters inscribed around the circumference of the platinum disc. "These Kanji are in the old style, but their meaning is clear."

"What do they say?"

"They say," Ted said quietly, "Here lies the dragon."

34

When the back wall of Alvarez's office slid open like the door to the bridge of the Starship Enterprise, Mobi knew he was back at the JPL he loved. Alvarez's anteroom was small, only about five feet deep and fifteen feet long, but it contained everything that her official office lacked: a secure server, pictures of her kids, and a well-used laptop which Mobi immediately cracked open. It was now obvious that the plastic alien out in the main office was a spare remote for the alcove, a key under the doormat in case Alvarez were to get locked out. He also realized that the alcove was probably built the way it was because even on a blueprint, nobody was going to miss that much space in such a large complex. No doubt the Director of Operations himself, a Caltech civilian to the end, had secretly authorized its construction because he didn't trust the DOD and their pet project below his facility. The tiny private operations center Mobi now sat within would have been an antidote to all that, a thorn in the side of the militarists who wanted to turn JPL into an extension of the Defense Department. Here,

Alvarez would be able to operate independently, secreted away from the watchful eye of the DOD. And here, if Alvarez had her way, Mobi would be able to do his thing as well.

Alvarez's laptop demanded a password and the mystery of the scrawled digits on the keycard fell into place. Guessing that Alvarez had kept it simple, Mobi typed in the first five digits and he was in. The last thirteen digits beginning with the 011 were no doubt Quiann's phone number. Mobi launched Alvarez's secure soft phone. He knew the data packets were trojaned to resemble standard internet traffic. Not untraceable to be sure, but given that he was about to share state secrets with a known traitor for the betterment of all mankind, it was better than nothing. Now, after untold hours of waiting around, Mobi was so excited to finally be doing something constructive that at first he didn't notice the door to Alvarez's outer office swing open.

"What are you doing here?"

Mobi literally jumped out of his seat. It was the blonde Air Force guy who was asking the question; the one who had slapped the handcuffs on him in the restroom. Mobi stood and stepped outside the alcove to meet his guest in the main office. He gestured nervously to the green alien he held in his hand. "Alvarez is a bit of a UFO nut."

"I said, why are you here??"

"Just, computing."

Mobi watched the cogs turn in the Air Force guy's head.

"I'd like you to come with me."

"Why?"

"Because I said so."

Tautology. If there was anything Mobi hated, it was tautology. Because he said so. The argument was circular. This ball-breaking bully was treating Mobi like a child. And in that moment Mobi did what he'd wanted to do to every ball-breaking bully he'd encountered since the first grade—he hauled back with the green alien and hurled it at him. Which would have been fine if the alien had been a sack of bricks. But given that it was inflated plastic, it simply bounced off the blonde man's square jaw. And only then did Mobi realize the mistake he had made. He'd made him mad. Worse than that, along with the alien, he'd thrown out the remote control to the retractable wall. Not quite the smooth escape he'd been looking for.

"You chunky prick."

The Air Force guy strode toward him. Now Mobi knew he was in trouble. He stepped back into the alcove and tried to think his way through the situation. He was in an alcove with a computer and a chair. Not much else. Just him, the Air Force guy, and a retractable wall. The retractable wall was, of course, the key. If it opened, it had to close. And Alvarez had to have a better way to do so than poking a green alien in the foot. Mobi searched the walls of the alcove for a panel or a button as his new friend approached. He found nothing. Was the wall voice activated?

"Wall. Close."

"Dream on, asshole."

"Close wall!"

The wall didn't listen and Mobi was fast running out of ideas. The blonde man had skirted around Alvarez's desk and was only steps from the alcove. Think what Alvarez would do. She probably used this space only occasionally, when she didn't want people to see what she was doing. Maybe when she was working in private. Maybe when she wanted to guard the contents of her computer. Mobi copped a glance at Alvarez's laptop. Its screen was open. He thought about it as his assailant drew a weapon from a hidden holster. It was worth a try.

"Hands in the air," the blonde man said.

Mobi risked it. He idly reached out one of his outstretched palms to his side in a slow motion wave and slapped Alvarez's laptop shut. He heard a relay kicking over. It was followed by a pneumatic whoosh.

"No you don't, fat ass," the blonde man yelled, diving toward him.

But it was too late. The wall had already closed. There was a click as it locked into place and Mobi found himself alone once again, only the glow of the server's LEDs lighting up the dark space.

35

Here lies the dragon. Michael mulled over the words. What they were looking for, what his father had been looking for, had remained hidden since the last years of World War II, despite repeated efforts by both the Chinese and a slew of foreign governments to locate it. Now, if what Michael had found buried deep within the old man's skull was what it seemed, they were about to find it, hidden alongside a river that hundreds, if not thousands of people traveled daily. It seemed impossible, and yet, in some strange way, it also seemed right.

"There."

Michael followed Kate's gaze across the bow of the boat. Perhaps a hundred yards ahead, nestled into a sharp bend of the river sat the double-peaked karst, rising like the devil's pitchfork out of the black waters of the Li.

Michael motored forward a few more yards before turning the tiller hard and cutting the engine. They drifted silently to shore, just the hint of the afterglow of a blood-orange sunset illuminating the loamy riverbank. Thirty feet up the rough river beach stood the limestone walls of the double-peaked karst. Michael hopped off the bow of the boat, pulling the long bowline up the bank to a crooked tree where he tied it off in a clove hitch. Kate followed Michael off the bow, Ted handing off a trio of climbing packs, each complete with a collapsible shovel bungeed to its back panel. Already, what ambient light was left in the sky had given way to a deep navy blue, the evening's first stars twinkling above.

Michael pulled out his headlamp and turned his attention to the base of the looming karst. The thought of scaling a mountain, though, especially a lush mountain like this one, brought back Peru. The kidnappers had abandoned their operation at the last moment and left him to die in that mineshaft. The physical toll as he perched there with burning legs and an aching back, the walls of the shaft pressing in all around him was one thing, and it was horrible. But what was worse was the mental torture. The doubt. What if his father, despite his best intentions, was just too late? It was the doubt that proved to be Michael's worst demon.

Somehow, Michael had been able to summon a deep faith in his own ability to survive and he had hung on. When his desperately relieved father finally poked his head down the shaft, extending his arms downward, Michael wasn't convinced that he wasn't hallucinating. It was only the roar of the helicopter when he was dragged out of the shaft that had finally snapped him back to reality. Michael was choppered down the mountain and immediately given medical attention. Dehydration had taken its toll on him, but once he learned just how hard his father had worked to find him, Michael felt ashamed that he had ever doubted him. But despite his love for his dad, he also knew that he never wanted to have to rely on somebody else for his survival. To that end, Michael refused to give up doing what he loved. He camped, he climbed, in fact, he threw himself into it with a vengeance, just as he did the martial arts and every other aspect of his life. Michael made it his mission to do anything and everything to never be the victim again.

Two years after the ordeal, he had attempted a technical assault on a little-known Rocky Mountain peak with some friends from college. This time the enemy wasn't doubt, but bad weather. A storm had prevented them from reaching the summit, but he had learned something from the experience, and no matter how much he tried to suppress it, two things about his current situation gnawed at him: one, you didn't try to scale several hundred unknown vertical feet in the middle of the night, and two, if you were foolish enough to try, you didn't do it with people who weren't climbers.

Michael was willing to throw the first point out the window because he saw little choice. This green karst was the key to what had happened to his father. The second point resolved itself with even less fanfare.

"Unbelievable," Ted said.

There would be no need to climb the mountain. At least not in a technical sense. In a marvel of Chinese ingenuity, a network of bamboo ladders had been fastened to the rock, all the way up the face of the karst.

Michael remained incredulous. "Let's rope together just the same," he said. "It may be a ladder, but it's a long way to the top."

• • •

Li tung toyed with the palm-sized detonator in his wrinkled hand. Despite the gravity of the situation ahead of him, he reasoned that he was nearer to happiness than despair. The American had left from the docks on a stolen riverboat not long before. Now, Li thought, if the risks of the next few hours could be adequately contained, he would be well on the way to achieving his goal. To that end Li quietly replaced the detonator in his pocket. He would remain guardedly optimistic, but cautious, always cautious. There was much yet to be done.

• • •

The bamboo ladder was cool to the touch in the night air. Michael estimated that he was already more than three-quarters of the way up the karst, and though he didn't glance below, he could hear both Kate and Ted on the rungs beneath him. He climbed two more rungs and made his way along a ledge of rock before taking hold of the next section of ladder. Whoever had installed this system had been thoughtful, but the more Michael thought about it, the more the ladders quietly crushed the hope he had felt not ten minutes before. A mountain that people would have seen from a passing boat was one thing, but a mountain so well traveled that it necessitated this kind of infrastructure was something else entirely. Nazi airplanes didn't stay hidden for decades in well-traveled areas. The odds were just plain against it. And this was an airplane that had been the object of years of searching. To find it here, now, a convenient ladder leading to its final resting place would be beyond absurd.

And yet the platinum plate, the most compelling piece of evidence Michael had yet seen, had pointed here. Michael knew he had no choice but to press on. Reaching the top of the ladder, he stepped onto a rock ledge a couple feet in width. This time, instead of proceeding along the ledge to what looked like the fourteenth and final ladder, he waited for Kate to show her head. "You ever play that game Chutes and Ladders?" Michael said.

"You mean the one where you roll the dice and you climb a ladder on the board, but if you hit a snake you go sliding back down?"

"That's the one."

"We call it Snakes and Ladders, but yeah, I played it when I was a kid. Why?"

"I don't know. Fourteen ladders in a row," Michael said, staring down at Ted below. "I can't help but think we're going to hit a snake."

36

Though the door of the alcove rattled in time with his aggressor's fist, Mobi did his best to remain unperturbed. After twenty minutes of effort he had finally managed to get Quiann to pick up the phone and he wasn't about to let the big bully outside ruin his moment.

"Hi, my name is Mobi Stearn. I'm a telecommunications engineer here at JPL in California."

"Who is this that continues to call?" the heavily accented voice demanded.

"Dr. Mobi Stearn," Mobi said, somewhat self-consciously. "Am I speaking with Dr. Jie Quiann?"

"Yes."

"I have an urgent matter I'd like to discuss with you, sir."

"Yes." Quiann paused. "I see you are calling from Deputy Director Alvarez's IP address."

"Yeah. I can explain that."

"I must speak directly to Deputy Director Alvarez."

Mobi saw that making friends might be harder than he had anticipated. "Well that's the thing, sir. She's held up and I'm kind of your go-to guy here."

Quiann lowered his voice. "I will speak only to Deputy Director Alvarez."

Mobi could see the call was going nowhere. If he wanted to save the day he'd have to pull a rabbit out of a hat and he'd have to do it now. "Look, sir, we've got a reverse-engineered cold fusion reactor with a secondary coil that's about to spray plutonium over half of California and figuring you to be a nice guy, I'm guessing that isn't the kind of thing you want to do. Now, I have no idea what kind of encryption algorithms you've tried to open COM with that thing and frankly I don't care. I don't think that's the solution. What we need are the original Horten files. Our copies are missing anything to do with the radio gear and if we're going to crack this thing, I need to start there and I need to start now. So what do you say? You want your next vacation to Disneyland to be in a Hazmat suit or do you want to dance?"

Mobi regretted the Disneyland part. He was pretty sure Quiann would never be granted admission stateside again thus rendering the comment moot, but still, he hoped he'd made his point. He needed Quiann's help and he needed it now.

"Are you the Mobi Stearn who won the millennial Caltech Athenaeum robo-war?"

"You Googled me?"

"It is very important that you are who you say you are, Mr. Stearn."

"Millennial champ. My bot carried a small-scale EMP I put together with spare parts from the Rutherford lab. Scrambled anybody who got close."

"Interesting. I would think that an electromagnetic pulse weapon would disable your robot as well."

"Nano-ceramic shielding."

"Clever," Quiann said.

The line was quiet for a long moment. "Dr. Quiann?" Mobi was sure he could hear typing.

"I do not have much time," Quiann said. "I am compressing the files now."

Mobi let out a sigh and said, "Thank you."

"Please, be discreet, Mr. Stearn."

The line went dead and Mobi heard nothing more.

37

Michael remembered clearly *when his father first taught him to trust his own opinion. He was supposed to write a book report. In the report he was supposed to talk about what other people said about the book. He was supposed to provide footnotes and a bibliography to support his work. But Michael didn't like writing reports. Especially when he thought what the other people had to say about the book was dumb. So his father made a deal with him. He told him to write what he thought about the book. He didn't need a bibliography or footnotes because he wouldn't be quoting anybody else. All he had to do was think about the book and write down what he thought. With this spin on it, Michael found the project interesting. He had a lot of things to say about the book. He chose his words wisely. He was proud of the finished project. He handed it in. And he got an F. The teacher wrote that what Michael had written was not scholarship. When he showed the graded report to his father, his dad said that the teacher was right. It probably wasn't scholarship. Then he asked Michael, what he had learned?*

"Not to do my own thing if I want a good grade."
"Yes, but what else did you learn?"
"Not everybody out there wants me to succeed."
"True, but what else?"
Michael thought about it. "I learned to think," he finally said.

WITH A FINAL heave, Michael summitted the karst. Up here, free from the shadows, he found himself bathed in the light of the newly risen moon, the surrounding peaks poking their heads from the clouds like islands in a deep dark sea. The vantage point was so intoxicating, so foreign, that it took a glance at the dark river below to remind him of what he was doing there. Michael took a fresh breath and refocused his gaze. There was a small shrine to the north of him consisting of a stone Buddha sitting amidst a stick forest of recently burnt incense. To the west lay the saddle between the two peaks of the karst, dense foliage covering the ridge. To the east and south was simply raw limestone, no defining features really, nothing to hide. Kate reached the top, Ted breathing hard behind her.

"It's a shrine," Ted said. "An old one by the looks of it."

"Long way up to pray."

"Local Buddhists believe that proximity to the spirit world could be found at the tops of mountains. Chances are that network of ladders has been there forever."

Ted dug into his pack pulling out what looked like the sensor to a fancy metal detector. He then opened up Kate's pack removing a portable LCD screen and a telescopic handle.

"When I heard you were in Yangshuo, I pulled in a favor." Screwing the device together he said, "Ground-penetrating radar. The rock in this region is extremely porous. Water tends to flow through it creating pockets and caverns over time. Anything like that, this girl here will pick it up." Ted tossed Kate a device about the size of a packet of cards. "Laser grid. It should help us map this out."

Kate clicked a switch on the device's all weather case. A red grid of laser beams emanated from all four sides of the device turning the peak into a life-sized chess board, lines of laser light delineating search quadrants.

"Sweet," Kate said. "Michael, are you seeing this?'

Michael turned his head and nodded. If the truth were known, he was more interested in the full moon than the red lines of laser light. There was something about the way the moon hung just above eye level in the eastern sky, something atavistic about its presence that made Michael want to dig deeper. This was a moon that held secrets. Secrets that for better or worse, could no longer afford to be kept.

Michael reached into his pocket and withdrew the engraved plate he had extracted from the old man's skull. Holding it up under the moon's pale glow, it looked somehow different than it had earlier in the day; its platinum surface seemed less harsh, almost organic. Michael studied the disc carefully. The actual engraving appeared exactly as it had before: a double-peaked karst before a rising moon— nothing more, nothing less. But Michael found it difficult to believe that this same metal plate that a Japanese surgeon had gone to such trouble to implant in the man's skull didn't in some way hold more significance than what he had seen so far.

Michael turned the disc over in his hand. The reverse side was smooth blank platinum. It remained as blank as he had remembered it, except for a little patch of dried brown blood that Michael had missed while washing the plate in the river. Later, when he had time, he thought, he'd have to clean that bit of blood off. Or would he? Michael felt his pulse race. He peered at the stain again. Had he been hasty in washing away the old man's blood? Had he dismissed the smooth back of the plate too quickly? One way to find out. Michael reached into his pocket and withdrew his Swiss Army knife.

"Kid?" Ted said.

Michael snapped open the surgically sharp blade. Messages had been hidden in relief before. It wouldn't be that different from the seam uniting the two halves of the capsule. It was there, you simply had to know where to look.

"Michael," Ted interrupted. "If we're going to do this thing, we need all hands on deck."

Michael ignored Ted and pressed the tip of the hardened stainless steel blade to his thumb. He felt a well of excitement churn in his stomach as the skin broke, a pearl-sized drop of blood pooling out. Quickly dropping the Swiss knife back into his pocket he traded it for the platinum disc, squeezing out more blood which he let fall to the smooth surface of the disc, spreading it around like finger paint. The result was predictable at first—just a mess of blood exactly as it had appeared when he had removed the plate from the old man's head—but as the thin layer of dark blood dried slowly before his eyes, he held the disc at an oblique angle and something else took shape. Though the blood stained the smooth surface of the disc, it was unable to penetrate what must have been a hairline engraving. As a result an image was forming, an image which Michael immediately recognized as a topographical representation of the peak they were standing upon. The drying blood revealed a series of contour lines reaching out like ripples on a pond, the farthest line aptly intersected by a bloodred swastika. Michael didn't hesitate. He didn't call Ted or Kate. He simply swung his pack over his shoulder and headed due west, down the craggy limestone path toward the saddle separating the two peaks. If the swastika meant what he thought it did, he didn't want to waste a second more.

38

MOBI SCANNED THE file Quiann had sent him, unsure
what bothered him more: the pounding at the door or
the high-pitched whine of a drill coming from the back
wall. Rand wanted him out of the alcove, that much was
clear, but whichever way Mobi looked at it, the time
for surrender had long past. Now all that mattered was
making his last stand pay. Quiann's file consisted of
background on the Horten and a link to a feed consisting of two streaming codes: one in red and one in blue.
The code in red was live data being transmitted up to
the satellite from China's Jiuquan South Launch Center.
The blue data was the satellite's response. So far Mobi
hadn't been able to discern a pattern in the streaming
codes, but he had established three things. Number one:
the original Horten had been equipped with powerful
radio transceivers to communicate with other aircraft
of its type. Number two: apparently the Chinese were
fine with this design because their satellite contained a
modern, but extremely powerful transceiver as well. And
number three: transmissions to and from the Chinese

satellite were encrypted at the point of origin and then re-encrypted before being returned to the base. As far as Mobi was concerned the crux of the problem lay in this final point, namely dual encryption.

Dual encryption was a risky business, especially when you were dealing with something as far away as a satellite. If something were to go wrong, if a single line of code was buggy on the space side re-encryption protocol, control would lose contact. That this had apparently happened begged two questions: A—why had Quiann been so obtuse in launching a dual encryption protocol, and B—what the hell was Mobi going to do about it when he was stuck down on Earth with a drill buzzing in his ear?

Mobi had to assume that the answer to the first question was an insane desire for secrecy, but in terms of what he was going to do about it, that was more complicated. So far no pattern had emerged between the data streaming up to the satellite and that which it was returning. Without a pattern, Mobi had no way in, only the unwavering conviction that the alcove door would soon be breached. He decided to risk an instant message to Alvarez. "Called our friend," Mobi typed. "You there?"

He hit send and waited. There was nothing. Only the whirring of the drill, punctuated by the syncopated thumping of what Mobi now suspected was a jackhammer. Then, the thumping stopped leaving only the drill. Mobi's screen chimed in response.

"Closer than you think."

"Where?" Mobi typed.

"Clear-code buried in data stream. Analyze."

Clear-code buried in data stream? Mobi read it again. Alvarez obviously had new information. He started to type again, but was interrupted not by a message, but a muffled voice.

"Mobi?"

Mobi threw his head back at the sound of his name.

"Mobi, it's me, Allison."

The voice was coming from outside the alcove.

"Deputy Director Alvarez?"

"It's me you've got to worry about, Stearn," Rand's baritone commanded. "Now how about you get your ass out here, and we can get on with the show."

"I am getting on with the show," Mobi said. "I'm figuring out how to get that thing out of the sky without blowing plutonium from here to Korea."

A pause.

"It's too late for that. Our platform is locked on. We're taking the Chinese bird out whether you crack the mystery of the flying foo dog or not."

Except there was something about Rand's response that told Mobi that it wasn't too late. Perhaps it was Rand's moment of hesitation or his surfeit of confidence, Mobi wasn't sure, but something was up. It was Alvarez who spoke next.

"You might as well just come out, Mobi. It wouldn't matter if that terminal in there was cat wired into every mainframe in the building. It's still just a laptop, and they'd still haul you out. Even a secure 4-EVR structure gets breached eventually."

Mobi listened, but what was she saying to him? A secure 4-EVR structure? What the hell was that? Some kind of brand name for a bank safe? And the cat wiring. If anything, Alvarez's terminal was optically linked to the rest of the facility. Alvarez would know that. CAT wire was a residential standard. But secure forever? Mobi thought it through. Was it that simple? Was she telling Mobi that this little room he was in was secure FOREVER, or at least long enough? Then why bring up the cat wiring? CAT WIRED. Mobi broke it down to its alphanumeric. 22894733. Is that what she was telling him? It was worth a shot. Mobi logged out of the operating system and keyed in 22894733 at the shell prompt.

Bingo.

Each of JPL's servers showed below the prompt, each open to his inquiries, each ready for his instruction. Mobi got it now. He understood what Alvarez was telling him. He wasn't locked in. They were locked out. Mobi controlled JPL's systems. And the best thing was, Rand didn't even know it.

Mobi's screen chimed again. The message read, "Check outgoing data packets."

"I'll give you one more chance, Stearn," Rand said through the door. "Open up, or we're coming in guns blazing."

But Mobi wasn't listening. Not really. He had access to the servers now. Isolating the outgoing data was a simple process. There was the usual space-bound traffic in the log, and the stuff to other research institutions, and the traffic to China. But the China traffic was more than just his conversation with Quiann at the Launch Center; it was a series of encrypted packets sent directly to a separate location that looked to be in Beijing, Xiyuan to be precise. Xiyuan, Google quickly told him, was near Beijing's Summer Palace. It was also the location of the headquarters of the Chinese Ministry of State Security—the country's spy service. Mobi wasn't sure what this meant, but he knew it was big. He was getting in deeper by the moment.

"Stearn," Rand yelled through the door. "You can't pull a paycheck in prison!"

"Like I'm in it for the money," Mobi said. Then he fished a pair of earbuds off Alvarez's desk and drowned out the racket with good old rock 'n' roll. Rand could huff and puff, but Mobi was the lone wolf in town. If anybody was going to have the last word about what went on above planet Earth tonight, it was him.

39

A SPARK LIT OFF the blade of his shovel as Michael thrust it into the rocky soil. He had been digging for less than five minutes and already he had hit a hard flat surface, maybe twenty inches below the grade. Now, instead of digging down, he began shoveling dirt to the side revealing that the surface he had hit was in fact an iron plate. Ted's GPR unit had confirmed that the spot where he now stood had a hollow beneath it, but in reality the technology hadn't been necessary. The contour map on the back of the bloodstained disc had been engraved to scale, the swastika perfectly marking the spot.

Kate and Ted hunched down alongside Michael to remove the earth from the metal plate's surface. Within minutes they had uncovered a four-foot-wide iron trap-door, hinged into aging concrete. A simple deadbolt key lock kept the plate fastened down, but one look revealed the mechanism was heavily corroded.

"Pass me the pick."

Ted handed over a lightweight climbing pick and Michael jammed the blade under the metal door at the hinge. The concrete was white and flaking where it had deteriorated with exposure to moisture over time. Holding the edge of the door up with the pick, Michael levered the blade of the shovel into the gap and popped it up with one swift motion at the hinge. The rusted metal let go almost immediately and Michael pulled the blade of the shovel out, moving on to the second hinge. This one was harder to jimmy, but ultimately let go with a groan. Ted moved in beside Michael and together they were able to lift the heavy metal plate up on end, letting it fall backwards into the fresh pile of dirt. They were left with a gaping hole into the darkness.

A flood of cool air rushed out, but from a standing position they could see nothing. Michael immediately laid down, focusing his headlamp into the depths, but still he could see only shadows. Michael didn't like it. The hole reminded him of the mineshaft. But he was close to finding his father. So close, he could taste it. "Pass me the rope," he said.

"Michael," Ted said, tossing him a walkie talkie, "There are other options here."

"Pass me the rope. I'm going in."

• • •

THE FLAT-BOTTOMED BOAT moved slowly down the river, not much faster than the current. Huang wanted it that way. In his view the American was on to something. And if this was the case, the worst thing he could do was get in the way, at least before he had led him to the prize. On this matter Huang was convinced—better to be the vulture moving in to feed after the kill than the leopard risking life and limb to make it. Add to that, the technical situation with the satellite appeared to be well on its way to resolution. Though not strictly his purview, Huang had it on good authority that the mole in the American Space Agency was providing actionable intelligence. The fallout from the situation would soon be contained. Still, Huang could feel the tension building up among his men. Yes, patience was good, but if the American didn't make his move soon, Huang knew that he would have to act. For now, though, he would follow. The time to lead would come.

• • •

THE CAVERN WAS as dank as it was enormous. An extra long six–hundred-foot top rope secured above, Michael had descended less than forty feet and already the Petzl descender was warm in his hand. As the cave opened up around him like a bell jar, he only hoped that he had enough rope to get to the bottom. He carried an extra three hundred feet of line with him, and though more rope would have been ideal, truth be told Michael was impressed that Ted had been able to gather the climbing equipment he had. It was all new, top-of-the-line stuff, making his descent into the depths of this cavern a lot more secure than it might have been.

He had descended at least a hundred feet now, the LEDs in his headlamp glistening off the wet cavern walls. And though those walls had expanded dramatically around him, Michael still could not see bottom. He was, in every sense of the word, dropping into the abyss. The aluminum descender he held in his hand had heated up to the point that he decided to give the mechanism a rest. He eased up on his grip, the descender's jaws crimping the line, and Michael slowly came to a stop, bouncing gently on the rope like a human yo-yo.

Surveying the space around him with his headlamp's beam he saw only darkness. The cave was big, so big he suspected that the entire double-karst was hollow: porous limestone that had succumbed to the gentle flow of water over millennia, yielding the enormous cavern in which he now found himself. He reached up and rotated the bezel of his headlamp, clicking it off. Then there was nothing. The only sound was the murmur of the elastic rope singing ever so quietly with his movements like a loose bass string. Michael was so entranced by its low murmur in the echo chamber of the cave that, for a moment, he didn't recognize the flapping. Then, seemingly out of nowhere, came the high-pitched squeal.

Michael knew what it was. He felt the wind rush by his face even before he switched on his headlamp. Bats. A storm of them engulfed him. Michael had no particular loathing of the winged creatures, but contracting rabies or histoplasmosis wasn't on his agenda either. He fanned his right arm and simultaneously gripped the descender, releasing its crimp on the rope. He felt the warm, furry mammals brush by his ears and face. Like wall-to-wall carpeting, they were everywhere. Fortunately their presence was fleeting. It took several seconds, but by then Michael had dropped through the worst of them and slowed his descent back to a crawl.

Michael checked his face and neck with his free hand. He felt no cuts or abrasions, meaning a trip to the hospital for a painful series of rabies vaccinations was unlikely. More to the point, as the remaining bats flew lazily around him, he reasoned that their very presence pointed to another entrance to the cave, perhaps an entrance large enough to bring in an aircraft. Michael gripped the descender, squeezing it tightly. As the rope raced through it, he knew he was testing the limits of his equipment, but found he didn't care. All that mattered now was that he get to the cavern floor.

The bottom snuck up on him like a hammer. Michael thought he saw a flash of something, an amorphous expanse of organic steel, and like that his feet slapped down and he was bending his knees to absorb the impact as he landed in a pool of water. The water was little more than calf deep and he quickly recovered. He then unclipped his harness, reasonably certain that the tingle in his spine had been caused not by his rough landing, but by the object he had viewed from above.

Though every fiber of his being compelled him to look upon the object, he took a moment to reflect. The aircraft was after all the reason he was here. It was the reason his father had spent a lifetime in China, and it was, in many ways, his last best hope of finding the man who had given him life. And so, hoping against hope, Michael cast his glance up at the amorphous expanse of aluminum above. And in that moment he understood. He understood the pull the plane must have exerted on his father and others like him. He understood why nations had covertly fought to find it for so many years. And he understood, clearly for the first time, what he had to do. Reaching into the pocket of his cargo shorts, Michael pulled out the encrypted two-way radio Ted had given him and pressed the talk button.

"Drop on down," he said. "The water's fine."

40

WITHIN MINUTES KATE and Ted had descended to the watery cavern floor, where they now stood alongside Michael, quietly amazed by what they saw. The aircraft was a flying wing: stealth technology from a bygone era. Like its blueprint, the bat-winged plane looked to have a wingspan of about sixty-five feet. It appeared amorphous not by design, but due to the decades-old accumulation of bat guano covering its surface. The underside of the plane was, however, clear of guano, and it was from this perspective that it began to take shape. Its fuselage stood perhaps seven feet above the cave floor on a tricycle landing gear. What appeared to be vertically mounted jets or thrusters poked out from its underbelly, suggesting that the plane was in fact capable of vertical take off. A metallic surface of a matte titanium gray sloped up forming a low cockpit between the wings, a swastika adorning the flat nose of the aircraft. It was a perfect life-size version of the blueprint—a crap-covered, decades-old, Nazi bomber.

"Shit," Kate said.

"Don't you mean, *Heil*?" Michael said.

"It was supposed to be a vertical lift, long range stealth bomber," Ted said. "Or so people think. Nobody's laid eyes on an intact example."

Michael noted that hundreds of bats still hung upside down from the underside of the Horten's fuselage, clustered around a series of three thrusters. What surprised Michael was that despite being covered in guano, the Horten appeared amazingly well preserved. There were no visible rust spots or outward signs of decay, just the bat crap which he suspected was, at most, cosmetic. Michael eyed the Horten's underbelly.

"There's got to be a way in."

"First things, first," Ted said, pulling out his smartphone. "We need a record of what we've found here."

Michael responded with a step forward, careful not to lose his footing in the calf-deep pool as he moved toward the underside of the airplane. As bats fluttered from their roost, he saw what looked like an egress on the underbelly of the fuselage, the smooth ridges of the gap between the door and its aperture as finely engineered as a classic Mercedes-Benz. Gazing upwards, Michael took another short step, locating the recessed handle that kept the door in place.

He reached up.

"Wait," Kate said.

Michael paused, arm in the air.

"The plane was hidden here in wartime, remember. It could be booby trapped."

Michael visually inspected the recessed stainless steel handle. If it had been tampered with he could see no sign of it. There were no external wires, no scratches or signs of forced entry. Of course Michael was the first to admit he was no expert in the art of booby trapping Nazi airplanes. It wasn't long ago that the notion would have never crossed his mind. But now that he had to seriously consider the possibility that the thing might explode, he found himself rejecting the idea. Put it down to common sense. Explosives tended to destabilize over time. With the care taken in hiding the Horten, he doubted those who placed it here would risk an accidental detonation. They wanted to preserve it, not blow it up. Still, there was only one way to be sure.

"Michael."

Michael ignored Kate and folded the handle down turning it clockwise. The mechanism was initially stiff but moved easily after the first quarter turn, responding with a smooth click. Michael thought about it for a moment. If he was wrong this would be his last moment of life. This would be when the whole thing went boom. But it didn't. There was a delay of about a second, and then the hatch opened with a pneumatic whoosh, easing down on a single hydraulically dampened arm as easily as it might have the day it was manufactured. Michael expelled the breath he had been holding, tasting the metallic bitter of adrenalin on his tongue. He scanned the dark interior of the hatch with his headlamp. There was a telescopic ladder bolted there. He pulled downward.

The ladder smoothly extended several feet allowing Michael an easy climb up into the fuselage. Climbing pack tight to his back, his head now in the ladder well, the first thing he noticed was that the air was predictably acrid inside. Taken in conjunction with the absence of cobwebs, Michael had to assume that good old German engineering had prevailed, ensuring that the interior of the aircraft had remained hermetically sealed for decades. He started up the ladder well, his headlamp casting its beam on what he could only assume was the gray metallic interior of the cockpit. Then, finally poking his head into the cockpit above, he simply stopped.

It wasn't the cockpit itself that threw him. The Horten's cockpit was what might be expected from an antique aircraft: a cramped space, all dials and switches and two harnessed pilot's seats. There was a control stick in front of each seat and a facetted windscreen provided a sweeping view over either wing, but again, it wasn't the cockpit that threw him.

It was the corpse.

Laid out in the rear of the cockpit directly behind the pilots' seats was a skeletal corpse, a molded rubber oxygen mask still strapped to its skull. The corpse's hand was outstretched, a shrunken elastic layer of skin pasted over its dead bones. There was no sign of any clothing. Whoever it was had either been naked, or stripped after death. The corpse was lying in an act of supplication, almost as though the victim had begged for mercy in the moments before death.

Michael pulled himself up into the cockpit and once there he could clearly make out a bullet hole in the corpse's skull. From what he knew of such things, he suspected that the lack of an exit wound indicated a small caliber weapon. In addition to the bullet hole, the blade of a bayonet was broken off at the blunt end and stuck directly through the corpse's heart.

Then, adjusting his view downward, Michael saw what the corpse held in its hand. Within its cupped mummified fingers were a series of titanium rotors. He couldn't immediately tell how many of them there were, but he knew exactly what they were for. Without a doubt, they were the missing element to the Purple Sky encryption device he carried in his backpack. As Kate had explained it, each of the three-inch rotors fit on a spindle on the back of the encryption device. They were used to mechanically scramble a message before it was transmitted. But they didn't matter for the moment. Not right now.

What mattered was the tiny pendant held tightly in the corpse's other hand. The pendant was small and silver and contained three small stars offset in a larger ring. It looked, Michael thought, like a misshapen face and its very presence filled him with dread. Because Michael had only ever seen one other pendant like it in his life. And it had hung around the neck of his father.

41

Jackhammers continued to bite at the armored alcove, but Mobi paid them no heed. He had larger matters to attend to, namely each of JPL's eighteen mainframe servers which were now under his command. Mobi fired code at them, his every instruction shooting through JPL's eighty-five-foot antenna and into space at the speed of light. His aim was to shut down the targeting system aboard the DOD's orbital platforms thereby rendering the weapons useless. Mobi's concern was that, though the ASAT platforms might try to eliminate the Chinese satellite, the more likely scenario was an indirect hit that would breach the satellite's core but not stop its reentry. The unknown effect of a cold fusion breach aside, the certain result would be the dispersal of atomized plutonium into the jet stream.

Such a dispersal meant that every man, woman and child on the planet would ingest a dangerous dose of radiation. Mobi knew in his gut there was a better way and if it meant sabotaging the Air Force's ASAT efforts, so be it. But it didn't take long for Mobi to grow concerned. There were two reasons for this. The first was another outgoing message to Xiyuan, China. Unlike the other messages, however, this one didn't emerge from the JPL servers and it wasn't encrypted. It was simply a routine e-mail sent to a numbered account that got caught and cached in Mobi's wireless sniffer. The message read, "Problem solved."

Since the message could have originated from any wireless device in the building, Mobi didn't have a lot to go on, but he couldn't say it left him feeling encouraged. It was the second development, however, that actually got Mobi worried: Rand's men had suddenly stopped making any effort to reestablish communication with their platforms. No test transmissions, no pleas for the system to let them in, nothing. And that, Mobi realized, most likely meant that Rand had quietly transferred control of the platforms back to Colorado Springs.

Mobi couldn't control the platforms if they were running them out of Colorado. What was worse, his screen showed a new high-velocity object in near Earth orbit confirming his deepest fears. Despite his best efforts, they had launched a missile. Mobi was so dismayed that he barely registered the jab of the steel jackhammer as it bit up through the concrete floor. Less than forty seconds later the first warhead hit.

42

Michael crouched in the Horten's cockpit, staring at the leathery corpse caught in its final act of supplication. There had been suffering, even torture, that much was clear. He didn't want to imagine his father's last moments like this. Not if he didn't have to. Kate pulled herself into the cockpit, finally breaking the silence.

"It's not him."

"His pendant, it's exactly the same."

Kate shook her head. "Look at the pelvis."

Michael redirected his gaze to the corpse's groin. From the way it lay half on its side the area was mostly hidden, the bones covered in an elastic, translucent skin.

"It's female," Kate said.

"Are you sure?"

"See how wide the hips are? This was a woman. A tall woman by the looks of her. But a woman. Not only that. The degree of decay is way off. Whoever this was has been here for years, most likely decades, not months."

Kate reached for the corpse's outstretched hand, but Michael beat her to it, pulling the handful of titanium rotors out of the skeletal outstretched palm and dropping them in his pocket. Kate was right. He had allowed his emotions to get the best of him. Even if the pendant was the same, there was no way this was his father. Still there was a connection. There had to be. Recovered from his initial shock, Michael took a second look around the cockpit, and as he did, he made note of a significant feature that he had missed in his initial shock.

The capsule.

Behind a low open hatch on the rear bulkhead of the fuselage was a metal capsule like the one they had found at Chen's. It was perhaps fifty percent larger, and it was difficult to see the whole thing, but it was obvious that this area behind the hatch was more than a hiding place. It was the reactor room.

"Kate?"

She followed his glance. "I'm with you."

Michael stepped over the corpse and bent down low, climbing into the reactor room. It was pitch black in here, even darker than the main cockpit where Ted's headlamp in the cave below had provided the occasional flash of light. But Michael's headlamp burned strong and he was able to see that the capsule was solidly mounted to the floor and connected to the rest of the aircraft through a series of anodized ducts. The whole assembly looked like a silver spider poised to strike.

Kate entered the reactor room behind him. Casting his glance back at her, Michael noticed a length of ducting running out of the capsule and along the reactor room wall to a hinged metallic surface with a recessed handle. Michael twisted the handle and what looked like a communications console eased out of the wall.

"You know what that is?" Kate said.

"I can make a pretty good guess."

Michael pulled the console out from its recess revealing an empty bracket. He then removed the green anodized box from his backpack and slid it onto the bracket. It was a perfect fit. He inserted the jumble of output wires from the encoding unit into the communication console's reciprocal socket.

"Purple Sky," Michael said.

With the installation of the rotors, Michael thought, they would have a full transceiver. But something else was also becoming clear to Michael. It hit him with the same force as those long hours in the mineshaft he had spent hopelessly waiting for his father to rescue him. As the corpse on the cockpit floor had so painfully demonstrated, there were no guarantees. No guarantees the transceiver would work and no guarantees that he was any closer to finding his dad. If anything the whole mess was beginning to feel like a dead end. He had located the Horten, but he hadn't found his father and he didn't know if he ever would. The thought sent a chill down Michael's spine. It was a chill so real that when Ted poked his head into the reactor room, an unseen gunman holding the barrel of an MP5 submachine gun firmly against the base of his skull, Michael could honestly say that he expected as much.

43

One weekend Michael's *dad had a surprise for him. They were going on a trip. Just the two of them. Vegas, baby. That was when his dad taught him how to gamble. True he wasn't old enough to legally sit on the casino floor, but gambling Chase-style had nothing to do with the tables. It was about people. They sat in the hotel lobby in front of the elevator banks wagering on the guests as they headed into the casino.*

"Ten bucks the woman in green is from Idaho. She's forty-two, has four kids, a husband who sells auto parts, and she's here on a girls-only trip."

"Forty-five, one kid, recently divorced."

Then to settle the bet they'd strike up a conversation and ask. Nine times out of ten Michael's dad was right. Even about the number of kids. But Michael got better and pretty soon he had picked up the knack. Not as well as his dad. But pretty well. Michael met a lot of people on that trip. And he learned two things. One, you could learn a lot about people just by looking. And two, he should never, ever, bet against his father.

THE CAVERN WAS illuminated by a row of battery-powered lanterns, their white light hitting the underbelly of the Horten where it sat above the cave floor. Michael knelt before the old airplane, up to his thighs in the cold cave water, Kate and Ted at his side. They were held prisoner by Huang's men, an MP5 to the back of each of their heads.

"Excellent work," Huang said to no one in particular. "My countrymen have been searching for this aircraft for sixteen years. You found it in two days."

Huang paced behind them, Kate's newly surrendered Glock in hand. Michael took the moment to cop a glance at the side of the cave, but was swiftly rebuked by a sharp tap of the MP5's barrel. He had seen what he wanted, though. There were five top ropes strung down from the mouth of the cave above. It explained Huang's sudden appearance. He had been following closely behind them, just as he was now.

"My men tell me the transceiver is in place, but it is missing parts. Vital parts."

"Really?" Michael said.

"I have yet to search your person," Huang said. "I give you the choice of retaining your dignity."

"That ship sailed back when you got me on my knees," Michael said, raising his arms. "Go ahead. Search."

Michael felt a nudge to the back of his head from the barrel of the MP5. Huang's men had done a preliminary pat down for weapons upon their capture, but not much else. Michael hoped his invitation to a search was enough to keep Huang at bay.

"Hands to your side," Huang said. "I do not believe you realize the severity of your circumstances. You are under my command and have been for some time."

"Am I?"

"Perhaps a demonstration is in order. Reach into your pocket."

Michael glanced down at his cargo shorts, his hems wet in the cave water. The worn cotton pockets sagged to the point that you could almost make out the bulge of the rotors he kept hidden in his pocket.

"Reach into your lower left pocket and withdraw a coin."

Michael carefully reached past the rotors, removing a Chinese coin.

"Recognize it?"

"Yeah. It's one yuan."

"Throw it in the water."

"You want me to make a wish?"

"I want you," Huang said, "to throw the coin in the water."

Curious as to what Huang was up to, Michael tossed the coin. It landed in the water with a small splash, sinking the twelve or so inches down to the cave floor. Huang walked in front of them and hit a key on his phone. There was a tiny pop, followed by several large bubbles migrating to the surface.

"Sarin gas. I've neutralized it with an alkali, but the seven other charges you carry within your front pocket are active. You have been a walking chemical bomb since my men approached you on the bridge, Mr. Chase. In addition to emitting a trackable beacon, each of the coins my agents placed upon you contains a lethal dose of nerve poison. Upon release of the gas you will experience nausea and difficulty breathing followed quickly by a complete and total loss of bodily function. Within three minutes you will suffocate to death in your own shit."

Michael considered the possibility. If there was one thing he was certain of, it was the fact that weakness would pay no dividend with this man. "Better than listening to yours," he said.

Huang snickered, revealing a decayed tooth. "Open your mouth."

Michael just looked at him.

"I said open your mouth."

Michael immediately felt a crack to the back of his skull, presumably from the butt of the MP5. He opened his mouth.

"Stick out your tongue"

Michael didn't like it, but when Huang racked the slide on Kate's Glock, shoving the barrel between his teeth, he saw little choice but to comply. He stuck out his tongue.

"Good." Huang withdrew a sarin chemical coin from his pocket and placed it on Michael's tongue. "Swallow."

"Fuck you."

Michael spit out the coin.

Huang's rebuke was as swift as it was brutal. He pulled back the gun and smashed Michael in the face with a left hook, his fist glancing off Michael's jaw like a wet hammer. Michael felt a rivulet of blood running down his cheek, but found he didn't care. He wasn't going to give this prick the satisfaction of seeing him wince. Not if he could help it.

"You are a spy, Mr. Chase. You are a spy like your father before you and you will suffer the fate of all spies. You will die."

"Yeah, I'm a spy. I'm a slacker Seattle spy come to kick your sorry ass."

"Michael," Kate said. "Stop it. It's not helping."

"The man has a right to know who I am."

"You're going to get yourself killed."

"Then I'll die with a clean conscience."

Huang was done punching. He pulled back the integrated trigger lock on Kate's Glock, extending the barrel of the pistol to Michael's head. The cave was silent for half a second, maybe more.

"Enough!" Ted said. "Michael, just give him the damn rotors."

Michael caught Kate's glance. She kept a near-poker face, but he thought he saw the hint of a crack in the façade.

"The sooner he gets them, the sooner we can all go home."

Huang seemed to have recovered his composure. "Please listen to your friend, Mr. Chase. I think you'll find you'll live longer if you do."

Michael weighed the odds. He didn't have much choice. Not the way this was going. Plus, he trusted Ted. He trusted him with his life. If this was how it was going to play out, this was how it was going to play out. He made his decision. MP5 still firmly planted at the base of his skull, Michael carefully reached into the front pocket of his cargo shorts and removed the handful of titanium rotors, holding them before him, palm outstretched. For a moment Huang looked like he was about to burst, unable to contain his pleasure. Then Ted rose from his tired knees, disregarding both the machine guns and Michael's eyes as he collected the rotors directly from Michael's hand.

Huang said, "You did well for an American."

"Don't push it," Ted said.

Michael was entirely silent.

"Ted?" Kate said.

"Sorry, Kate. Had to be done." Ted dropped the rotors into a small nylon stuff sack before addressing his attention back to Huang. "I've got it from here."

"Very good. Be sure to thank Mr. Chase before you shoot him."

Without a second glance Huang marched off to the hanging belay ropes and harnessed into the compact automatic ascender dangling there. Michael heard an electric hum and the ascender began to move upward, pulling Huang with it like a worm on a hook. Kate couldn't contain herself. She glared at Ted.

"I knew you were all wrong."

"After I left the Agency I had some time on my hands."

"So what's the MSS paying these days? Better than the CIA I hope."

"Just zip up and stare straight ahead."

"Oh, come on. You want me to make this easy for you?"

Ted nodded to Huang's men who stepped forward and circled around so that they were facing the kneeling prisoners. Even in the cold cave Michael saw the sweat on Kate's brow. Then Ted glanced at his watch. Michael's mind raced. This was it. This was the moment. He glanced at Kate. Then he saw nothing at all but an intense blast of white light. It was followed, what seemed like an eternity later, by incredible percussive force, slapping him to the rock below, din and flame tearing through the cave like an angry act of God.

44

THE SCREECHING BLADE of the circular saw provided a pretty good indication that Mobi's fast times in Alvarez's indestructible alcove were about to come to a screaming halt. The first ASAT missile appeared to have detonated somewhere near the Chinese satellite, but as Mobi predicted, it had not resulted in the total destruction that Rand had desired. The system was too buggy for that. Instead, the Chinese bird had ceased transmitting. The good news was that transmissions had now resumed. Mobi attributed the lapse to the EMP effect of the warhead, but regardless of the cause, the fact that the effect had been temporary had Mobi stoked. He might be on his way out, but he was still in the game.

Of course, he knew he wouldn't be in it long. Sparks from the saw were literally dancing off his keyboard. Add to that the fact that there was obviously a mole within JPL passing secrets to the Chinese and things were definitely not looking up. Mobi took a moment to rest his eyes. It was time to reassess, or at least examine his fundamental assumptions. He had grown uneasy with the fact that Alvarez had put him in contact with

Quiann. What was she really doing talking to a known traitor? She had given him no explanation for this. Could she be the one sending the messages to the Chinese? Putting Mobi onto those messages would certainly be an easy way to deflect suspicion from herself. Not to mention that what Alvarez was saying didn't make sense. Mobi had assumed that what Alvarez had identified as a hidden clear-code would effectively reset the system allowing normal communication between the Chinese satellite and control. But so far he had found nothing even vaguely resembling a clear-code. Was the answer even in the data stream?

Mobi remembered a magazine article he had once read profiling Quiann. The article was written several years ago in conjunction with one of China's higher profile space launches. Mobi recalled his impression of the Chinese technology being woefully behind the curve, but what stuck in his mind was something the article had said about Quiann. Something about his alleged earlier involvement in a quasi-cult organization. Mobi thought it had been called the Green Dragon Society. He had dismissed the tidbit as being largely irrelevant at the time, but it occurred to him, what if Quiann did have some kind of weird allegiance to a secret society? That kind of thing could be enough to throw logic right out the proverbial window. What if Quiann deliberately sabotaged the satellite? What if he wanted it to crash down? Over his old alma mater no less? What if crashing the satellite provided the perfect cover for destroying the cold fusion reactor it held? Because Quiann and his cronies wanted to keep the technology secret. Secret from the world. No, Mobi thought, he had been staring at the data too long. Quiann was a man of science. Of course, so was the Unabomber.

"Stearn!"

Mobi heard his name called but paid it no heed. The thought was burnt into his head. If Mobi were to proceed on the premise that Quiann didn't want him to reestablish communication with the satellite, then he might have sent him bad data. Data that was real enough to look legitimate, but corrupt enough so that Mobi could never crack it. What if Quiann's whole point, and by that measure Alvarez's, was to get him off the scent? Mobi wasn't sure what happened next. He felt a sudden lurch in the floor below him as though the whole alcove was going to fall to the bottom of the building, followed quickly by the cold metal of a nightstick thrust against his throat. But Mobi didn't struggle. He didn't even move. Because he had a hunch. Now all he had to do was prove it.

45

THE PERCUSSIVE IMPACT of the blast brought Michael to the floor atop Kate, chaos unfolding all around them. All he saw after the initial blast of light was blackness and all he heard was a terrible ringing, so piercing that when the second and third detonations hit, he heard nothing at all. Michael coughed because the cave was now filled with billowing clouds of dust, but the strange thing wasn't the grit in the air or the ringing in his ears, but something else, something like the rush of water.

Michael had no idea how much time actually elapsed between the final detonation and the wall of water that followed it, but he knew that what felt like hours may well have been less than a second. In that time, Michael could sense the wave that was coming to take him away, he could feel the rush of moist air, and then the wall of river water simply picked him up, propelling him under the Horten and toward the back of the cave. He felt arms and legs flailing about, arms and legs that definitely didn't belong to him, and at the same time he felt Kate beneath him. Somehow she had been able to grab ahold of him.

Michael struggled under the rushing tide, desperately hoping that the water would recede, but instead it continued to push them farther and higher, until finally they both hit the back wall of the cave. Then miraculously enough, the river water began to recede, dragging them with it, until Michael grasped a slippery rock and held onto to it like he'd never held onto anything before. The current ripped at them, but in the end relinquished its tug, pulling back until they were left wet but alive on a low ledge on the far recess of the cave wall.

A battery-powered lantern must have floated to the surface, because a dim light was now cast through the cave and already Michael could see Huang's men picking themselves up. There was shouting. Even though Michael couldn't hear it, he could see it. But that wasn't all. Something else had come in with the torrent of water —a hail of gunfire. And though Michael couldn't see who was shooting, he could see Huang's men being cut down, even as they searched the waist deep water for their weapons. One by one they collapsed, only Ted escaping the hail of bullets as he wrenched himself to cover under the Horten.

Michael shared a glance with Kate. She was as beat up as he was, but the unspoken communication was clear. They would lay low until they knew what they were up against. As Michael broke eye contact with Kate he saw a single bright light entering the cave. It looked like a cyclops, or a train in the night, except its luminosity betrayed an airy quality, almost as if the light itself was floating on the air. The light grew in intensity, floating toward them like the great white beacon at the end of the tunnel of death. At that moment, Michael didn't care what was on the other end of that light. What mattered to him was that it represented a release from the black bowels of the bat cave and for that he would be grateful.

It didn't take long, however, for Michael to recognize that they were not the focus of the light's beam. In fact their very presence seemed incidental to the men who leapt off what was now identifiable as a Zodiac rigid inflatable boat. Michael watched as the men, whose faces were all but obscured by shadow, rounded up Ted with the frightening efficiency of seasoned professionals. Ordering him to raise his hands above his head, they zip cuffed his hands from behind and led him at gun point through the chest-deep waters to the waiting boat.

Michael carefully craned his neck out of the recess in the rock for a better view. Once Ted was aboard, the focus of the men in the water changed. They set their sights on the Horten which, though standing in several additional feet of water, appeared undamaged from the blast. Their first order of business was to call a command into the dark reaches of the cave. Another spotlight glowed bright white and within moments a second Zodiac containing another crew of men purred in. They bumped up against the base of the Horten and the crew began unfolding mounds of black rubber from their boat. There was little light to make out the proceedings and Michael's left cheek was level with a cold wet rock, but from what he could see, the men were placing the black rubber under the fuselage of the Horten, all to the chorus of a muted popping. Michael knew his hearing still wasn't right and that the popping sound was no doubt the sound of the rubber slapping the water as it was unfolded, but before he could confirm it, he felt Kate nudge him.

Michael mouthed the word, "What?"

She pointed above, pantomiming a gun. Michael got it. The popping he heard wasn't the slap of rubber on water but gunfire echoing from the karst above. There was a shooting match going on up there even as the men below proceeded with their task, unrolling the rubber tubes like snakes beneath the Horten. Michael began mouthing another word, but Kate motioned him not to talk. It didn't matter. It was obvious that the question on both their minds revolved around their next move. The wall of water that had deposited them so high up on the cave's wall had given them an excellent vantage point, but it also made them sitting ducks. It would require some tricky climbing to get down, and getting down without being noticed would be even more difficult. For now it was best to stay put.

The bravado that Michael had felt in the face of the Chinese agent's interrogation had been mostly washed away by the wall of water. Now all he felt was wet. Wet and cold and glad to be alive. He took the moment to empty his pocket of the sarin-laced coins, placing his change on the ledge beside him. They were better there than in his pocket. Except as he placed the final two coins on the slippery rock beside him, he caught his wrist on the pile. One of the coins began to roll. He reached out to catch it, but he wasn't quick enough. The coin bounced down and hit a rock which it again bounced off before hitting the black water below.

It was a tiny splash really. Nothing to get excited about. But someone must have taken notice. Because the powerful spotlight which illuminated the Horten began a slow arc over the cave wall. Michael and Kate lowered their profile as much as possible, doing their best to blend into the rock. It seemed to work at first because the spotlight passed right over them. Then the beam retraced its path backward, shooting past them again before returning to bathe them in a white focused light. Michael knew his hearing was back because he clearly heard the Cantonese chatter drifting up from the cave floor below. Whatever the merits of laying low, they didn't much matter now. They had been discovered.

46

Mobi's extraction from the alcove was brutally efficient. Within minutes of being subdued he was transported to a glass-walled holding cell. They had cuffed his hands, but there had been no interrogation, only Rand and Alvarez arguing heatedly outside the cell. Mobi could hear nothing, of course, as the cell was completely sound proof, but what surprised him was that he didn't care. What he cared about was following up on his hunch—a hunch that told him that he had just wasted a whole lot of time barking up the wrong tree.

If Quiann was trying to get Mobi off track it would be something simple. As far as Mobi knew, Quiann had no way of knowing he would contact him. Therefore if Quiann had wanted to mislead Mobi, it had to be done quickly. After all, the data had arrived soon after Mobi had phoned. There wasn't a lot of time to alter it. Quiann would have wanted Mobi to believe the data was real, yet he didn't want it to be real. That meant the changes would be slight, yet significant. And a rigorous scientist like Quiann was nothing if not a perfectionist.

Even if engaging in an act of subterfuge, Mobi assumed Quiann would go for the elegant solution. Simple, but systematic. To Mobi, it suggested one thing: that the damage could be reversed. But if his premise held, if the data stream had been altered, the bigger question was how to bring it back to its natural form. Mobi considered this point as the glass door to the cell slid open behind him.

"Mobi?" Alvarez said softly.

Mobi didn't react, but simply stared at his reflection in the glass wall, his thoughts churning.

"Mobi, it's me."

Mobi heard the Deputy Director this time around, but continued to stare at his reflection.

"Mobi, damn it, I'm the only thing standing between you and the three hundred forty-two pages of the Patriot Act. Talk to me."

"You know there's somebody sending messages out of this facility."

"I'm the one who told you about it."

"That person would need access."

"Of course."

"That person might even want me to waste my time with Quiann."

"Mobi," Alvarez said, uncomfortable with the suggestion, "whatever you're thinking you need to put that aside for the moment and focus."

"Why?"

"Because you can still help."

Mobi looked to Alvarez. He didn't want to doubt her, but it didn't change the fact that he did. Regardless, she was right. He could help. Even if he wasn't sure which side he would be helping. "Quiann wasn't square with us," Mobi finally said.

"What do you mean not square? Why?"

"The why I'm not sure about," Mobi said, eyeing his reflection in the glass, "but the how is obvious." He turned to Alvarez. "And I know how to fix it."

47

FROM THE MOMENT the spotlight found them on the cave wall, it was clear to Michael that there was only one course of action—to come down. The man with the Uzi submachine gun below had an unobstructed line of sight and what was more, there was nowhere to go. The cave wall above the ledge was too smooth to climb. A brief glance at Kate had confirmed that her thinking matched his and they scaled the slippery cave wall back down to the cave floor. Their circumstances, however, had rapidly deteriorated since their descent. Both Michael's and Kate's hands had been bound behind their backs with plastic zip cuffs. They stood upright, chest deep in the cave water, held hostage by a muscular Uzi-wielding man in the Zodiac.

Kate was silent, but she didn't have to speak. Michael could tell that she recognized their captor's Tiger-Snake tattoo just as he did; he was another Tiger Snake Boy. Shortly after they reached the cave floor, a compressor had been turned on and the rubber tubes beneath the Horten had begun to inflate. Four men fit the pontoons together with a tubular steel frame. As the pontoons took on a cylindrical form, the Horten actually rose above them like a water bug skating on a pond. A roughly circular fifty-foot hole had been blasted into the cave wall from the riverfront. How the Horten had gotten into the cave was still a mystery. It could have been sealed in with a similar explosion years ago or it could have come through an as yet unseen tunnel. But how it was going to get out was obvious. One look at Kate told Michael that she, like he, understood exactly what was going on. The Tiger Snake Boys intended to float the Horten downriver.

It was a good plan, Michael thought, if getting a Nazi war plane out of a bat cave was on your to do list. Not foolproof, maybe, but good. A cry of protest erupted from Michael's right and he redirected his attention to the farthest corner of the cave. There, where the newly blasted cave opened to the river, Ted was being forced into the second Zodiac by two gun-wielding men. Several shouts of protest were followed by a short growl as the Zodiac's twin outboards purred to life. The man at the helm made a quick turn forcing Michael to stand on his toes to avoid swallowing the second Zodiac's wake.

"Where are they taking him?" Michael said.

His words were answered by a sudden silence. The compressor had been shut down. Apparently the machine's work was complete because the Horten had risen so high on its inflatable pontoons that it was actually floating now, drifting toward where they stood at the bow of the boat. Michael listened carefully as the men who had been working to inflate the pontoons waded back to the

Zodiac, each carrying a three-quarter-inch polyethylene tow rope. He could hear the receding purr of the second Zodiac, but not much else as silence enveloped the cave. Michael knew it was the calm before the storm. The quiet might last another minute or two, but it wouldn't last forever. You didn't blow a hole in the side of a mountain just to enjoy the view.

"*Kah!*"

Michael recognized the Cantonese word for "go" and felt the twin Yamaha outboards snort to life. A second man grabbed them by their collars and within a few seconds the bow of the Zodiac swung gently around pulling Michael and Kate with it. They soon lost their footing, hanging from the bow of the boat in the deeper water, barely able to hold their heads above the surface. Michael was so cold his body was numb now. He felt the slack in the polyethylene ropes being taken up as the Zodiac moved forward, churning the dark cave water behind it. The Horten was no doubt floating behind them, but Michael directed his attention to keeping his head above water as they steered toward the newly blasted hole in the cave wall.

One thing Michael had learned from Peru was that in the long run, you had no idea what curves life might throw at you. You could plan, you could visualize, but in the end, you had no idea. Michael had done almost everything wrong when he was captured on that mountainside in the Andes. He had wept, he had screamed, and he had panicked. And yet, when it was all over, the one thing that he had done right was to not lose faith in himself. Even in his darkest hour, when he was clinging to that ledge in the mineshaft, he had told himself that he would make it out alive. Even if his father didn't save him, even if nobody saved him, he would survive. It might have been misguided, but he credited this blind faith with saving his life. Now, thousands of miles away and many years later, he suspected he was going to need to tap that same faith again.

"Kate?" Michael said.

"Yeah?"

A wave came up and swamped both their heads as the Zodiac slowly motored out of the cave into the open water of the river. Michael struggled to get his head back above water.

"When I had you in that submission hold back on the plane, when you were lying on the cargo floor, how did you know I wouldn't break your neck?"

"Don't be stupid."

"How did you know?"

"It doesn't matter now."

"Everything matters."

"Because," Kate said.

"Because why?"

Kate gulped down a breath. "Because you're not a killer, Michael."

A second wave crashed over the bow and submerged them both. They must have hit a whirlpool because this wave didn't recede. Instead, it became more vicious, white water sucking them down. Michael felt the powerful arm that was holding him struggle to retain its grip, but it did no good. Kick his feet how he might, Michael couldn't keep his head above water. His body was numb, his world nothing but liquid blackness. Starved of oxygen, the roar of the river displaced his every living thought, until finally, when rescue came, Michael couldn't be sure if he was living or dead.

"Mr. Chase." the name was heavily accented but clear.

"Mr. Chase," the voice said again.

A pair of strong arms fished Michael from the river, dragging him into the boat. Kate was already sitting there, waterlogged and breathing heavily. Michael sucked in the night air. They were several hundred yards downriver from the cave, the Horten bobbing faithfully behind. Shaking the water out of his eyes, he peered sideways at the dignified old man who had spoken his name. Michael recognized the man from the limousine outside Chungking Mansions. He didn't have to be a mind reader to see that Kate recognized him too, and however much she might try to hide it, she didn't look happy at the turn of events. She looked afraid.

"Allow me to formally introduce myself," the old man said, offering Michael a towel. "My name is Tung. Li Tung."

48

Mobi studied the Chinese satellite's trajectory on Mission Control's overhead display, both Rand and Alvarez silently waiting on what he had to say. When Mobi thought about it, he didn't know if he could trust either one of them, but it didn't matter. He was on planet Earth's side tonight. Politics be damned.

"Quiann reversed the stream."

"I'm not following," Alvarez said.

"Quiann didn't want me to decode it, so he reversed the stream."

"If he didn't want us to have the data," Alvarez said, "then why send it at all?"

"Because he was scared. Scared I was going to find a way to contact it anyhow."

Rand was unimpressed. "If your boy doesn't start making sense in the next five seconds, he's back in his cage."

"Mobi," Alvarez said, "for you own sake, speak clearly, from the beginning."

"Okay, here goes. Quiann wanted me to fail. I don't know why, but he did. He sent me a mirror image of the data. Combined with a common cipher it proved to be a simple but effective cloak. But now, looking at the data stream the way it was meant to be seen, now I get it. I can stop that satellite from falling out of the sky."

Mobi sat down at his workstation, quickly entering his password with his tightly cuffed hands. He hit a key and the data stream appeared on the overhead screen.

"Look. All those scrolling numbers are just two things. The Chinese saying to their spacecraft, 'We're down here, please talk to us,' and the spacecraft calling back, 'I'm all alone up here, why don't you talk to me?' And both sides are doing it again, and again, and again."

"And you have to lock yourself in a closet to figure that out?"

"Well, yeah. It didn't make sense until I figured out that Quiann cooked the data. Now look at this." Mobi went to work on the keyboard, the numbers on the screen realigning into their mirror image.

"So?"

"So watch when I factor out the noise." Mobi hit a key and again the numbers on the screen changed, cycling through a series of permutations, before finally settling like the wheels on a slot machine. "There." Mobi grinned proudly. "Quiann disguised it as well as he could on such short notice, but now that it's been turned around and cleaned up, you can see there's a subroutine buried in the loop." Mobi pointed, jerking both cuffed hands. "The digits in the middle. Those are the clear-code. They would have been designed to reboot the system in the event of a problem."

"So do it," Rand said

"What do you mean do it?"

"Send the code."

Mobi just looked at Rand. "I can't send the code."

"What are you talking about?"

"This thing's a closed system. This is just a window. Not a way in. The Chinese have to send the code."

The corners of Rand's mouth turned up into the same nasty smile Mobi now knew well. "Perfect. The Chinese have to send the code."

"Is there a problem?" Mobi asked.

"No, no problem unless you consider the fact that as of fourteen hundred hours today we confirmed a massive explosion at China's Jiuquan South Launch Center. Preliminary intelligence indicates sabotage. Probably an inside job. Even if the Chinese could communicate with that thing, their facility has been destroyed. There's nobody left to send squat."

49

BLACK KARSTS ROSE like sentinels from the riverbank. By Michael's estimate they were now several miles downriver, but there had been little talk and no change in their circumstances. Michael and Kate were kept cuffed at the bow of the Zodiac until finally the helmsman eased them around in a wide arc lining up the load they pulled with a gravel boat ramp on the riverbank. Michael could just see the black boxy form of a tractor-trailer with all but its front wheels backed into the water. Then, a flash of light from the riverbank was returned by a like signal from the Zodiac.

As they neared the bank, Michael saw men up to their waists in the water. The helmsman shut the twin outboards down, their four-stroke purr replaced by an electric hum as the engines hydraulically tilted up from the water. A moment later the bow of the boat ran gently ashore. The men in the river wasted no time taking hold of the tow ropes, guiding the inflatable pontoons supporting the Horten up onto the back of the submerged tractor-trailer. The Horten was now sideways, its wings lined up with the length of the trailer. The men pulled tie straps from a large utility chest and began securing the fuselage down.

"Off," the sinewy helmsman said.

Michael glanced at Kate, who rose, stepping off the Zodiac's inflated rubber bow onto the muddy riverbank. Michael got up as well, his wet clothes clinging to him in the night air. Then, Tung's stocky enforcer marched them at gunpoint to the tractor-trailer which unceremoniously belched smoke and black soot as its diesel engine turned over. Michael risked a glance back at the Zodiac where Li Tung and one of his lieutenants were deep in discussion. He gained only a sharp tap from the barrel of the Uzi. Redirecting his gaze ahead, Michael watched as the big truck pulled slowly forward, the Horten rising from the river like a behemoth from the deep.

• • •

MEANWHILE, HUANG BRISTLED at the indignity of it all. He had made it safely up the top rope to the peak of the karst. His backup team had greeted him as planned. And then, in one short moment, his entire operation had fallen apart. It started with the explosion below. The whole peak shook. At first Huang feared an earthquake, but he soon realized that what had befallen him was no natural disaster. He immediately dropped to the ground bellowing out an order for his men to do the same, but it wasn't enough. Before the rumbling from the explosion had even subsided, Huang saw the muzzle flash. He knew at that point he was foolish not to have expected it. There had always been other forces at work in China. It was a wonder they had not interfered earlier.

Huang ordered his men to retreat, but by the time the words had left his mouth, the bullets were already flying. The assault appeared to originate from the south side of the peak. His agents attempted to return fire but their assailants were well covered behind the rocks. With nowhere to run, his men were sitting ducks. And Huang would have been too if not for a simple piece of luck. He was still wearing his climbing harness. Rolling to his side, Huang was able to clip back into his top rope and lower himself over the far edge of the cliff. There he had found a rock outcropping in the lee of the karst. And there he had patiently waited while his men were slaughtered above.

• • •

Michael was running on pure adrenaline. All he could say for certain was that both his and Kate's hands were zip cuffed behind their backs as they rumbled down the road in the rear cab of an eighteen-wheeler towing a Nazi airplane. Tung's sinewy enforcer held the wheel while another member of the Triad crew rode shotgun. Apart from these few facts, the only other thing that was clear was that time was running out. Michael was thinking big picture, spy style now. If the Chinese satellite was still in the sky, it wouldn't be there for long. The boys in tech needed to find the clear-code. And if they found it, Michael needed to send it. Regardless of his personal motivations, that was his mission now. That was why he was here.

It was for this reason that Michael knew it was time to act when their truck slowed, rattling to a stop alongside an open fire on the road. Craning his neck toward the driver's side window, he was able to see that they had pulled up beside a corrugated tin shack home to several men drinking tea around their roadside campfire. Tung's enforcer removed the keys from the ignition, clipping them to his belt, and along with his wiry companion, they opened the vehicle's doors to exit the cab. But before Michael was able to even formulate a plan, he felt Kate's feet on his back shoving him forward. He tumbled ahead, face-first into the long gearshift between driver and passenger seats, unable to break his fall thanks to his tightly cuffed hands.

The move evidently took Tung's enforcer by surprise as well, because instead of twisting aside to avoid Michael's fall, he was set off balance and shoved halfway out the door. His accomplice reached for his weapon, but the Uzi hanging from his left side got caught up in the wheel well. He hesitated and Kate rolled through the gap between the seats. She hauled back with both feet, booting him from the cab. On Michael's side the driver regained his balance, taking hold of Michael's hair and yanking him toward the door. Chin down on the seat, Michael eyed the truck keys dangling from the man's belt as he was pulled inexorably out of the vehicle. Kate must have been thinking the same thing because he felt her slam her body against the backs of his legs, screaming one word.

"Key!"

Michael felt what he thought were Kate's lips on the back of his wrists. Then he heard an enormous groan.

"Pull!"

Michael wrenched at his wrists, finally realizing what Kate was doing. She was biting through the plastic cuffs. Michael could feel them weakening, Kate's hot saliva dripping down as he stretched the cuffs between his wrists. The plastic was stretching beyond its breaking point. Kate bit down again and the cuffs snapped. Tung's man was still yanking Michael by the hair, but Michael's hands were newly free and he reached for the man's crotch with his left hand and the truck keys with his right. As he did so, he felt Kate kick like a dolphin with both feet out the passenger-side door. Her blow must have knocked the Triad guy off his feet for the second time because he heard a moan even before he squeezed the driver's balls. Michael slammed the door and threw the keys into the ignition.

Kate screamed, "Drive!"

Michael fired up the truck and whatever Kate said next was lost in a burst of machine-gun fire. It didn't matter, though. Michael's feet had already found the pedals. Still lying low, he popped the big rig into gear and hit the accelerator, lurching blindly into the night.

50

Mobi wasn't disappointed, he was devastated. If the Chinese Launch Center was destroyed it meant they had no access to an appropriately encoded transceiver. That in turn meant the clear-code was useless. Which ultimately meant that a lot of innocent people would die. And they would start dying soon. In silent acknowledgment of this fact, Mobi slumped forward and closed his eyes, burrowing his forehead into the metal desk. There was nothing he could do now and he knew it. Rand's men had re-cuffed his hands behind his back, seating him as far away from a computer terminal as they could get him. They had then taken up position outside Mission Control's open exit doors.

To make matters worse, Mobi was now convinced that Alvarez was the mole. Rand had access as well, but Alvarez was the one cozying up to Quiann. Mobi wondered why she had put him in contact with Quiann. Was it to implicate him in her web? Alvarez, meanwhile, stood near the front of Mission Control, sucking back a soda as though she didn't have a care in the world. He wished he understood her motives, but it didn't really matter, not anymore.

At least, Mobi thought, he had no family in California. All of his friends were right here at JPL and he hoped they would be able to get on the freeway and out of town, even though he saw no such option for himself. When it was all over, people would be looking for a scapegoat. He'd be dead, but it wouldn't stop them from blaming him for the dispersal of plutonium into the atmosphere. Or for incinerating half the state. These and a thousand other thoughts plagued Mobi even as he felt the tap on his head. He thought the tap felt like freezing rain. Or hail. No doubt they'd blame him for global warming as well. All on the back of one stupid satellite.

Mobi felt another tap and opened his eyes. But it wasn't hailing. In fact the only thing that was different was that Alvarez stood much closer than she had before and there were two ice cubes melting into a tiny pool on his desk. Mobi opened his mouth, about to ask Alvarez why she was lobbing ice at him, but instead he followed her gaze to the guards watching them from either door. Alvarez then took out her phone and checked her voicemail, letting the phone hang down in one hand as she walked past Mobi. Mobi had no idea what to think until he read the phone's screen: "Transceiver acquired. Clear-code?"

Mobi just shook his head. If what Rand had said was true, the clear-code was useless. Then why keep bothering him? Mobi looked away. And in that moment Alvarez tripped, spilling Diet Coke all over him.

"I am so sorry," Alvarez said. Then she whispered, "We have an agent on the ground. Give me the clear-code, you stubborn-ass, Caltech dork."

Was she serious? Was she actually bullying him? Still, something about the way she said "dork" made Mobi smile. She might be a traitor, but what kind of traitor talked like that? Maybe he was wrong about her. Mobi just didn't know. But he did have the clear-code. If there was even a chance he could do some good with it, he decided in that moment it was a chance he would take. Hoping against hope, Mobi dangled all ten fingers behind his chair and carefully signed the seventeen-digit clear-code to Alvarez who now stood at the back of the room.

Less than twenty seconds later Alvarez left Mission Control. A minute after that the code was relayed through two commercial communications satellites and back down to an encrypted mobile device in Guangxi Province, China.

51

SOME OF MICHAEL'S *dad's lessons weren't lessons at all. Like when he taught Michael about family. Family was everything in the Chase home. Even if their home was unconventional. Mom ran most of the show because Michael's dad had a pretty intensive travel schedule. But when Michael's dad was there, he was all there. They did things together. They hiked. They swam. They went on family trips. Once, Michael remembered, his dad flew back overnight from Japan, just to see him play Lacrosse. Michael didn't think he was flying that far just to see him at the time, but when he woke up the next morning, his father was gone. His mom explained that his dad had a very important job to do, but Michael was more important than the job, and he wanted to be there for the game. It was the same thing when Michael broke his leg skiing. His dad was there the next day. Ditto for when he got his appendix out. So even though his dad couldn't be there all the time, he was there when he needed him. Always. And Michael knew that he would always be there for his dad too. Whatever it took.*

Kᴀᴛᴇ ʜᴜɴɢ ᴜᴘ the phone. Tung's man had left it plugged into the dash of the truck and though convenient, Michael was certain it wasn't secure. Kate, however, didn't seem overly concerned.

"My people gave me the coordinates of a meeting place not far from here," Kate said. "A reservoir about ten minutes up the road. They'll meet us there."

They had been driving through the night for over half an hour now. There had been no talk of Ted's betrayal and no talk of what was to come. Kate seemed to have retreated inward and though Michael didn't mind the silence, it did nothing to set his mind at ease. A satellite was falling out of the sky and he was anxious. Anxious that he would have blood on his hands. Anxious that he had come all this way to fail. And anxious that he would never find out what had happened to his father. For the tenth time in as many minutes Michael hung his wrist out the window to get a signal lock. His GPS indicated that they were still headed southwest toward Vietnam.

"What then?" Michael said.

"What do you mean?"

"You said that if we found the Horten there was a chance we'd be able to communicate with that flying bomb up there. Well, we found the Horten. When we get to the reservoir what happens? What then?"

"They said they'd update us as the situation developed."

"Is that it?"

Kate could see the pleading in Michael's eyes. "They said they had information. Information regarding your father."

Michael was silent for a long moment. "What kind of information?"

There was no reply.

"I said, what kind of information?"

"I don't know, okay? Ow!" Kate screamed grasping her ear. A high-pitched hum filled the cab. Working her thumb and finger into her left ear, Kate managed to pull out something that looked like a wax ball. "It's a sub aural receiver. Standard issue. The water in the cave must have shorted it out."

Kate started to put the receiver back into her ear when a tinny mechanical monotone began echoing a series of numbers as clear as a bell.

"5-6-9-1-2-3-6-8-1-4-6-6-1-7-2-4-3." The numbers stopped.

"Was that what I thought it was?" Michael said.

"The clear-code," Kate said. "My people are telling us there's still a chance we can keep that bird in the sky."

52

HUANG WAS WELL aware that his operation had careened dangerously off track. He had no doubt that many of his men had been killed, others had been taken prisoner, and his objective, the Horten's unique reactor, had been snatched from his grasp. But none of this meant that the mission was lost. Not yet at least. He still had good intelligence on the American efforts to destroy the satellite. More important than that however, he believed he knew who the gunmen were. Even before setting out, he had been warned that a particular Triad organization might have a vested interest in the Horten. And now, given the evening's events it was obvious that the warning had held true. Huang had seen the Horten barged out of the blasted cave and down the river with his own eyes. Now it was time to do something about it.

Still in possession of his secure Motorola, Huang's first action had been to contact Guilin Station. From there a Bell 460 helicopter armed with an M27 mini-gun had been dispatched to pick him up. He had then made a second call to place informants on all the riverbank landing points for a hundred kilometers south of Yangshuo. Huang knew it would be suicide for the Triad to travel the river in the light of day. They would be seen and hence had no choice but to leave the river before daybreak. And given that there were no rail lines within convenient reach, to leave the river meant a tractor-trailer large enough to transport the Horten.

In a stroke of good fortune, Huang's quick response to the situation had already garnered a hit—a suspicious truck had left the river following the old Guangxi Highway south. Satellite services had since identified that it was carrying a wing-shaped load approximately twenty meters in length. What this told Huang was that he had effectively reacquired the Horten. And even as he tried to not be unduly influenced by the optimism welling within him, he felt his pulse quicken. The American spy wouldn't get by him again.

53

THE LAST MILE or so had been uphill. Michael and Kate had turned off the main artery onto a dirt road leading into the hinterland. The road had deteriorated to the point where it was little more than a dirt track. Then, that too had given way, leaving them in a rolling meadow surrounded by karsts. Michael stopped the truck, checking the coordinates Kate had given him against his GPS. They were there. An emerald-shaped reservoir, indistinguishable from a natural lake, lay just below them. They were alone up here, or at least they appeared to be.

"You say we're going to meet your people here?"

"That's what they said."

Michael knew that time was running out. And he knew he had a mission to complete. But he also knew that this was the moment he had been waiting for; his single best chance to finally learn what had happened to his father. He would be a fool to turn his back on that opportunity now. Michael decided he could manage the risks. Leaving the headlights on, he pulled the keys from the ignition and followed Kate out of the truck and down the bank to the water's edge. Given the course of the last few hours, he was well aware that the bucolic beauty around him could erupt into a bloodbath within seconds and as such he did everything in his power to remain vigilant.

"They said wait?"

"Wait and they'd meet us here," Kate said.

Michael glanced at his watch. The cicada's song carried over the cool lake breeze did little to calm him. If he had to wait much longer, it would all be over.

"Your father was a worthy adversary."

Michael spun around. The words hadn't come from Kate who remained beside him, lips pursed shut, eyes wide in the moonlight. They had come from the bank above, near the truck. Michael craned his neck, but could see nothing in the darkness.

Kate put her arm out, barring Michael's movement. "Follow my lead," she said quietly.

But the only lead Michael was following was his own. He pushed Kate's arm aside, striding up the bank toward the truck. Not much of anything was visible in the shadows even with the headlights shining. Then the woman walked into the light. Michael had seen her before, but now he was seeing her with new eyes. Young, pretty and innocent, it was their bicycle tour guide from Yangshuo. Ester. Michael noted that she didn't appear to be holding a weapon, at least not one that was drawn. He took a moment to slow his racing pulse.

"What do you know about my father?"

"I know that he was good at his work."

"What else?"

"I know that he did not choose his friends wisely."

"And?"

"I know that neither do you."

Michael was within ten feet of Ester now. He watched her eyes. They were young and dark, but they weren't focused on him. Not even close. They stared beyond Michael. Through him really, back down the bank to Kate. Michael turned to her. Her gaze conferred a softness he had not yet been privy too.

"I'm sorry, Michael."

He turned back to Ester. She had taken a step forward and now aimed an antique German Luger straight at his chest. It was an old weapon to be sure, but it still shot standard 9mm rounds. An encounter with it would be fatal.

"What do you want?" Michael asked.

Ester motioned him toward the truck. The steel plate utility box sat nearest the cab, bolted to the I-beam frame of the trailer.

"I want you," Ester said, "to get in the box."

Michael, unsure if he had heard her correctly, didn't move. Ester repeated herself.

"I said, get in the box."

Michael risked a backward glance. The utility box was perhaps six feet in length and two and half in width, a couple feet deep at most. It was made of forge-hardened, diamond-plate steel and one thing Michael was absolutely certain of was that he would not get inside of it. Not without a fight anyhow. But he needed a plan. He needed to buy time and already Ester was backing him toward the box where it sat welded to the frame of the trailer immediately below the leading edge of the Horten's wing. As Ester backed him up, Michael noted that in addition to the Luger in her left hand, she carried a double-barreled sawed-off shotgun, a twelve-gauge by the looks of it, hanging from a leather shoulder loop inside her coarse wool jacket.

"The old man in the village. You shot him before he could talk."

"Yes," Ester said.

Michael considered the implication. "Is that what you did to my father?"

Ester smiled. "Your father was a brave man. That is all you need to know."

"Where is he?"

There was no response.

"Shoot me if you want, but you will tell me where he is."

Michael's command was answered by a cellular beep. Ester carefully ended the ring with a touch to the phone on her belt.

"There is no time. Turn around."

Michael was loathe to do so, but he didn't think she was going to execute him. Not if she was still talking about the box. He risked turning ninety degrees and as he did, Ester reached into her pocket, removing what looked like a flash memory card. She held it in the air.

"The account details are saved on the card," she said to no one in particular. "They will be useless without remote activation which I will provide upon the successful completion of my mission."

Kate stepped up the bank. "That wasn't part of our agreement."

"You were to deliver the aircraft alone."

Ester stepped to the side and jabbed the barrel of the Luger into Michael's back. He found himself wishing she'd stuck it in the back of his head. His father had always told him that contrary to popular opinion, the back of the head wasn't the worst place a gun could go. With a gun to the back of your head, a quick turn to the left or right, dramatically increased the odds of a flesh wound, the bullet skirting your skull mostly harmlessly. With the gun in his back, Michael knew that his soft organs would be vulnerable if he tried to move. An escape attempt now would result in at least a pierced lung. Probably worse. He stalled for time.

"What was it, Kate? Why'd you sell me out?"

"Make it easy on yourself, Michael. Do as she says."

Michael stood tight against the trailer now, the cold steel utility box at eye level. He still felt the Luger at his back, but he was hopeful. She couldn't keep the gun parked there forever, not the way he saw it. He placed both hands down and pulled himself up onto the steel frame of the trailer. The semi-trailer had no deck, only two long I-beams which composed the length upon which cargo was fastened. The box was welded down where the I-beams met an orthogonal strut.

"Lift the lid."

Pistol still trained on him, Michael forced any thought of Kate from his mind. If he was going to survive he needed to focus. He knew that. It wasn't the time to consider how he had gotten into this situation—it was the time to get out of it. Michael reached down for the lid of the box. It was heavy as he expected. Inside was a collection of the tarps and fasteners used to secure cargo. Michael could feel Ester's gun trained on his back, but he thought if he could leap across the width of the trailer, from one I-beam to the next, he might be able to take cover behind the Horten's landing gear. It wasn't a perfect plan, but it was something. Still, he needed a diversion. Anything to buy him another second.

"You're a coward, Kate."

"I'm a survivor."

"Silence!" Ester said.

And Michael seized the moment. He leapt diagonally across the I-beams toward the wing of the Horten. He knew it was hard to hit a moving target with a handgun. Especially at a distance in the dark. For a quarter second, maybe even half, all was well. Michael felt himself sailing through the air. Then he felt a nimble hand take hold of his rear foot, using his momentum against him. Losing his balance, he was unable to stop himself from tumbling backwards the way he had come. He managed a split-second glance at Ester on the ground below the trailer before his remaining forward momentum was redirected against him. Then he fell shoulder first into the hard steel utility chest, his forehead grazing the sharp corner as he landed. The heavy lid crashed down and even though he sprung up with all the ferocity of a coiled spring, it did little good. He felt the snug hold of metal on metal and knew that the lid was already latched. Michael found himself alone in the dark. No room to roll over. Stuck in the box.

54

ESTER MOVED QUICKLY over the steel I-beams of the trailer. She had bolted the utility chest shut, but now had bigger fish to fry. Her mission was a simple one—to destroy the Horten before it became too late. She had hoped it wouldn't come to this. The Horten had remained hidden since the Japanese retreat near the end of World War II. The Dragons wanted it that way. They couldn't afford to have its technology made public. There was too much at stake. Overnight, massive hydroelectric projects would become obsolete. Oil fields would become no more valuable than desert sand. Wind power projects that had eaten years of capital would have no hope of turning a profit. The Dragons were too heavily invested in the current energy infrastructure to allow a technology like cold fusion to wipe it out. Not before they were ready.

Ester had been inducted into the Green Dragon Society by way of her late mother's sponsorship nearly ten years ago. She knew that outsiders might find it odd that she belonged to a Japanese organization; the Japanese were after all the same people who had brutalized her ancestors, but Ester understood that the importance of the Society easily outweighed any lingering ethnic tension.

Ester's mother had told her that in the beginning it was simple. Back during the Cultural Revolution the waves of spies had been easy to detect. They hid under the cover of diplomatic missions and covered their tracks poorly. But later, as the years progressed, foreign governments' appetites for the Horten's cold fusion technology increased. Wave after wave of foreign agents had come. Even in the relatively short decade Ester had been tied to the Society she had personally dealt with Israelis, Russians, French, even Saudis, all looking for the Horten with her famed propulsion technology, all looking for a leg up in the energy game.

Even Ester had initially thought it absurd—foolish foreigners searching China for an archaic aircraft. She was studying to prepare for university at the time. If not for her mother's counsel, Ester would have turned down the seemingly harmless, middle-aged Japanese man in an instant. She wanted to earn a degree and move to the city, not keep tabs on the local tourists. But her mother had insisted that Ester give the man a chance and finally Ester had relented. All the man had asked was that Ester keep a lookout for foreigners in the area and report back any behavior she regarded as suspicious. At first she simply sent information about the various tourists poking their heads into the local nooks and crannies, but the more she looked, the better she was able to recognize those visitors whose interests weren't so benign. With time, she was able to identify the many operatives of foreign governments who came to Yangshuo searching for what her Japanese employer referred to only as the reactor. Though she did not understand its worth initially, as the waves of agents descended upon the region over the years, Ester came to realize that whatever the reactor was, it had to be very valuable indeed.

Her work for the Japanese man went on for years like that. Even her mother refused to tell her more, saying only that she was doing good work. Ester received a monthly stipend that grew with her responsibilities. Then, immediately after the fourth year of working for the Japanese man, she was invited on a trip abroad. The necessary travel documents were secured for her, and within a few days she found herself in Tokyo meeting with a man who identified himself as Director of the Society. It was during this trip to Japan that Ester the Freelance Operative became Ester the Believer.

In the month she spent with the Green Dragons, she learned of their global energy interests and the new world order they were proposing. A world without borders. A world driven by limitless green energy. A world with equal opportunity for all. More importantly she learned why they were protecting the Horten and why the world was not yet ready for its bounty; not until all the pieces were in place. In the space of a week, Ester vowed to protect the Horten not for money, but for the very sanctity of her soul. She knew that many others, even the famous Doctor Jie Quiann, father of China's Space Program, had also taken such a pledge. It was up to believers such as themselves to protect the others.

Now, nearly ten years later, Ester faced the spear tip of that pledge. She had eliminated Chen, the factory man, who in his foolhardy production of the dangerous trinket had risked exposing the Society. She had eliminated the old man in Yangkok. But despite these things, the Horten had been discovered. Both the American and the British spy had laid eyes upon it. At this point she didn't know who else might have seen the Horten, but it no longer mattered. All that mattered was that it be destroyed before further damage could be done. To that end Ester removed the three kilograms of Semtex explosive from her shoulder bag.

Ester separated the cellophane-wrapped Semtex blocks carefully from each other. The detonators were kept apart, in their own Ziploc bag, to prevent the possibility of an electro-static discharge. The procedure was easy really. She simply had to mold the Semtex blocks into position at intervals around the Horten's airframe and insert a detonator into each block which would be hardwired to a single timer. The timer would give her ample time to escape to safety, providing all went according to plan, and so far, given that the discovery of the Horten had prompted a worst-case scenario, things were proceeding along remarkably predictable lines. The American had been neutralized and when containment had proved impossible, the British spy had delivered the aircraft as contracted. Now all Ester had to do was place the explosives and her duty here would be done.

Her phone rang, cutting her rumination short. "Yes?" Ester answered.

"Is it done?"

Hayakawa's strong voice was familiar to Ester. The great Japanese man didn't have to introduce himself and she could tell he was in no mood to waste time. "I am applying the putty now."

"The British?"

"Paid."

"The American?"

"Neutralized."

"Excellent. Report back to me upon completion."

The man hung up and Ester reflected that he had not greeted her or said good-bye. This did not bother her, though. Only the cause mattered now. The world was not ready for the Horten and its promise of clean green energy. The change would be too swift. Governments would collapse. The social order would dissolve. Capital, the same capital the Dragons would one day use to usher in a better world, would be destroyed. And what would rise to take its place? Chaos. Certainly a new world order would eventually be drawn along new lines, but the concomitant damage would be horrific. The Dragons' goal was to avoid this. The Dragons' goal was to usher in a golden age of limitless peace.

With that comforting thought, Ester affixed the first block of Semtex to the wing of the Horten. She inserted the detonator noting that she had chosen a spot on the wing directly above where the American had been laid to rest. No matter, she thought. It was more merciful this way. There would be time to atone for her sins once her journey was complete.

55

IT WAS THE nightmare all over again. Michael was back in the mineshaft. Back on the ledge. He couldn't move more than a few inches in any direction and nobody had come for him. No water, no light, no food. He'd been left to die. Above him just beyond the reach of his fingers was the iron trapdoor. Below him, beyond the rock ledge, God only knew. Only this time, he wasn't on a ledge. This time he was in China. In a metal box. And there was no chance of his father saving him. Because he had come to save his father.

Michael beat on the lid of the box, but it did little good. Already he felt the familiar claustrophobia settling in. The way Ester had said "neutralized" had chilled him, the walls of the chest closing in, spiraling around. All in all, Michael thought, his circumstances were dire and were getting worse by the moment. He questioned the decisions that had brought him here. He cursed the fact that he had said yes to the man who had approached him after the terrible news about his father. For what had he come to China, he asked himself? A metal coffin? Round and round he went fighting back panic with the left half of his brain while the right half fanned it on. He was certain that it was over, that he had been too lucky for too long, that he had bitten off more than he could chew, when a single fleeting thought gave him pause.

What if?

What if he died right there in the box?

What if no one ever heard another word from him?

What if his last breath was here, seven thousand miles from home?

His heart would stop beating. He would cease to be. But what then? Michael didn't consider himself to be a spiritual person. He had no firm beliefs regarding what would happen to him when he died. He had no idea whether he would encounter a white light or a black void. But what if the cosmic coin flip came up void? What then? If death meant that he would simply cease to be, then there wasn't a lot to lose. Which meant that there was everything to be gained. And with that thought the steel walls of the chest began to spin a little slower. It was an odd notion, he thought, finding comfort in the void, but Michael appeared to have found it. Michael reflected back on his training; not just the training his father had given him over the years, but everything that had happened since his dad's disappearance. Closing his eyes, Michael was able to center himself, moderating his breathing inside the cramped space. As his heart rate slowed and his spinning head came to rest, he found that faith. Faith in himself.

Michael took stock of his situation. Survival, he knew, depended on one thing: his ability to stay calm. He reached out tentatively with his fingertips. He hit the walls of the metal box right away. He estimated that he had a little less than two inches play on either side of his shoulders. His legs were bent up slightly at the knee for lack of room to fully extend his six-foot-three-inch frame. Reaching above his head to the top of the box, he guessed he had five inches of space. Not roomy to be sure, but it was something.

Michael took an inventory of his general physical condition. He had grazed the side of his head in the fall, but he didn't think he was concussed. On the contrary, since the initial panic had subsided he was now thinking clearly. Though his shoulder hurt from the impact of the fall, he also observed that the bottom of the chest was remarkably soft. There were canvas tarps in here. Tarps with hard lumps which Michael guessed to be tools below him. Looking above, he saw a flash of light through the seam in the chest's lid above the hinge. Like that, Michael knew what he had to do. Now he just had to do it.

56

MICHAEL'S FATHER'S GREATEST *lesson to him wasn't a lesson at all. It was inherited. On the gene. Michael's father was a man who knew how to take the bull by the horns. When something needed to be done, Michael's dad did it. No questions. No fuss. And no whining. Like at the accident. They were driving to the grocery store one day. Just a normal day, when a big truck coming in the opposite direction lost its brakes. Michael's dad was able to swerve out of the way and maintain control of the car, but the guy in front of him wasn't so lucky. He veered right off the road, rolling down the embankment and into the river.*

First Michael's dad asked if he and his sister were okay. Then he jumped out of the car and headed for the guy in the river. The guy's car was floating by this time, being sucked away by the current, but Michael's dad was able to jump atop the hood and pull the unconscious driver out. He saved the guy's life. They waited for the ambulance to get there and then went to the grocery store. Just a normal day. Like nothing out of the ordinary had happened. Michael always hoped that if it came to it, that he had that part of his dad in him. That he could do something like that too.

THIRTY SECONDS EARLIER Michael had told himself that getting out of the box might just be possible. Now he wasn't so sure. He had turned onto his side and reached under the tarp to pull out the hard object he was lying on top of. Extricating it from beneath him, Michael discovered that he now held a tire iron. That was the good news. The bad news was that maneuvering the tool in the tight space proved next to impossible. It was shaped like a cross, each of its arms of equal length, and the harder Michael tried to pull it up and over his body, the harder it seemed to get wedged like an anchor in the corner of the box. Finally Michael changed tack and let the tire iron fall back down to the floor of the metal box, arching his back so that he could fish under his body with his left arm and pull the tool beneath him. This time he was just able to get the tool out of the tight corner and above him.

Michael took a deep breath celebrating his first minor victory. He held the tire iron against the lid of the box for a long moment, resting his arm. Then, the muscle burn gone, he wedged the flat end of the iron into the crack where the lid of the chest met the hinge. He pushed, but he applied too much force and quickly lost purchase, the blunt end of the tool skidding down the seam.

"Damn it," Michael swore under his breath.

It was then that he heard a sputter, followed by a roar.

• • •

ESTER HAD FINISHED applying the last of the Semtex before she hit the switch. She had been explicitly instructed to fire the aircraft's auxiliary jets prior to completing her operation. To do so she had climbed into the Horten through the bottom hatch and attached a simple booster battery with remote switching device to the leads below the control panel. It was not known if the antique jet engines would operate, but the Society leaders had determined that it would be worthwhile to at least attempt to open the fuel gates prior to detonation. Ester's understanding was that the open baffles to the fuel reservoir would greatly enhance the initial Semtex charge thus assuring that the destruction of the aircraft would be complete.

The safe operation of the aircraft was, of course, in no way guaranteed after so many decades of dormancy and Ester had thus retreated a safe distance before she activated its vertical-lift jet engines and their integrated afterburners. To her considerable surprise, the vertically mounted jets fired nearly immediately, hot flames shooting out of their exhaust ports and hitting the trailer below.

If one thing was certain, Ester thought, it was that the American wasn't long for this world. The British spy had already retreated to the shore of the reservoir to verify the integrity of her payment. In Ester's mind, the Brit was worse than the American. She believed only in money, but the American believed in something more. True, he would never find the father he was looking for, but at least he had tried. Ester almost felt sorry for him, cooking quietly inside that metal box under the hot flame of the afterburners, but she quickly turned her attention to the task at hand. For the good of the Society, sacrifices had to be made.

· · ·

The box was hot and getting hotter, but Michael had no intention of being anyone's sacrifice. The intermittent yellow light that he had seen through the crack of the lid now glowed red, the roar of the jet engines deafening him. Michael smelled an acrid odor and realized only belatedly that it was his own hair, singing where it touched the metal chest. It was now obvious that he faced not one, but two challenges: first, getting out of the box and second, actually surviving once he was out there. To that end he knew he was going to need more than a tire iron. Arching his back, he lifted as much of his body as possible off the metal floor of the box and pulled on the tarp below him. It came slowly at first, but he was eventually able to extract a corner of the thick canvas tarp out from under him and pull it over himself.

Then he reached into his lower cargo pocket and withdrew the compact folded space blanket that he kept there. Unfolding the blanket along its length, he covered himself with this too, careful to keep the shiny side out. Sweat poured off of his forehead stinging his eyes. He knew that even if the afterburners weren't firing directly down on him, he wouldn't be able to take much more. Cocking his head to the left, he wiggled the blunt end of the tire iron into the gap again. This time he levered it back and forth gingerly until its leading edge was well within the crack beside the hinge. But just when he thought he had it firmly in place, it slipped out again.

It went without saying that to admit defeat now would spell the end. The way the box was heating up, he was looking at his last chance. This time he had to mean it. With that thought, Michael took a breath, centered himself, and let out a loud karate-style *kiyah*, letting the thought of a perfect hit guide him. It worked. In one solid motion he sent the blunt end of the tire iron directly through the gap. He levered the iron up and down, once, then twice, listening to the hinge creak and groan until on the third downstroke it popped.

Michael wasted no time, sticking both arms under the cover of the tarp and pushing upwards on the lid, bench pressing the hot steel like a strongman. He didn't know if it was the heat or his overpowering desire to escape that had made the metal soft, but he didn't care. All he knew was that he sprung up, into the flames, the tarp and blanket covering his body. He took a running step forward leaping out of the box and launching his body through the fire and exhaust.

Blind under the tarp, all that Michael was certain of was that the ground seemed much farther off than he had remembered it. When he finally hit the cool earth, he rolled to a rest several feet down the embankment. Doing a quick check of his motor functions, Michael found that all his body parts were still working; the reflective space blanket together with the heavy tarp had protected him from the searing heat. It did nothing, however, to mask his astonishment when he pulled the smoldering fabric from his eyes.

The Horten was hovering in mid air. It wasn't just the Horten, though; it had taken the entire length of the semi-trailer up with it as it hung there, above the meadow, only the front wheels of the truck still touching the ground. Michael estimated that it was pitched at a fifteen-degree angle as it attempted to lift off with its heavy load, jet engines thundering down in the night. Michael quickly returned his attention to the tactical, checking his periphery. As far as he could tell he was alone on the embankment. As he began the climb back up the bank, however, he was able to make out Ester's figure carefully watching from the other side of the craft. A closer look at the Horten as it hovered restlessly revealed what looked like a faintly glowing red necklace around its cockpit. It took only a moment for Michael to place the red LEDs as the signature glow of the detonators. He now knew that the situation was much more dire than he had initially suspected. A Semtex explosion would likely breach the Horten's reactor. At that point all bets were off.

57

Huang's MSS gunship was a dozen kilometers to the east and closing fast. The pilot had locked in the GPS coordinates of the suspect truck, but really there was no need; the Horten's plume of smoke and fire could be seen across the valley. There were still gnawing concerns, chief among them why the Triad gang which had ambushed them would be interested in the Horten, but Huang took the matter in stride. Most likely they were interested for the same reason criminals were interested in anything: money. As to their immaculate timing, Huang had never doubted the sophistication of China's criminal gangs. He knew that they were quite capable of getting what they wanted. But he also knew that the element of surprise no longer rested with the Triad. It now belonged to him. Huang rose from his crouch and made his way up to the pilot to relay his commands. Already he could smell the burnt jet fuel through the open chopper door. It was time.

. . .

Nᴇᴀʀᴇʀ ᴛʜᴇ ɢʀᴏᴜɴᴅ, the roar of the Horten's auxiliary thrusters echoed off the surrounding karsts creating a cauldron of sound. Crouched low, Michael skirted around the front of the truck. Though the deafening jets gave him cover, they also reminded him of how bad things could get. If Ester was allowed to detonate the Semtex there would be no escape—for himself or California.

Ester stood arms akimbo, staring up at the Horten as Michael approached. He arced far and wide, approaching from directly behind her, certain that her peripheral vision would kick in if he did anything less. Michael noted that she held something in her palm, undoubtedly a remote detonator. He was only feet away when something deep inside Ester alerted her to his presence. Michael sprung forward in a low tackle, but she sidestepped, firing her Luger as he rolled across the soft dirt. Michael knew she had missed, but not by much. He found himself hoping the antique gun would be slow to chamber a round. It didn't matter, though, because even if running face first into a bullet wasn't his first choice, he saw little alternative.

Ignoring the weapon, Michael launched his body upward, lodging his left shoulder in Ester's gut while sweeping her legs out from under her with his arm. Michael's gamble paid off. Ester fell hard and he turned his efforts to wrestling away her weapon. He managed to palm the Luger easily, but only because Ester's energy was directed to the remote she held in her left hand. By the time Michael had realized his mistake it was too late. He grappled her left wrist and reached for the device, but the moment was lost. Ester clicked the remote.

The first thing Michael noticed was the relative quiet. The roar of the Horten's auxiliary jets ceased almost immediately as the hot orange flames were sucked back into the thrusters. The Horten hung there in mid air for a moment before dropping back down to the ground with a bouncing thud. Then, Ester allowed her wrist to go limp, the remote falling to the earth below. Her stoic stare spoke volumes without her lips uttering a single word. Michael looked past Ester to the LED atop the remote trigger. It blinked.

"No!"

Michael sprung off Ester and grabbed the remote. It had begun a countdown from fifty-five seconds. He examined the remote, but found nothing in the way of a reset button, not even a battery compartment. Just a single trigger and the LED display. Michael heard a powerful low thumping in the sky. There was no time to dissect the mechanism. He glanced up to see Ester detaching the sawed-off shotgun from her shoulder loop. He reacted with a flying front kick, booting it from her grasp before she could level the gun. It tumbled down the bank and in that moment rotor wash engulfed them, minigun fire strafing the earth. One of the bullets must have found its mark because Ester jerked suddenly, collapsing to her side. Michael needed no further encouragement. He sprinted for the Horten like a bat out of hell.

• • •

HALF A MILE away, Li Tung told his driver to step on it. They weren't far from the meeting place now, but he could take no chances. His welfare, and more importantly, the welfare of his only son, depended on it. Behind his limousine followed two Mercedes-Benz G-Class sport utility vehicles. An off-road motorcycle led the way in front. The ten-man crew could have fit easily in the two SUVs, but Li insisted on the second truck in case something should happen to the first. What worried Li was that at even this distance, a good kilometer from the site, he could see the spotlight of a helicopter and hear automatic weapons fire in the darkness. It could mean only one thing—the MSS had managed to arrive before they were in position. Li picked up his walkie-talkie and pressed the talk button as he had been instructed.

"You must hurry," he said.

Before Li could say another word, the two powerful SUVs overtook the limousine, accelerating past it on either side of the narrow road. They would get there, Li silently prayed. There was no other way.

• • •

MICHAEL GRUNTED AS he hauled himself up the ladder into the cramped cabin of the Horten. The LED read forty-five seconds and counting. Three quarters of a minute. Enough time to microwave a burrito. Or froth a couple of lattes. Or maybe, if he was very, very lucky, do what he had come to do. Michael stooped through the hatch into the reactor room and opened the communications console. The green anodized encoding machine was there, just as he had left it. He removed the machine's back cover and took out a stuff sack from inside his cargo shorts. Emptying its contents into his lap revealed the items wrapped in the towel Li Tung had handed him—the code machine's eleven rotors complete with a variable-voltage power source. In hindsight, Michael wished he had used the rotors immediately after receiving the clear-code, but he wouldn't have been able to forgive himself for jumping the gun, not when he had been so close to solving the puzzle of his missing father. Of course hindsight was twenty-twenty. In retrospect, he would have had Tung deliver a pistol and maybe a blow torch too.

Though the rotors hadn't felt great hidden in his crotch, Michael was happy to see that they fit onto Purple Sky's spindles. He carefully lined up the numbered rotors in the correct order at the zero marker on the ratchet. Michael knew the correct re-installation was essential. Without it, any attempt to communicate with the Chinese satellite would be a failure, and as such, he took an extra second ensuring each of the rotors was snapped firmly into place. With the final rotor positioned, Michael latched the code machine's back cover with an audible click.

Now came the moment of truth. Michael knew the auxiliary jets had been fired which meant there was a chance, however remote, that the ancient lead-acid batteries would have picked up enough of a charge to sustain a transmission. The lithium-ion power pack with its dual alligator clip leads had been provided for this contingency, but Michael would have to wire it and right now he just didn't have the time. So he did the next best thing. He flipped the switch.

At first there was nothing. Michael glanced down at the blinking LED on the detonator. Nineteen seconds. He reflected without humor that if he didn't get a snap or crackle out of old Purple in the next few moments, things were definitely going to go pop. The next two seconds seemed to last an hour. It was as if time had attenuated to the point that it had actually stopped. Nothing happened. The cockpit was perfectly still. And then Michael heard his snap. It was more of a click accompanied by a low buzz, really, but there was no question that the code machine had sparked to life. Michael didn't waste any time verifying the code he had received. He had heard the seventeen-digit number clearly through Kate's ear piece. And he had remembered it, just as he remembered most everything else: 5-6-9-1-2-3-6-8-1-4-6-6-1-7-2-4-3. He entered the digits, feeling the whole craft shudder. Then he hit the return key, literally launching his body through the hatch before his finger had even left the keyboard. As he moved he caught a clear glimpse of the man who now stood outside on the Horten's bat-shaped wing.

58

THE DAY HE *was old enough to drive, Michael's dad taught him how to handle a gun. His father told him that both a car and a bullet could be lethal, the difference was the car had another reason for existing, the bullet existed only to kill. If you picked up a gun you had to be willing to use it. That was the nature of a gun. They went to the local gun club, both to the rifle range and the handgun facility. Michael liked the rifles. They suited his personality. You could shoot from a distance and be precise. You could be very exacting about what you intended to do. But he was decent enough with a handgun too. He practiced with a Browning 9mm. His dad explained that in general terms most 9mms were fairly similar. Their accuracy was greatly reduced over the rifle, but they made up for it in portability. They were weapons designed to incapacitate or kill your fellow man. You had to know that before even picking one up. You had to understand the circumstances under which you would use such a weapon—when your own life or the life of someone you loved was in danger. And you had to stop thinking about it right there.*

What Michael liked about his father's instruction was that it took the gray area out of it. There was no debate. The gun came out to protect your life. If someone tried to take your life from you, it was your duty to protect it. Period. Michael believed that. He would never pull a gun if he wasn't sure he could pull the trigger. But that didn't mean that he had to pull the trigger. Not if there was a better way.

THE MAN ON the wing was dressed in a black Novex jumpsuit, but even in the low light Michael couldn't mistake the glint in Ted's green eyes. He was working quickly, systematically removing the Semtex charges from the wings of the aircraft. Michael slid down the polished rails of the Horten's ladder and ran for cover. The gunfire that had pierced the night air had been replaced by the eerie rhythm of heavy breathing and boots on gravel. Huang's men were running as well. Michael could only hope that Ted, who had been so busy ripping the Semtex off the wings of the Horten, had a plan for its disposal. His answer was a scream.

"Chopper!" Ted yelled.

Ted lobbed what looked like a rucksack at Michael. Michael caught it like a football, and knew that the game was now in his hands. Michael had left the countdown timer in the cockpit of the Horten, but the time left made very little difference now. He was holding at least twelve pounds of wired Semtex. He had to throw it and he had to throw it fast. Swinging the rucksack like a sling, Michael extended his arm allowing the rucksack a full rotation in the air before letting it fly. For a fraction of a second he felt certain that he had waited too long, but he could do nothing about it now. Huang's men streaming down the hill toward their helicopter, Michael hit the dirt.

A moment later, the world was awash in blinding light. The inevitable blast of hot air was followed by the roar of the explosion. As the echo dissipated, Michael heard the crackle of fire which he guessed to be the burning helicopter, followed by two high-pitched tones. They sounded like an angry elevator buzzer, or the whine of a circular saw, or perhaps, he thought, a beacon to indicate that the code had been sent.

Michael pulled himself up from the ground. Huang's men had hit the deck long before reaching the chopper. There were two new sets of headlights on the scene now with another following. Michael disregarded them. He had more pressing concerns.

"Ester?"

There was no response.

"I know you're there. I can see you."

Michael crawled forward until he was able to recognize Ester in the darkness. She moved toward the Horten without acknowledging him. Ester grasped at her side where the bullet had hit her, a widening stain darkening her blouse. Before Michael could call out again, her telephone chirped.

Ester said two words. The first was in Japanese. The second was, "Yes." Ester then entered a number into the phone and tossed it to the side.

"Wait!"

Michael recognized the voice. It belonged to Kate. He heard her breathing behind him. A magnesium flash fizzled from Ester's mobile, self extinguishing before it had time to land on the ground. Ester pulled a short hand-hewn blade from its sheath and sank to her knees.

"No!" Michael screamed.

Ester was close now, not more than ten feet away, but despite Michael's protestations, there was nothing he could do to stop her. He watched her bite down, detecting a bitter almond odor as she did so. Michael hadn't smelt it before, but he thought he knew what it was: potassium cyanide, the choice of both Hitler and Eva Braun before her—a fast-acting poison to take the edge off what came next. Michael saw only a brief flash of polished steel as Ester plunged the blade through her white buttoned blouse into her abdomen. She worked the blade from left to right and then abruptly up. By the time Michael reached her she was barely breathing, a dull beatific look in her eye. He knelt down beside her and took her by the shoulders.

"My father. You know where he is. Tell me."

"The damage is done."

Michael pushed on, even as the life ebbed out of Ester's body. "Where is my father?"

"Gone."

Ester said nothing more, the dull gleam in her eye replaced by the stare of the dead. As she slumped forward, Michael thought that this woman whom he had worked so hard to find, this woman who had taken his father from him, had just taken one final thing—her secret to the grave.

"Is she dead?"

Michael nodded, reaching for what was left of Ester's mobile phone with his left hand. He knew there might still be viable data on it, as did Kate, who stood behind him, no more than six feet away.

"Give me the phone, Michael."

"Why?"

Kate laughed. "Call me an optimist. She didn't send me the activation code for my payment. I'm willing to bet the data is still on her phone."

Michael turned to see that Kate now held Ester's shotgun. "I want answers," he said. "She knew him and you knew him and I want to know where he is."

"Dead."

Michael bit his lower lip. "Why do you say that?"

"You know why."

"No," Michael said, "I don't."

"Your father's video clip had to be months old. It's the only way to explain it. It was taken while he was still in their custody. I don't know how he managed to send it or why it had that time stamp, but it doesn't matter. There's no way he's still alive. Not with them."

Michael stood slowly, reaching into his pocket for the Luger as he did so. Kate must have seen the outline of the gun.

"Hands in the air, Michael. Above your head."

Michael complied, palms open.

"I liked you. And I liked your dad. But like isn't enough in this world. You need to survive. And dollars are the currency of survival. Your father was a spy. He knew the game. They made me an offer and I did what I had to do."

"Which was?"

"I didn't kill him if that's what you think."

"I didn't say you did."

"I handed him over to the Dragons. That's it. He would have done exactly the same to me if he'd been in my shoes. So would you."

Michael was silent for a long moment.

"No, Kate. That's where you're wrong. I wouldn't do the same to you. Not for money."

Michael's words were punctuated by a burst of sub-machine-gun fire from the bank below. Hidden behind the Horten as they were, Michael thought the chances of them being hit were remote, but it didn't stop Kate from casting her glance in the direction of the shots. It was the split second Michael needed. He lunged forward and came up in a hard open-handed block, pushing the shotgun to the side. Kate fired, but that's what Michael wanted. He knew the double-barreled weapon only chambered two shells at a time. He took hold of the barrel, pushing it away from himself, and Kate fired again. Before the hot exhaust had left the second barrel, Michael was able to wrench the weapon from Kate's hand. He tossed it aside. The move was perfunctory. He was fairly certain Kate had no more shells, but regardless it seemed to confer the appropriate psychological effect. Kate backed away.

"It was never personal," she said. "Not with your dad, not with you."

Michael drew the Luger. Kate's eyes were wide and wet with emotion, but Michael could see the calculation behind them. He could see the cogs turn.

"I'm going to walk away now," she said.

Michael raised the Luger, training it squarely between her eyes.

"You're not going to shoot me."

"Keep telling yourself that."

"You're not a killer, Michael."

And with that Kate turned and walked slowly away. He had a clear shot the whole time. He could have brought her down. She certainly deserved it for what she'd done to his father. To him. But he didn't shoot. And he couldn't fault her logic in thinking he wouldn't. Because she was right. He wasn't a killer. Not if there was a better way.

59

THE SECOND-TO-LAST THING Michael's father taught him was how to deceive. He said it was different from lying. The way a symphony is different from a single instrument. To be able to lie was a useful skill. To be able to deceive was a brilliant one. He told Michael right off that the business of deception was just as serious as handling a gun. If you were going to deceive you had to do it for the right reasons. And you had to be ready to bear the consequences of failure. Hopefully you wouldn't fail. But if you did, you had to man up and take it. The difference between deception and a gun was that the tools were more ethereal. Any idiot could buy a gun. Most could lie. But to deceive, to meticulously concoct a web of lies, that was an art.

His dad wasn't content with theory, though. He wanted Michael to understand how it worked in the real world. So he brought Michael to a fishing lodge. He told him that they were going to tell all the other fishermen that they were brothers on vacation from their assembly jobs at the auto plant. Their goal was to gain one of the other fishermen's trust so that they could borrow some equipment from the medical lab he worked in. Their excuse was that they needed to test a car component—to make sure that what the company was selling was safe. The setup sounded preposterous to Michael. Nobody would believe they were brothers. Nobody would give them access to their employer's expensive equipment. But the fisherman did. And it was easier than Michael thought. All they had to do was appeal to the fisherman's sense of justice. People want to believe, his father said. They're trained to believe what they're told from a very young age. You just need to give them what they want.

Michael thought he heard an engine start, most likely a two-stroke, probably a motorcycle, but with the onslaught of vehicles cutting through the night he couldn't be sure. What he was sure of was the fact that Kate was not going to be happy when she found out about him. But that wasn't his problem. Not anymore. Within seconds of Kate's departure, Michael was flanked by two Mercedes SUVs. A pair of men dove out of each. Two of the men laid down cover-fire in the direction of the burning helicopter while the other two pulled Michael into the cab of the tractor-trailer. That the men were Triad was evidenced by the tattooed tigers wrestling snakes on their thick necks. The taller of the two men took the wheel and seconds later Michael found himself leaving the reservoir as quickly as he had come. Five minutes after that they were headed south, hellbound down the Guangxi Expressway for Vietnam.

• • •

HUANG WAS REELING. Not only had he lost the Horten, but his own helicopter had gone up in a ball of flame. He had no transportation, he had no radio, and what looked like a terrorist attack at the Jiuquan South Launch Center had taken his satellite phone offline. His men, as far as he could tell, had escaped the inferno, but the lack of casualties was of little consolation to him. Put simply, he had lost the war. His mission objective had been seized from him not once, but twice in one evening. He would not be granted a third reprieve. In his heart of hearts Huang understood that only one man was to blame for the debacle his mission had become and that man was the American spy. In that moment Huang decided that the American would pay. He would pay if it was the last act Huang committed in the service of his country. He would pay personally. And he would pay regardless of the cost.

· · ·

MOBI, MEANWHILE, SIMPLY stared at the overhead screen and waited. There was nothing to keep the Chinese satellite up, which meant that it had to come down. But after several minutes it didn't. Mobi watched as the seconds ticked by, sure that his calculations were off. Maybe he'd misassigned the entry angle or perhaps the velocity data had been compromised. Then something occurred that Mobi thought he'd only see in a dream. The satellite moved into a new orbit entirely. And that could only mean one thing—the bird had power. Somehow, somewhere, someone had sent the clear-code. The bird's systems had rebooted. It was going to be a good day.

Alvarez entered Mission Control, a pair of scissors in hand. "You see that?"

"Yup."

"You ever see anything so beautiful in all your life?"

"Nope."

"Are you going to talk to me?"

"Depends."

"On what?"

"Quiann."

"I can't really talk about it. Let's just say our government asked me to contact him and I did."

"Did they ask you to deliver the clear-code too?"

"Yes."

Mobi looked straight at her. "Are you a traitor?"

"No."

"Then who is?"

"Watch."

Alvarez indicated the open door to Secondary Ops where Rand stood with his two security men. It didn't take long before a group of uniformed military police approached. Rand raised his hands in protest, but he didn't run. Perhaps he knew that there was nowhere to go. Within moments he was cuffed and led out of the room.

"Hainan Island?"

Alvarez nodded. "They think that's where he was recruited. He's been trading secrets for money for years. Worried about his retirement, I guess. NSA wasn't sure until they tapped the transmissions coming out of this facility."

"Are you sure you're not an enemy agent?"

"I'm sure."

"Totally sure?"

"Hundred percent."

"My bad."

"No, Mobi. You did good. Really good." Alvarez snipped Mobi's plastic cuffs with the scissors. "Listen," she said. "You want to get some chicken or something?"

"Yeah," he said. "Some chicken would definitely be nice."

• • •

MICHAEL SHIFTED UNCOMFORTABLY in his seat. Compared with the evening's earlier events, the border crossing had been uneventful. Prior to crossing, the Horten had been tarped over like any one of a dozen wide-loads leaving the country that evening. Michael had then slipped into a specially designed compartment below the rear bunk in the cab of the truck. It was a tight fit, but compared to the tool chest, it felt like a protective cocoon. A few minutes later they were waved through the Friendship Pass and into Vietnam. With that, China was behind them. The driver had signaled Michael with a knock and he had slipped back out of his hiding place to find that they had just passed through the Vietnamese border town of Dong Dang. Now, less than ten minutes later, they had reached their rendezvous.

The driver pulled over beside a paddy field at a fork in the road. Before they even reached a full stop the doors on either side of the cab were opened from outside. Michael and the two Triad gangsters shuffled out and two new men, each of them wearing a coiled earpiece, took their places in the truck. They smiled and nodded coolly and Michael nodded back. Then, they closed their doors behind them and drove off in the truck, headed east this time, toward the Gulf of Tonkin.

Michael watched as the truck's red lights disappeared in the darkness, but he knew that he too had to go. There were two cars idling on opposite sides of the road a hundred yards up. Walking at a brisk pace alongside the truck driver and his companion, Michael approached the nearest vehicle, a midnight-blue BMW 7 Series sedan. Michael stopped outside the rear passenger door, staring down the tinted rear window in the moonlight. He considered knocking on the glass, but thought better of it when the window descended of its own accord.

Li Tung sat there, obviously fatigued, but relaxed, the makings of a smile on his thin lips. His normally perfectly coifed gray hair was slightly askew, but the dishevelment was more than made up for by the vibrant color in his cheeks. Michael thought that he looked years younger than he had that night outside Chungking Mansions.

Li looked Michael in the eye and said, "It is now I who owe you the favor, Mr. Chase."

He then raised his window and the BMW quietly drove out of sight. The purr of the car's engine still hung in the air as Michael heard his name called out in the darkness.

"Chase?"

"Yeah?"

"Time."

Michael crossed the road toward the man's voice and got into the rear seat of the second vehicle, a black Volkswagen Jetta. His work for the evening was done.

60

KATE DIDN'T GET as far as she had planned. Not because the motorcycle that was hidden in the hills near the reservoir didn't start easily. Not because her route out wasn't well planned. Not even because the trail had been blocked at one juncture and she'd been forced to detour en route to the airfield. No, Kate didn't get as far as she had planned because she'd miscalculated. When she'd reached the airfield, the Bombardier Global Express jet waiting to transport her per her deal with her employer was parked cold, dust covers still protecting the engines.

At first, Kate considered the jet's lack of readiness a small matter. She got off the motorcycle and entered the compact cinderblock control building proceeding with caution, but not alarm. True, the exchange of the Horten had not gone as planned, but upon consideration she didn't believe that this in and of itself was enough to derail the deal. The Society, after all, had a reputation to maintain. Bad news traveled quickly in the Intelligence community. If the Society wanted to continue to use independent contractors it would need to honor its bargains. This, coupled with the fact that Kate had already proven her trustworthiness by delivering Michael's father seven months earlier, shored up her resolve. The Green Dragon Society might not like it, but it was in their best interest to follow through with the promised fee and transport her safely out of the country per their agreement. It was as simple as that. But what Kate failed to consider was that her problem tonight might not rest with the Green Dragons. Because she had other enemies, enemies who were closer than she had thought. Kate heard the high-pitched whistle of the dart a millisecond before feeling its insect-like sting. It was only when she regained consciousness, however, that she realized the trouble she was in.

"Hello, Kate," a male voice said.

Kate heard the words before opening her eyes. When she finally managed to lift her heavy eyelids, her head throbbing in pain, she found herself cuffed to a metal chair. Though she couldn't yet see her interrogator, one thing was clear: the job had the Company written all over it. From the abrupt takedown to the barracks-style interrogation room she now found herself in, Kate saw the CIA's signature everywhere. Though she realized that by this point she could be anywhere in the world, her location was irrelevant, at least for now. The important thing was to make herself useful to them. She was after all in form, if not in spirit, still an MI6 Agent. The Americans, she calculated, would have to work through the logistics of that set of loyalties before pressing her too hard. And that thought gave Kate poise. But from the moment her interrogator revealed himself to her, she knew she had calculated wrong.

"I'm pleased to see you," the man said.

The man was middle aged with a finely lined face and a fashionably short hair cut. Kate immediately had the unsettling feeling that she knew him, but she couldn't quite place him. Then, he spoke again, this time in a high-pitched squeal and Kate knew exactly who she was dealing with. The hair was different, and the nose, but the voice was the same. It belonged to Larry Wu. Shanghai Larry.

"Surprised to see me again so soon?" Larry asked.

This was the man who had died in a pool of blood in Michael's arms, the man who had given him the cell phone message, the man who had solidified her interest in Michael as an asset. He was absent the prosthesis, but there was no doubt about it. It was him.

Larry's voice dropped a full octave and he said, "I know I'm glad to see you."

Kate felt a pull in the pit of her stomach. If Larry wasn't dead, then his death had been faked. And in the spy game there were only a couple of reasons to fake death. One was of course to enable a subject to disappear, but another was to foster credibility in a mark. And if this had been a case of the latter, then one more thing was clear. She had been set up. Kate forced herself to remain calm. What mattered now was not the duplicity, but the extent of it. What they wanted was for her to panic. If she could retain a cool head she might still find a way out.

Then the battered metal door opened. And Kate felt the pull in her stomach drop into a free fall because this time her old backpacker pal Crust entered the room.

True, he was clean-shaven in a crisp suit, his dreadlocks neatly tied back, but it was Crust, there was no question about that. He carried a Beretta semi-automatic in one hand and a mobile phone in the other. He tossed Kate the phone. It landed in her lap, a video clip already playing.

Kate looked down. She recognized the clip. It was the message from Michael's father. Only this time she noticed something that she couldn't possibly have recognized before. The interrogation room. She glanced around the bare space in which she sat. The concrete walls were the same as the walls in the video clip. The battered metal door was the same. The lone incandescent bulb, the gray metal table, the very chair she sat in, it was all the same. There was no doubt about it, the video had been recorded here, in this room. This was bad news. About as bad of news as she could get. It occurred to Kate that things had not been as they appeared for some time. Michael had not been as he had appeared.

She thought about his naïve blue eyes. About the way he arrived in Hong Kong, earnest, but eager for answers. She thought about how she had extricated him from the bloody scene in Chungking. How she had wanted to help him, but more to the point, how she had seen how he could help her. How what his father might have told him could be a potential asset in her work. But what she hadn't considered at the time were the inconsistencies. They were subtle, but they were there. Like the fact that Michael seemed reasonably comfortable under pressure; the kind of comfort that comes only with training. Or the fact that he never fully relaxed, not even when they made love, not really. Or even the fact that after what she had done to him, after what she had done to his father, he had simply allowed her to walk away. No one could do that, no one could be that forgiving. Unless he knew she was walking into a trap; unless he had set the trap himself.

Kate flashed to the temple cellar where she had first interrogated Michael. "I'm a spy," he had said. She hadn't thought much of it at the time. It was just bravado, a civilian coping mechanism to deal with an impossible situation. But then when Huang had held them at gunpoint in the cave, he had said it again. "I'm a slacker-boy spy come to kick your sorry ass." Again, it had to be bravado, or was it? When he wasn't talking about Mata Hari being his prom date he was kidding about espionage being a 24-7 game. Was it that obvious? Could she really have missed it? Kate felt an involuntary shiver run through the length of her body. Then she felt the bile rise from the back of her throat. It tasted bitter on her tongue. It was the taste of deception.

"Where is he?"

"That's what you're going to tell us," Crust said.

"Not the father," Kate said. "Chase. Where is Michael Chase?"

61

CIA SAFE HOUSE HANOI, VIETNAM

MICHAEL'S FATHER'S FINAL *lesson to him was no test. It was an act. He sent Michael a message. It was on a radio frequency that Michael had never heard of, encoded in an algorithm that Michael couldn't possibly break. And it had come through Ted. But that didn't diminish it in any way. Because the message said that his dad needed his help. And Michael did what he had to do. He went to find his father. That's when Michael learned what his dad had been teaching him all along. From being brave, to reading strangers, to the art of deception and everything in between, his father had been teaching him one thing. The family business. Michael now knew that from his earliest memory, his father had been teaching him how to be a spy.*

HE AWOKE TO the rhythmic sweeping of a straw broom outside his window. Slowly opening his eyes Michael watched as the morning sunlight danced on his pillow. It had been a hell of a night. Now it was time to see if it had all been worth it. The safe house was a simple two-story affair, just far enough outside the city center of Hanoi as to be unobtrusive. From the outside it was merely a well-maintained compound amidst a series of similar compounds; a neighborhood for the city's well-heeled. Inside, however, it was a sanctuary, and within its walls Michael felt the simple luxury of letting his guard down without the fear that someone might discover that he was more than he pretended to be. It might not seem like much, but to Michael, who had been diligently maintaining his cover since before his arrival in Hong Kong, it was the world. Allowing his eyes to wander to the bedside clock, he was surprised to see that it was nearly nine a.m. He'd gotten less than four hours of sleep, but they'd been good hours. Debriefing had been scheduled for 0900 sharp. He noticed that a fresh pair of jeans and a short-sleeved shirt had been left neatly folded on the edge of his bed. It was time to meet the man.

A quick shower and change of clothes later and Michael ambled down the stairwell to the smell of freshly brewed coffee. The first doorway on his right revealed a bright kitchen off of which sat a garden view breakfast room. Inside he was greeted by the Hanoi Station Chief, Sam Grolling. A tall man with a long chin and deep worry lines etching his face, Michael had briefly met Grolling back at Camp Peary in Virginia. His presence felt noteworthy to Michael because in some small way it signified completion, at least of this leg of the journey.

"Good to see you safe and sound, Agent Chase."

Michael pulled up a chair. There were three others at the table: a dark-haired petite woman whom Michael had never seen before, Song, the bubbly Australian who palled around with Crust, and Ted, his gray ponytail knotted in a clean bandanna for the occasion.

"I believe you've already met Song."

Song rose briefly and curtsied. "My liege."

Grolling went on. "This is Aimie, our program co-ordinator, and of course, Mr. Fairfield."

"Ted," Michael said. "Glad you made it."

"I could use about fourteen hours under a hot shower, but yeah, I made it."

"Well then," Grolling said, "shall we get started?" He took the quiet around the table as consensus and continued. "As of 0800 this morning the Horten had been transported via a local fishing vessel out of Ha Long Bay and into international waters where it was picked up by the Frigate USS Kingfisher. A CIA science team has already begun the initial examination of the plane and barring bad weather, it should be stateside for further study within ten days." Grolling paused for emphasis. "Given that the recovery of the Horten was your primary mission objective, Langley is pleased with the outcome."

"The incoming satellite?" Michael said. "What happened?"

"The clear-code you transmitted reinstated standard operating protocol. It self-corrected its course as of 0300 China Standard Time."

"So you're saying it worked. After all that time the transmitter actually worked?"

"We'll know more once the Horten is examined, but yes. For all intents and purposes the transmitter seems to have functioned perfectly, which is fortunate because we got word late last night that the Jiuquan Launch Facility was sabotaged, most likely by one of their own senior people. They couldn't have reestablished communication with that thing even if they did figure out how to do it. It's a national embarrassment. I think unofficially the Chinese were happy for the help." Grolling took a sip of coffee. "In addition, you'll be happy to hear, Li Tung and his merry gang of thieves are pleased as punch with what we've done for them."

"Which was?" Ted asked.

Grolling looked to Ted. Everybody here, especially a long-standing agent like Ted, knew that information was doled out on a need-to-know basis, and this item was not, strictly speaking, need to know. However, Grolling thought, the mission had gone well, and in all fairness, he had brought it up.

"Which was help Mr. Tung with a particularly worrisome problem his only son was facing stateside. In return for the help he extended us within China's borders, we agreed to extend our help within ours."

Ted smiled. "So let me guess, we sprung his little boy from an as-yet-unnamed facility."

"In so many words. Yes."

"What about the other reason we're here?"

Ted was not one to mince words, but still the directness of the question hit Michael like a knife to the heart. He wanted to ask if there was any more information regarding his father. He had wanted to ask since he awoke. The only reason he had even considered working for the CIA back when Ted had approached him a few weeks after his father's funeral was to get closer to the mystery of his dad's disappearance. But now that there might actually be some solid information, Michael didn't want to hear it at all. He didn't want to listen because he didn't want to be disappointed.

Grolling wavered. "The secondary mission protocol was less conclusive."

Michael finally opened his mouth. "How much less?"

"A lot less."

"Hold on," Michael said. "I risked my ass delivering you Kate Shaw. I want to know what you've found out."

"Not so fast, Agent Chase. We're questioning Ms. Shaw as we speak. We're following up on the information she provides."

"But?"

"I didn't say 'but.' We're following up." Grolling turned away from the table. "As far as your mission is concerned, the Director and I have agreed, we would like you to keep operating here in the field. Your backpacker cover is intact. There's no telling where we may use you."

Michael nodded. He knew he was tangling with the bureaucracy of the world's most powerful spy agency. He knew that they would let him know what they had learned when they were good and ready to do so. And he knew that the best way to hold his cards was quietly and close to the chest. But he also knew that he didn't give a damn. This man, Grolling, had made his case to him over six months ago when his dad had been missing only four weeks. He had told Michael that the country needed his help. Grolling had personally fast tracked Michael's path through the Farm. He had guaranteed that if Michael would help with the very sensitive mission of investigating his father's disappearance, Michael would be given priority clearance. And most importantly, Grolling had said unequivocally that in return for his help, Michael would never, ever, be left out of the loop. And now it looked like that loop was closed. Protocol be damned. It was time for the CIA to pay up.

"I went along with recruitment to find my father. I trained at your facility to find my father." Michael looked the Station Chief directly in the eye. "Then I risked my life finding your Nazi airplane and stopped a Chinese satellite from blowing up half the West Coast. I've paid for my ticket. Now you're going to tell me what you know or I'm done here."

"Think about what you're saying."

"I already have."

"Michael," Ted said, but Michael rose from the table regardless.

Grolling said, "We thought you might feel that way." He reached into the pocket of his jacket and retrieved a letter-sized envelope, handing it to Michael.

"What is this?"

"You know your father's video message was a digital composite. We faked it to acquire the target's interest. But it was based on a real intercept from eight days ago. The waypoint that led you to the factory, that was real." Grolling turned his gaze to the garden where the rich pink peach blossoms were blooming. The others around the table were silent, waiting for him to go on. "We don't know where your father is. We don't know if he was captured and managed to escape or if he's still in their custody. We're not even certain precisely who they are, not yet anyway, but thanks to your work bringing in Kate Shaw, we're closer than we were."

"So again," Michael said, holding up the envelope. "What's this?"

"Open it."

Michael tore open the envelope. Inside was a slip of paper no bigger than a grocery receipt. It consisted of a string of numbers which Michael immediately recognized as a GPS waypoint. He committed the waypoint to memory. From the look of it, it was a location in Turkey, Istanbul most likely.

"An NSA analyst picked it up last night. It was identified on the same frequency where we found the first message."

"So you think it's him again?"

"It's no more than a series of digits so it's impossible to be sure. But it's his assigned frequency. And the coordinates were encrypted in his preferred algorithm. So yes. We think it's him."

Michael sighed. The news was not definitive. But it offered hope. Real hope that his father was still alive. And Michael would go to the ends of the Earth for that.

"You're willing to have me investigate his whereabouts in my current capacity?"

"Yes, we are."

Michael sat there, considering what Grolling had just said. "Same rules apply? Special liaison to the CIA. Current cover. No long-term contract?"

"No long-term contract," Grolling said.

"And full disclosure regarding any new messages or intelligence as to where he might be."

"Yes."

Michael didn't need to think about it. He could feel it. Before that fateful day, just over half a year ago, he had been floundering. Even before his father had gone missing he was unsure of his course in life, bouncing from option to option, waiting for something that felt right. That his purpose had been revealed to him in the horror of his father's disappearance was unfortunate, but it didn't have to be tragic. Even the events that had marked him so many years ago didn't need to be seen through that lens. His experiences had changed him. But they had also made him stronger. He knew that now.

He also knew in his gut that his father was still alive and that working for the CIA offered the single best shot he'd have at finding him. Plain and simple. But he didn't have to make it easy for them. Not if he got even a hint that they were holding back. Still, almost in spite of himself, Michael felt a smile growing on his lips. At some point over the course of the last few days he had become something. He had become an intelligence operative. And for this small moment, in the confines of this room, he didn't care who knew it. Ted must have known the feeling because he lifted his cup.

"Kid," Ted said.

"Yeah, old man?"

"Welcome to The Circuit."

About the Author:

A former television writer, Lars Guignard is a graduate of both McGill University and the American Film Institute in Los Angeles. Ever since attending high school in the Indian Himalayas at the age of fourteen, Lars has been an avid backpacker and traveler. Lars currently makes his home in the Pacific Northwest.

Connect with Lars online:

www.larsguignard.com